THE
INSATIABLE
MOON

By the same author

Masks & Shadows

THE INSATIABLE MOON

MIKE RIDDELL

HarperCollins*Publishers*

HarperCollins*Publishers*

First published in 1997
This edition published in 2010
by HarperCollins*Publishers* (New Zealand) Limited
PO Box 1, Shortland Street, Auckland 1140

HarperCollins*Publishers*
31 View Road, Glenfield, Auckland 0627, New Zealand
25 Ryde Road, Pymble, Sydney, NSW 2073, Australia
A 53, Sector 57, Noida, UP, India
77–85 Fulham Palace Road, London W6 8JB, United Kingdom
2 Bloor Street East, 20th floor, Toronto, Ontario M4W 1A8, Canada
10 East 53rd Street, New York, NY 10022, USA

National Library of New Zealand Cataloguing-in-Publication Data

Riddell, Michael.
The insatiable moon / Michael Riddell.
Previous ed.: 1997.
ISBN 978-1-86950-859-3
I. Title.
NZ823.2—dc 22

Cover design by Louise McGeachie
Cover image by Violaine Barrois
Typesetting by Springfield West

Printed by Griffin Press, Australia

50gsm Bulky News used by HarperCollins*Publishers* is a natural,
recyclable product made from wood grown in sustainable
plantation forests. The manufacturing processes conform to the
environmental regulations in the country of origin, New Zealand.

*For Rosemary,
who believed . . .*

I

Arthur pauses at the top of the street. He turns to look back. The Waitemata winking blue, the bridge standing guard. Pohutukawa on fire in their summer frocks. The sky goes on and on and on. In the distance, bush, freckled with houses, tumbling to the water. And the sun is washing everything clean. Arthur breathes in, and the trees dance. He exhales slowly; a sweet warm breeze plays along the footpath. White silk wings fluttering somewhere.

A woman passing, bent with the climb, towing her shopping trolley.

'It's a beautiful day, isn't it?'

'Thank you,' says Arthur, beaming.

The traffic bitches its way along Jervois Road. A big scruffy man watches it. He's playing games; locking his eyes on certain cars and slowing them down. Arthur loves puzzled faces. He concentrates on the traffic lights, changing the cycles. If only they knew.

It's early still. Arthur up all night again, about his father's business.

God never sleeps. I wish he'd let me, though. The burdens of divinity are not widely recognized. But today, today my world is wonderful, and my life shines through it. I will do many miracles today. My heart is sore with aroha. I am becoming who I must be.

Arthur lights up the dairy with his grace. It's a small shop, but it's doing its best to fit him in, to accommodate him.

'Morning, Arthur. How's it going?'

'As well as it can in these times.'

Arthur notes that the shopkeeper's eyes don't follow his smile; the man's mouth opening like a cash register.

'What'll it be this morning, then?'

'You got any of those, ah, disposable nappy things?'

'Nappies? You're a bit of a dark horse, Arthur. No offence, like.'

'They have a purpose.'

'A purpose? Yeah, well, I suppose you're right there. They're over on the back of that shelf. What size do you want?'

'Big ones. For a boy.'

'The ones on the bottom then. Anything else?'

'Tobacco. Port Royal.'

'Right you are. I don't suppose you'll be paying cash?'

'My father has need of them.'

'Yeah, well, my father has need of a few things as well. Like a son who doesn't go bankrupt. This is the last stuff you put on account before you pay the bloody bill, all right?'

'Be calm, my friend, be calm. There are many things you don't understand as yet, but they will become clear to you.'

'All right. No more bloody sermons, Arthur. Just put your mark here, and pay the bill by next week or that's it.'

Arthur pauses before he leaves, offering a gift to a sad shopkeeper.

'The time will come when you will look for friends, and the earth will be full of those you cannot trust.'

'Yeah, see you later. Bloody psych patients. I don't know why I bother.'

Margaret is doing the lunches. She cuts the bread in triangles. She used to cut it straight across, but now she cuts it diagonally. It's a little innovation, a mark of originality. Like the parsley. She puts a sprig of fresh parsley on top of the sandwiches before wrapping the clingfilm around them. The little flash of green on top of the packet pleases her. The kids don't appreciate it. They chuck it straight in the rubbish; half the time the sandwiches follow.

But Margaret is careful to cut evenly. So that the triangles are regular. *Isosceles*, she thinks. *It doesn't*

matter if anyone else notices. It's important for yourself.
Penny laughs at her for ironing the sheets. *I like to do things properly, that's all. I do it for myself, not for anyone else.* She arranges the bread, places the parsley, wraps with a deft movement. *There.* Admiring her own handiwork. *Well, you might as well take pride in your work. No-one else will.*

'Your lunches are ready!'

Mark and Stephanie are blank-eyed in front of the television. The presenter is unnaturally cheerful.

'Come and get them! It's time to leave.'

'Oooh, Muuum.'

Mark waits with his finger over the remote, extracting the last seconds of inanity. Finally he relents, the screen implodes, they come to life again.

The lunches are passed like sacraments, with a kiss.

They leave, the slamming door the end of a trail of noise leading down the passage. Margaret giving the obligatory sigh.

Brian is silently consuming the newspaper. Whatever he's looking for doesn't seem to be there. Every day he looks.

'Brian?'

'Hmmm?'

'Will you be home for tea tonight?'

'Uh, doesn't look good. I'll ring you.'

'You're very busy these days. I think you should take a break.'

'Someone's got to pay the mortgage and keep you in clothes.'

'I wasn't criticizing, Brian. I just miss you, and the children do too.'

'Hmmm.'

'I think I'll go out for lunch today. Penny's been wanting to take me to a new café in Ponsonby.'

'Fine.'

'I'll be home in time for Mark and Stephanie, unless I have an affair.'

'Fine. I better get going. Have a good day, love.'

The silence is the worst part. The silence and the emptiness. A great lurch in her stomach as the car accelerates away. The house crouches, menacing. Margaret doesn't linger long. Tidying, dishes, cleaning. The rituals of exorcism. Black demons hovering, waiting. *I will keep busy. I will be strong.*

She switches on the radio. Moanback, Brian calls it. They're all so bigoted and insular. *So why do I listen?* Voices are voices. They help to fill the hollowness.

At the bottom of the street, the big house lurks in the shadows. It reeks of stale grandeur. Arthur greets the house as he comes up the drive.

On the veranda are John and Pete and Sandy. They're waiting for something.

'Morning, Arthur,' calls Pete.

'Tena koe.'

John never speaks.

Sandy's suckling at a bottle in a brown paper bag. Sandy was once a seaman, who travelled the world. He could tell a story or two, but he doesn't. Arthur is smiling, bestowing grace on them all. A soft yellow light slants across them, so that they seem to brighten.

'What you got in that plastic bag, Arthur?'

'Supplies, Pete. I'm storing stuff in the shed. Things that I need for my job.'

'Jeez, Arthur, you're the only one here has a job. How about a loan?'

'I'll give you a smoke, e hoa.'

Arthur sits on the old sofa, next to Pete. Pete had a wife, possibly still has. He takes pills three times a day and screams in the night.

The tobacco and papers are shared among them. Sandy's hands are shaking, so that the sweet brown tobacco falls to the floor. Arthur takes it from him, rolls a smoke and passes it over. Together they blow smoke into the air. It curls and snakes. Arthur is watching, looking for any patterns, messages. Sandy pushes the bottle at them, offering. None of them's game. But to show there's no offence, Arthur places his great hand on Sandy's shoulder.

'You'll do me, Sandy.'

And he feels the power going out from him.

Today will be a day of many miracles.

From inside the house comes the sound of the

12

television. Children's programmes. Five or six men are watching. Not speaking to each other. Some will be upstairs, sleeping. The rest are out on the streets, on patrol. Twenty-seven men. Six bedrooms and the garage out the back. It's a family of sorts.

Pete was with Arthur in hospital. They have the bond of indignities shared. Arthur has hopes for Pete. *One day he might understand. Who I am. What my destiny is.*

'D'you know what's happening in this world, Pete?'

'I don't even know what's happening in Ponsonby, mate. It's this gammy leg. I can't get out much.'

'It's passing away. That's what's happening. The old is shrivelling up like your balls, and the new is coming. I'm going to bring it in.'

'Is that a fact? How're you going to do that, Arthur?'

Pete knows what's coming, but he likes Arthur, and he's smoking his tobacco. A matter of courtesy, really.

'My father has told me what I have to do. I can't tell you all of it, because some of it is secret. But the main thing is, I have to tell people who I am. And wait for the word to spread.'

'What's that?'

'That I'm the second son of God.'

Arthur's voice is hushed, secret-sharing.

'Fair go?'

'I've been appointed to bring in the new age. See this packet of nappies here?'

'Is that what they are?'

'They're for a baby.'

'Yeah, they mostly are.'

'But this is a special baby, not yet born. I'm to father a child with the Queen of Heaven. But careful who you tell that to.'

'Who's the Queen of Heaven?'

'I'm not sure yet. That's my next job — to look out for her.'

'Well, if you need a hand, just sing out. Me and John and Sandy are always out here. We could keep an eye out for her.'

'You're a good man, Pete. But it's not for you to know her or find her. That's my job. My father will reveal her to me.'

'Jeez, mate, I hope she's good-looking. I suppose she would be with a name like that.'

Arthur is silent now. He is seeing the picture of a starving Indian child. *Soon I will be feeding the hungry. I will gather you little ones to my side and give you shelter. Don't be afraid. I am the one who has been sent to you.*

From the dark interior of the house there's a shout, announcing a pot of tea.

He calls into being a blue heron, watches it beat its way across the sky, and follows the others inside.

It takes a few moments for Penny to answer the door. She's arranging flowers in a vase, keen to get them right. *Too sensible to be artistic, that's my trouble.*

Margaret knocks again. *Did I get the wrong time?* The anticipatory smile slips a little. Pangs of anxiety corroding the confidence. But here are the footsteps and the door opening and 'Penny, Penny, how good to see you.' A warm, breasty embrace, genuine pleasure.

Penny holding her at arm's length, drinking it all in.

'Marg, are you all right?'

'Fine. Fine. You look great.'

And they're strolling up the street, arm in arm, almost as they once were in another place and time. Laughing and stumbling over each other and Margaret holding just a little harder than she needs to. The narrow villas and cottages joining in the merriment, jasmine and lavender waving behind picket fences.

Ponsonby Road is a technicolour ribbon, streaming in the breeze. They're wading into the current, drifting with it. Human confetti. The street singing to itself, enjoying the sunshine. Penny leading the way to her secret place. The café is brimming over at the edges. Glossolalia presiding. Penny has a booking, a table out on the footpath.

They're looking at each other instead of the menu. Air thick with the scent of shared memories. The music is playing. And then Margaret's crying, and

15

she can't stop. Tears dripping off her chin. Reaching for tissues, hiding in her handbag, sobbing in silence.

Oh shit oh shit oh shit.

And Penny's holding her hand, stroking it, and her eyes are wet as well. The waiter's pretending not to notice, keeping his distance.

'What, Margaret?'

'I don't know, I don't know.'

'Is it Brian?'

'No! . . . Yes, maybe. I don't think it's anyone else. I'm all right — honest I am.'

'You look great. C'mon, Marg, what's happening?'

'I'm scared, Penny. Scared that I'm slipping down some black hole. I keep reaching out to grab hold of things to stop me going down, but sometimes it doesn't work. I'm sorry, here we are out to have a good time and I . . .'

'You apologize and I'll beat you to death with this menu. Oh Marg, you're so sad.'

'But I shouldn't be, I shouldn't be! I have healthy children and a good husband and a beautiful home.'

'In Howick?'

'There's nothing wrong with Howick!'

'You used to call it Wasteland.'

'That's when I was young and stupid and nothing mattered. I have no excuses, Penny. Everything I wanted I've got. It's just some stupid emotional bog that I've got myself into and can't get out of.'

16

'D'you really think that's all there is to it? Get some antidepressants and clear it up?'

'Yes, as a matter of fact, that's exactly what I'm going to do.'

Here she is crying again, and shredding tissues between her fingers. The waiter makes a tentative bid for an order, and Penny provides it. There is comforting and consoling, and calm comes with the food. Penny teases and makes stupid jokes and points out the more ridiculous pedestrians. One by one the demons depart.

Most people miss a lot. They're walking along and not looking, not taking it in. Smokes, for example. Any time of the day you can find enough for a roll-up. What's wrong with it? The tobacco's been inside the paper. You just pull the old stubs apart and empty the contents onto a new paper and before long, there you are. A good smoke for the price of a paper.

That's just for starters. Arthur keeps an eye on the rubbish bins as well. Not to go digging through them right to the bottom like some of the guys do. Just noticing things as you go past, that's all. It becomes a habit after a while. You don't even think about it.

It's probably why Arthur's got his head down today while he's walking through the shops. Why he sees the $50 note under the seat of the bus stop. That's probably why. But Arthur knows better. He knows that this is a gift from God, that it's appeared here for him and him alone. This is a great day for miracles, you can just tell.

He's praising God now as he walks along, his rumbling voice out of tune. *Then sings my soul, my Saviour God to Thee, how great Thou art, how great Thou art . . .*

This is a sign that I'm getting closer. The times are coming. I must be about my father's business. Today is a given day.

Here's Digby. Leaning next to the bank door, where he always leans, asking for change as people come up.

'Kia ora, Digby.'

'Arthur.'

'How you doing?'

'Yeah, not bad. Couple of dollars. Early yet.'

'It's a good day for miracles, Digby.'

'Is it? Haven't seen any round here.'

'Today's your day; today's your day. Have a look at this.'

'Fifty bucks! Where d'you get that?'

'God, Digby. I've told you I'm the second son of God.'

'You can be the Queen of bloody Sheba if you like for fifty dollars! You dirty lucky bastard.'

'I'm going to make a miracle, just for you. You want a miracle?'

'If it's got anything to do with fifty bucks I do.'

'Watch this, then.'

Arthur's stretching the note out flat, stroking it. Now he's holding it up to the light. What's he doing? Checking the watermark? No, he's saying something. Thanking God. Now he's changing his hold on it. And tearing it. Right down the middle.

'You mad bastard! What are you doing?'

'This part is for you, Digby, and this part is for me. We will share God's gift.'

'But you need both halves to spend it, you silly bugger.'

'Don't question the ways of God. You just keep the note in your pocket, and love in your heart, and when you come to spend it, it will be whole. This is the word of Arthur, second son of God.'

'What a load of cobblers. Thanks for nothing, mate.'

'Don't thank me, thank your father in heaven.'

'Not the fucking phone again!' Under his breath. Wouldn't quite be the thing for one's parishioners to hear. *Should I ask God for forgiveness? Nah, bollocks, God can take it.* None of which stops the phone ringing.

'Kevin Connor . . . Yes, that's right . . . No, just the morning I'm afraid . . . Eleven a.m. . . . You'd be most welcome . . . Bye.'

Don't know why people come to bloody church in the first place. Make my job a lot simpler if they stayed away. Bunch of whingers most of them. Grovelling before God to try and squeeze some extra benefits out of life. What do they think I am? An ecclesiastical bellboy?

Two angels are present; one on top of the filing cabinet and the other lounging in an armchair. They're enjoying themselves. This assignment is pure pleasure.

The minister of St David's is writing a sermon. It's his task to announce to the assembled congregation the word of God. This is an ambitious task. He's surrounded by screwed up pieces of paper.

Who asked for this ratshit job anyway? You know I don't belong here. You know I've got nothing to say to these people. Unless it's to take a running jump at themselves. So come on, come on, come through for me! I'm sick of staring at this blank bloody page. Give us a break, you great cosmic egotist, before I walk out altogether.

The angel in the chair lights up a carefully constructed joint and sucks it down. The other one has a toke, then descends beside Kevin's chair. She bends over and blows in his ear.

Yeah, well, there's a thought.

The vicar's scrawling on his paper. He can see something, and he races to get it down before it goes. He thinks he can hear laughter, but then again, maybe not.

Margaret's dabbing at the corners of her mouth, making sure there are no crumbs remaining on her face. Penny's watching her.

'Do you ever . . . have regrets, Pen?'

'Some. Mostly I just wonder how things might have been if I'd made some different choices.'

Margaret's simpering at her latte, a taster for poison. It's the way it makes a froth moustache. *The huge cups aren't necessary, are they?* She's looking into a private vision. Different choices. Life without Brian. A body before children. Opinions. Passion. Time to soak in the bath. Nobody else's hair in the plughole. *I used to be interested.*

Penny's all mother-heart and refuge. The sound of her voice is massage with body oil, slow. Which once, a life ago, it was.

'Remember when I was living in that awful old place in Grafton? You used to bring your own cup when you came round. I was with Rog, well, most of the time. I had all that money from Mum, and I wanted to travel. But Rog needed to stay here for his job. I didn't know what to do. We went for a walk in the Domain, remember? I think you just wanted to get out of the flat. I poured it all out for you, asked you what you thought. And you said something to me which I've never forgotten. You said stay true to yourself.'

'We were young, Penny.'

'I can still see the tree we were under when you said it. Stay true to yourself. It just all fell into place in the space of a few seconds. The next day I put in my resignation and bought the plane tickets. Rog got evil, threatened me with all sorts of things. It all happened very quickly.'

Margaret is pushing crumbs around the table with her finger. She's deeply interested in them.

'I didn't know what to say to you, Marg. I couldn't cope with your hurt as well, so I just cut and ran. But it was never you that I was running from. We never talked about it . . .'

'The day you left I drove out to Muriwai. There was hardly anyone there. I walked along the clifftops until I found a spot on my own. I watched the waves smashing on the rocks for hours. I decided then that I wasn't going to have anything more smashing into my life. I was going to build a breakwater, make a safe little harbour where the water was always calm. It was very cold and calculated. Three weeks later I met Brian, and I knew what I had to do.'

'You loved Muriwai! You were always hassling me to go out there.'

'I've never been back since.'

'I'm sorry. I'm so sorry.'

'It's just the way life is. There's no point in apologizing or regretting; you just have to get on with it. There's always the children and the mortgage.

I had to grow up, and that day at Muriwai was when I did it. I made my harbour, and now I live in it. And most days it's safe and beautiful.'

Penny's quiet now, fascinated by the coffee residue in her cup. The question hangs there in the space between them, massive and unanswered. It's just the way life is.

He's walking up and down outside the building, reluctant to go in. Arthur's in two minds about churches. All this emphasis on the first son of God, and none of them interested in the second. But he knows his father has something to do with them; he's seen the light often enough. If the word's to be spread, that's the place to start. In the night God had said to him, 'Arthur,' he'd said, 'I want you to go to my house.'

So he's reading the billboard outside. Vicar: Rev. Kevin Connor. The building is squat and brick. It looks more like a toilet block with a big roof. Arthur's walking up the pathway to the door marked 'Office'. A bird launches into song. Arthur acknowledges this welcome, pronouncing a blessing on his feathered brother. He's knocking at the door.

Arthur wants to take his shoes off. But his socks aren't great, and Pakeha have no sense of tapu anyway.

'Shit!'

That last carefully honed theological point dissolves into the fog with the knocking on the door. *It's like Coleridge with Kubla Khan*, he thinks.

The angels, mellow, find the priestly presumption amusing.

He takes a step back as he opens the door. A huge Maori is filling the frame. He has a head like a lion's; oversized and menacing. The hair is long and tangled. The fingers of both hands are stroking their respective palms. Head tilted; licking of the lips. Classic side effects. A psych patient.

'I was wondering if I could talk to you.'

Is this some sort of joke, God? I ask for some peace and quiet, and you send me a bloody psych patient?

'Come in. I'm Kevin Connor.'

'Arthur.'

The handshake is warm and firm. For no reason at all Kevin sees a huge oak door opening, feels the weight of it swinging on its hinges.

'Have a seat, have a seat.'

The angel moves to sit on the desk.

Arthur nods in acknowledgment. He's looking around the room. Wall-to-wall books. Certificates hanging like ancestors in black frames.

'You read all those books?'

'Well, most of them at one time or another.'

'Maan, you must be pretty smart, eh?'

'I do my best. Now what can I do for you, Arthur? I'm afraid the drop-in only runs in the afternoons.'

'I've got something I want you to do. God sent me here to tell you, to give you a job to do for him.'

Arthur's foot is rocking up and down. To tell you the truth, he's a little nervous. Even the second son of God gets nervous from time to time.

'What sort of job have you got in mind, Arthur?'

'Can you keep a secret?'

'It's part of my job. Anything you tell me is in complete confidence.'

'You know how the Bible talks about Jesus as the son of God?'

'Yes, that's right.'

'Well, I'm the second son of God.'

'I see.'

'I've been sent for a reason.'

'I'm sure.'

'I can't tell you everything about it, but the time has come when I'm to be revealed to the world.'

The angels are paying attention. They're always interested in picking up a bit of gossip about divine intentions. After all, angels are the last to know anything.

'And how would you like me to help you?'

'I want you to announce it to your people here. You got a big group?'

'About a hundred and fifty, I imagine. What is it

exactly that you'd like me to announce?'

'That Arthur is the second son of God, and the time has come for him to be revealed.'

'Look, I don't mean to be rude; but what exactly makes you think that you're the second son of God?'

'Well, the first has already been, so that makes me the second.'

'Quite. But why, specifically, should you be the son of God as opposed to me, for example?'

'You think you're the son of God?'

'No, I was just suggesting it for argument's sake.'

'When I was in Oakley, there were seven people who thought they were Jesus, and two who said they were the devil. So that just proves it.'

'Proves what?'

'That I'm the second son of God.'

'I see. Look, to be perfectly frank with you, Arthur, I don't think I'll be able to help you out. I'm not sure that I'd feel comfortable announcing anything like that.'

'You don't believe me?'

'It's not that; it's just that I don't know for certain whether you are or not. I can't go telling the congregation things I'm not sure about.'

This creates great mirth in the angels' corner.

Arthur is looking into Kevin's eyes, reading him.

'You can just say if you don't believe me. It was God that sent me, but I'm used to people not believing

26

me. The Catholic priest threw me out and said I was a blasphemer.'

'Have you ever thought that perhaps we are all the children of God?'

'Do you know what God's got in mind for this world in the next few years?'

'No, I can't say that I do.'

'Then you're not the son of God like I am, are you?'

'Evidently not. Look, I'm sorry I can't help you, but I wouldn't feel comfortable making that sort of announcement in church. Now, if you'll excuse me, I have a sermon to finish.'

'There's just one thing.'

'What's that?'

'I don't suppose you could see your way clear to lending me twenty dollars till next week?'

Kevin's sighing deeply. He's hunting in the bottom drawer for the cashbox where he has a special discretionary fund for the poor. He unlocks it, removes a $20 note and passes it to Arthur.

'Next Tuesday,' he says.

'Next Tuesday,' says Arthur. 'If the world's still here. Nah, just joking.'

The angels find it very funny.

A day of many miracles, thinks Arthur.

The waiter's casting distressed looks in their direction. He wants his table back; they've been lingering over empty cups for half an hour.

They're speaking of children, and other easy topics. Margaret's enjoying the sun on her back. The Ponsonby people are promenading, seeing and being seen. Underneath the cacophony, café music struggles to make a presence. A catchy chorus burrowing into the subconscious.

A stillness in the movement is catching her eye. An unkempt bear of a man, standing and staring. One of the street people. His eyes like the nose of a dog. She's feeling uncomfortable. But his face is fascinating. A huge, strong, leonine head, noble and gentle.

An image is playing on her private screen. A huge wave, shooting the gap between the rocks. Hovering for a second with the undertow. Crashing in a frenzy of whiteness and energy; glorious salt-spray exhilaration.

She's shaking her head, dragging herself up from unfathomable depths. Breaking the surface and gasping for air.

Walking and listening and looking. Arthur is doing his beat. Praying for those that he's passing on the street. He's aware that his radiance creates a space around him that no-one else can enter. They move to one side as he approaches.

I must be about my father's business. Today is the day of the beginning of the end. I have seen what I have seen.

Roslyn is sitting on a bench, nursing her bottle. The flesh has fallen away from her frame because she neglects to eat. She sits carefully erect, maintaining her dignity. Her lovely long hair is grey and matted in places.

Arthur is greeting her with aroha. He knows her from the boarding house, where now and again she comes to share her warmth with one of the men. Sometimes they'll give her a little money for a drink. Bob, the manager, doesn't like women around the place because of the fights, but he tolerates Roslyn.

He knows what he must do. Already his fingers have found the $20 note given by the minister. The second son of God pronounces a blessing upon it as he slips it quietly into her hand.

She isn't so ungracious as to acknowledge it. She keeps her head high so that her lovely hair will cascade down her back. A Mona Lisa smile brushes her face as she returns Arthur's greeting. He is moving on.

You are my beloved son. In you lies the seed of the future. My will be done through you, and the fruit of your loins.

The pavement is bathed in a golden glow. Awash with glory. Arthur's feet do not touch the ground as he walks. He is stepping into destiny, into the intersection. Choirs are singing, harmonizing on the sounds of the street.

Then there is total and absolute silence.

A face leaps from the sidelines, a sad, beautiful face. Blonde hair lit by a halo, shining like the moon on the water. Eyes of longing.

He stops dead, drinking from the wellspring of the future. This is the day of miracles, and this is the miracle of miracles. He has been waiting so long for this moment, seen this face every night. She is seated upon her throne, and the nations are gathered before her. But she has eyes only for the king.

Praise be to you, my father, for your great wisdom and love.

The man is coming towards her. She is both fearful and calm. Penny's aware that she's slipped off the edge of conversation.

'Margaret? Marg?'

Penny turns her head, following the tracks of the gaze. A giant bearing down upon them, with hand outstretched.

'Don't give him anything, Marg. It's best not to start.'

In Arthur's hand is a scrap of paper. He holds it in front of her, and nods once. Margaret cannot help herself. She reaches to receive, hand cupped. The man places it on her palm so gently. He says nothing.

She says thank you, but the words don't make it. Arthur hears, nevertheless. He nods again, steps back, plunges again into the river and is gone.

She looks down to discover a crumpled half of a fifty-dollar note.

'Bloody nutters,' says Penny. 'Ponsonby's full of them since they emptied out Carrington. What's that he gave you?'

She holds it up for inspection.

'I'm not sure what I should do with it.'

'Nothing much with that. I wonder where he got it from? Perhaps you should leave it for a tip.'

The die is cast. What has been purposed in the heart of God will come to be. On the side of a road in the city of Auckland the wheel continues its spin.

They're strolling back, arm in arm. Margaret is washed out, exhausted. But glowing with some post-coital flush. Penny worries for her.

'D'you think you should talk to someone?'

'Mmmm? Oh no, I'll be all right. If I want to talk to someone I'll come to you.'

'I'm not sure I'm much help.'

'I don't want help, Pen. I just want you to be around when I need you.'

Digby's at his station, beside the bank. He's just shared a smoke with Roslyn, who might come to see him tonight. If she remembers.

Two likely prospects are approaching. One with

dark hair and eyes, the other blonde, frowning. Comfortable casual look of the unruffled rich. Digby and Margaret were born in the same year, but she's twenty years younger.

'Can you spare a couple of dollars?'

Penny has already averted her eyes, knowing what was coming. But Margaret is filled with uncharacteristic compassion. She holds out her hand, still cosseting the crumpled banknote. Not till they've gone past does she think of the cruelty of it.

Digby can barely bring himself to compare the numbers on the two halves.

'Well, I'll be buggered; I'll be buggered.'

In heaven they're playing reggae, and the joint is jumping.

The last paragraph of the sermon pleases him. He reads it over to himself:

So how to live? Well, in the words of Ecclesiastes: 'In the morning sow your seed, and at evening withhold not your hand; for you do not know which will prosper, this or that, or whether both alike will be good.' Make a habit of avoiding self-preservation, and in the important times you will be able to bear the risks. The one certainty is that God is calling to us through all of our small decisions, summoning us to risk more and

*so to become more, to give more and so to live
more, to sow more and so to reap more. God is
an adventurer; life was his idea in the first place,
and death God's constant enemy. Let us enter the
future with a commitment not to observe the wind
or regard the clouds, but to press on from life to
life.*

The angels applaud, with just a hint of sarcasm. He
already thinks that the ideas are his. Humans are so
egocentric. Still, that's what makes them such good
entertainment.

Kevin can't quite clear his mind of Arthur. He's
psych, for sure. But there's something special about
him. A strength, a winsomeness. *I should never have
given him that money, though. There'll be a queue of
them tomorrow.*

The trees are offering a standing ovation. They clap
their hands and sway in time to the music. Arthur
alone sees this. It is his gift.

Pete's with him on the veranda, sharing a smoke
and a cup of tea.

'Great day today, Arthur.'

'Ka pai, my friend. Ka pai.'

'How's your search going? For what's her name —
the Queen of Heaven?'

'It's over, Pete; I found her.'

33

'Fair go? You don't waste your time. What's she like?'

'When I was a boy up north, I'd sometimes get up early and go down the beach on my own. The sun was just up, and I'd be the only one there. The salt spray would get right inside your head, and the waves seemed to break on top of you. Everything was fresh and brand new — nothing had been touched or handled. She's like that.'

'Go on. You going to bring her round to meet us?'

'At the right time. There are signs which will come first, and then it will be time.'

'You're all right, Arthur; I hope it all works out for you. I never did very well with women.'

'This is what has been written from the beginning of time. My father sent me here for this.'

'I don't doubt it, mate. I don't doubt it.'

The calm of evening is settling over Shelly Beach Road. Arthur sees the faint white shadow of the moon against the sky. Everything is at peace, because he is.

He pronounces a blessing, and a thousand kahawai leap from the Waitemata. Somewhere in Howick, there is an answering sigh.

2

The angels have been redeployed. Kevin looks at his watch again, checks his shoulders for dandruff. He's waiting for the woman from television. A presenter. He couldn't quite pick up what it was about on the phone.

Still. The big chance. You have to make the most of your opportunities. He's selecting a book from his shelves to leave nonchalantly on his desk. He changes his mind. Puts it back and tries another one. Better.

A knock on the door. He counts to ten before opening it. A power-dressed young woman with briefcase and purply-black lipstick.

'Kevin Connor. Come in.'

He offers his hand. She looks at it, as if to say quaint. A brief squeeze and then she takes over.

'Yes, hello. I'm Karen Bligh-Farnsworth. I spoke to you on the phone. Mind if I take a seat?'

'No, sorry, of course.'

'Let me get straight to the point, Mr . . . Connor. We're doing a one-off doco on community care of psychiatric patients. We hear you run a drop-in here at the church. What we want is the life stories of a few people. Tragic stuff, preferably. You know — turfed out of hospital, nowhere to go, no-one to look after them, attempted suicide, that sort of thing.'

There's a statue on the wall behind his head. It's a man pinned to a wooden cross, like a butterfly in a display case. She finds it distasteful.

'Think you can help out?'

'Well, Karen, St David's does run a drop-in three days a week, though it's not only for psychiatric survivors. We take whoever comes, and these days that includes a whole range of people, some of them with multiple disabilities . . .'

'But some of them are psychs, right?'

'Yes, a good proportion . . .'

'Some of those must have horrific stories?'

'I guess so. But you understand that we can't share any information without consent of . . .'

'Look, total confidence. We'll distort their faces, change their voices, that sort of thing. And we do pay rather generously. We just want to tell their stories so that the public can see what's happening out there. We're on their side, absolutely.'

'How soon do you want these people?'

'Yesterday. But our schedule is stuffed anyway. So if you could give me some names by tomorrow morning, that would be marvellous. Can do?'

'I'll do my best. Now presumably you'll want some

background about the drop-in . . .'

'I don't think that'll be necessary just now, Kieran. If you can just come through with the names and give me a bell when you've got them, that would be marvellous. Anything else we need we'll pick up as we go along. OK? Well, thanks for your help — you're doing a great job here and we're right behind you. We've got a programme on food banks in the can at the moment.'

'Well, actually, we don't have . . .'

'Excuse me if I dash. Busy morning this morning. Thanks very much, and I'll look forward to hearing from you, shall we say by ten tomorrow? Don't bother getting up, I'll let myself out. Nice meeting you, we'll be in touch. Bye.'

That little figurine on the cross is oppressive. Quite gruesome really. *All this religious hocus-pocus gives me the shits.*

Kevin picks up the book *Gospel and Media* and places it back on the shelf.

One pile is growing at the expense of the other. It's one of her favourite jobs these days, though she hated it when she was younger. But very satisfying now. The whoosh of the steam, the smell of starch, the weight of the iron. And most of all, making everything smooth. Taking out the creases that shouldn't be there and creating fresh, sharp, clean ones where they should.

It's a ritual, a domestic ceremony to lay the ghosts. Every stroke is practised and competent. Today it isn't working as it should.

The dream lingers like a hangover. She doesn't need to close her eyes to see it. A field of wheat, stretching off white in every direction. It's flowing in waves as the wind broods across it. She is naked, somehow floating on top of it. Even though it's the middle of the day, the moon is shining, four times its normal size. She is ebbing and flowing with the waves, feeling the pull of the moon.

Panic. The sense of slipping below the surface, not able to keep afloat. She calls out, screaming for help. But no sound is coming from her throat. Desperation.

But then the sound of hooves. Growing closer, ever closer. The most beautiful white horse galloping towards her. Only it's not a horse, it's a unicorn. And the face of the unicorn is brown and strangely human, and those great lion eyes are caressing her. Magnificent strength and purity and . . .

She cannot allow herself to follow it any further. Already she is moist between her legs, humiliated by her own body. She irons vigorously, pressing out the memories and making the fabric smooth.

In his night watch Arthur is seeing things. He sees the city of Auckland spread out before him like a blanket. Everywhere the roads are jammed as people stream towards the centre. All of them are weary and ragged. They head towards Ponsonby, drawn by the sound of the voice. There, from the balcony of the post office, Arthur is calling to them. His voice is the voice of God, speaking in words that none of them knows, but all of them understand.

He raises a hand and the Waitakeres burst into song. The other hand, and Rangitoto is singing descant. One Tree Hill sulking.

'Have no fear. I am with you, and the time has come.'

'Arthur,' a voice is calling from the bed next to his. 'Go to bloody sleep.'

'Sorry, Pete.'

In a villa with polished floors, Kevin is contemplating the ceiling. He hates waking in the night. His wife is snuffling beside him, gloriously untroubled.

Something is happening at some subterranean level. He has no idea what. *What did I eat tonight?*

Wind and the Holy Spirit have common indicators.

But the voice continues to echo.

This is my beloved son. Listen to him.

Outside his window, Ponsonby is humming an old spiritual.

Arthur has created another beautiful morning. He brushes it through his hair, rejoicing. The heavy fragrance of summer is a little overdone. Like an ageing whore. Perhaps less tomorrow.

He's making a gap in the traffic so that he can cross the road; fording the river. You have to brace yourself against the current.He's hauling himself up onto the far bank, where Point Erin Reserve lies open before him. A tui is dripping gold from a tree branch. Arthur stops to listen, and the ancient pohutukawa bursts into flower. How could it not?

Across the way the public toilets squat. They have a lobby, currently occupied by Norm. Norm is sometimes an alcoholic, and always an evangelist. This morning he's lying in bed, reading his Bible. His bed is functional; a thin mattress with a plastic sheet and newspapers for a blanket.

Norm's a special friend of Arthur's. Arthur brings him food and money.

'Kia ora, e hoa.'

'Arthur, me old mate. How are you on this wonderful morning?'

'Full of life, Norm, full of life. Had a good breakfast?'

A flick of the eyebrows at the empty miniature beside the pillow.

'Fire in the hole, Arthur.'

'What you reading, man?'

'I'm reading from the prophet Joel. It's good stuff.'

'Read me some.'

'OK, you'll like this bit. "And it shall come to pass afterward, that I will pour out my spirit on all flesh; your sons and your daughters shall prophesy, your old men shall dream dreams, and your young men shall see visions. Even upon the menservants and maidservants in those days, I will pour out my spirit."'

'What's that — menservants and maidservants?'

'Hell, I don't know, Arthur; poor people like us, I suppose.'

'OK — read some more.'

'"And I will give portents in the heavens and on the earth, blood and fire and columns of smoke. The sun shall be turned to darkness, and the moon to blood, before the great and terrible day of the Lord comes. And it shall come to pass that all who call upon the name of the Lord shall be delivered; for in Mount Zion and in Jerusalem there shall be those who escape, as the Lord has said, and among the survivors shall be those whom the Lord calls."'

'Nothing about Ponsonby?'

'Not a sausage.'

'Or the second son of God?'

'I've told you before, my friend, there's nothing in here about that.'

'I don't understand that Bible. It's right about most stuff, but it leaves a whole lot out.'

'It's an old book.'

'True enough, Norm. But I can't write.'

'You sure about all this? I mean what's going to happen and all that?'

'I've seen it. I wouldn't have seen it if it wasn't going to happen.'

'Fair enough. Only I saw a passage in Genesis yesterday which I thought you might be interested in. Let's see if I can find it now — yeah, here it is. "When men began to multiply on the face of the ground, and daughters were born to them, the sons of God saw that the daughters of men were fair; and they took to wife such of them as they chose."'

'I've found her, Norm. It's all started. Next thing will be the child.'

'You must have got to know her pretty quick.'

'I've always known her; I had to wait till the right time to find her.'

The sun is shining on the two men at the entrance to the lavatories. A Herne Bay matron notices and guzzles on her disgust.

Shopping is the excuse she makes. So much better in Ponsonby. *I saw a candleholder that would be perfect for the dining room.*

Is it all right if I take the card, Brian? I won't spend much.

That's why she's coming off the motorway and drifting down through Freemans Bay. Past the Noddytown houses. Ascending the hill, as pilgrims

42

are wont to do. Attaining at last the rollicking ridge, the churning cappuccino channel.

She takes off her sunglasses and unclips her hair. The wind lifts it; she enjoys its nuzzling at her neck. Brian likes her hair down, which is why she normally leaves it up.

Now what am I looking for?

The trouble is that in some secret place she knows the answer.

The angels have rearranged their schedule. Eternity has its perks. They have a sense that this is where the action is going to be.

He's taking a coffee break. Getting out of the office means the phone doesn't ring. The coffee shop being right across the road from the church makes it hard to resist. He chooses a seat outside, near the procession. What's a show without an audience?

He's thinking about Karen whatshername. In a most unvicarly way. Particularly the crossing of the legs. *Well, God, you gave me an imagination.*

One angel whispers in the other's ear, and both laugh.

The more immediate problem, of course, is her bloody TV programme. Where to find a few psychs for opinion fodder?

John is walking down the street, touching things as he goes past. He is repeating a silent litany.

I love you, lamppost. I love you, rubbish tin. I love you, shop front. I love you, tree.

Everything he touches lights up and glows, but only the angels and John can see.

Kevin's watching one of the nutters from the drop-in doing his rounds. He considers John as a candidate, then remembers that he doesn't speak. *What I need is someone with a story.*

How about the guy that came to see me yesterday . . . what was his name? Arthur. That's it. He owes me. But how to get in touch with him?

There's a queue in the bank. Arthur doesn't mind. He's used to queues from the hospital — lining up to get pills so they can drug God out of you.

He is calling down a blessing on the people around him, and asking that their eyes may be opened. So that they might know who it is who is among them.

A frail woman in front of him sighs. She has very white hair. She's clutching her bankbook as if it were a passport.

'I'm glad I made my will before I came. I'll probably die before I get to the counter at this rate.'

'Are you getting your benefit too?'

'Benefit? No, I'm on the pension. I've got to line up for the miserable few dollars this bloody government has deigned to give me. Bunch of thieving crooks they are.'

'I've never met them. Where's your family?'

'Family! They don't want to bloody know me. All too busy buying things for their fancy houses. I'm lucky if I get a phone call Christmas and Easter. My husband upped and died on me five years back, so I'm on my own now.'

Arthur is seeing a picture of two chooks shut in a small cage together, pecking each other to death.

'Do you miss him?'

'Now and again.'

She's thinking of the double bed, and how big it seems.

'What will you say when you see him again?'

'Oh, I've got no time for all that nonsense. If I see him again I'll probably ask why he didn't insure himself so I didn't have to line up for the bloody pension, that's what.'

'You will see him, I can tell you that.'

'Can you now? What makes you so sure of yourself then?'

'I'm the second son of God. I've seen things that I know.'

'Yeah, and I'm the Virgin bloody Mary. You want to get a hold of yourself, lad; stop talking all that rubbish. It'll do you no good.'

Arthur feels the tears brimming in his eyes, and turns his head away so that she won't see.

His day is making itself felt as he comes out of the bank. Heat booming from the pavement. Great washes of frangipani sweetening the air. The lid is off the sky, all the way.

If only they knew, if only they saw, if only they heard.

'Arthur!'

From across the street. The man from the church, with his angels.

Arthur's wading his way through the traffic again, reaching into his pocket for the new banknotes. He's peeled off a $20 note by the time he reaches the café table.

'No, no. There's no hurry for the money, Arthur. Have a seat. You know, I was just sitting here thinking about how I could get hold of you.'

'Before you ask, my father has heard.'

'Pardon? Oh yes, quite. Look, Arthur, you know you were wanting me to, ah, spread the news about you the other day? Well, I've got a little proposition you might be interested in.'

'You're going to speak to your church?'

'Better than that. I've got this woman who wants to interview you on television. I need to know today if you'd be interested.'

'On TV? Would this be right across the country, sort of thing?'

'Absolutely.'

The same shocked look is on the face of the angels, though for different reasons. Arthur, with the joy surfing his synapses, is reaching across to hug the man. Kevin is discovering that there's no way to be discreet when a rough giant embraces you on the street.

'Karen, ah . . . Bligh-Farnsworth, please. Thank you.'

'Karen, I've got someone for you to talk to; a man who lives in a local boarding house. His name's Arthur.'

'Yes, just the one I'm afraid. But I'm sure he'll be able to put you on to some of his friends.'

'Well, I think so, yes. He's been in and out of psychiatric hospitals for years, and now he's out on the street — well, in the boarding house actually. But it's a terrible hovel, more than twenty men crowded into very unsanitary conditions.'

'Suicide? I don't know. You'd have to ask him.'

'Yes, quite tragic. I'm sure your programme will help to open the eyes of the community.'

'Thank you. The name's Kevin, actually. That's all right. Now he'd like me to be there to introduce him, as it were.'

'Yes, that's fine with me. I'll look forward to seeing you.'

It's as well that only the angels can see the images flashing through the vicar's mind as he hangs up. They might be shocked if they lived up to angelic stereotyping. Instead the one without breasts is getting that hot and heavy look in his eye, and the other is smiling.

Margaret is trying to get a grip on herself. *This is entirely ridiculous.* But today the retail therapy isn't quite hitting the spot.

I don't even know his name. He's a psychiatric patient, he's Maori, he's untidy and probably smelly. I've never even spoken to him.

She's shopping with a passion. Turning things over, pushing and prodding at them, peering at the price as if it were in a foreign language. She welcomes the attention of shop assistants, toying with them, leading them on before deciding not to purchase. Delayed consummation brings greater pleasure. She sucks at the edge of the plastic card while pondering; it's like scraping your nails down the board.

Outside the urban symphony is into its second movement. A flatulent bus is playing bass to the massed motor vehicles. Plainsong of voice ebbs and flows, the occasional contralto shriek lifting above it. There's a humming of something — a waiata? And the inevitable sirens hemming the borders.

Arthur conducts it with his fingers as he walks along. Mostly it follows his lead.

This is my appointed hour. Stand and watch my will unfold.

There they are. Face to face on the footpath. The

music has gone into remission. All heaven is watching on the big screen. A small aeon stretches itself in the interim.

'Hello — I'm sorry, I don't know your name. You gave me that note the other day. Remember?'

'I'm Arthur. And you're the Queen of Heaven.'

'No, Margaret actually. I'm just over in Ponsonby doing some shopping. Hello, Arthur. I haven't bought anything yet. It's very busy, isn't it?'

She's babbling like the neurotic she's scared of becoming. But his great brown eyes are huge and bottomless, and she can't feel anything under her feet.

'I have much that I have to speak to you about. My father has brought you to me.'

'Your father? Does he live locally? My father's in a rest home. Quite sad. We visit him on Sundays of course, and it's a very nice place . . .'

'Don't be afraid, Margaret. Did you see the moon?'

'The moon? Sorry, I'm not quite with you — the moon? No, well, I'm not sure what you're talking about. I did have a dream . . .'

Now she's blushing over her whole body, remembering the dream with him standing there. She feels like crying but his voice is soft brown sugar. Everything below her mind is basking in a soothing white light.

'Let's go somewhere we can talk. There's a little

park just a few streets down . . .'

She's allowing herself to be led away by this strange man to a park. And it's the most natural thing in all the world.

The small patch of green is tacked on to the city skyline. The great religious turrets of commerce suffer no competitors. Arthur knows there'll be no-one else there. They sit on a park bench, spectators to the brash bronze towers. The trees huddle around them.

'Arthur, to be perfectly frank with you, I've no idea what I'm doing here. I hope you don't think . . .'

'Do you like the day?'

'What — you mean the weather?'

'No, the day. The whole of it.'

'Yes, it's perfect. Except that I'm a little flustered at the moment . . .'

'I made it for you.'

'Pardon?'

'I made it for you; the day.'

'Oh my goodness, this is ridiculous. I'm not in the best space I've ever been in, and you're obviously not one hundred per cent either. I think I'd better leave.'

Arthur is raking her soul with his eyes. Some people learn to read books. Others find their knowledge elsewhere.

'When you were young, you wondered if there

was a God. Your parents couldn't help, your friends weren't interested, but you wanted to know. So you made a little test. You wrote a letter to God, asking him to send you someone special to tell you the truth. You waited and waited, but no-one ever came. So you gave up on God.'

'I . . . How could you possibly know that?'

'You just had to wait a bit longer than you thought, Margaret. God always turns up three days too late.'

There's a ripple of laughter rolling through heaven at the old joke.

'I've been looking for you for a long time. You might find this difficult to believe, but I'm the second son of God. One of the reasons I'm here is for you.'

'But Arthur, you're . . .'

She's too polite to finish.

'A psychiatric patient? Yeah, you're right. I see things. Other people don't see them. I try to point out to people what they're missing. For that I got locked up. Four years in Oakley. Another three in Carrington. I have a lot of pills I'm supposed to take. But they stop me seeing what I want to see.'

There's a sadness as old as the hills, as deep as an ocean. She succumbs to it, feels herself sinking. She reaches out a hand and discovers that it's found Arthur's.

At the touch there is a tearing and a shifting in the depths. Liquid lava rolls into caverns. Huge black seas boil and hiss. A land mass heaves itself into existence. The archangel Michael stands a round of drinks. In truth it was his end of a wager.

'So what is it you want from me?'

'I can't tell you that yet. Some other things have to happen. Why don't you tell me a little about yourself?'

Someone has undone the latch on the wardrobe and it all begins to tumble out in a heap. There's no shame in it, that's the strange thing. As if you were sharing secrets with the person who slept in the same room as you. Much of this hasn't seen the light of day for a long time. But the brown eyes shine with aroha and something more; and all is well, and all is well.

The two cold sausages left by Arthur make a good breakfast. The white congealed fat lines the stomach. Norm's washing them down with a hit from the bottle.

He's reading the Bible. He loves the stories and the punch lines, especially the way the good religious people keep getting tipped on their arses. The stuff about the end of the world is fascinating. He doesn't mourn for the passing of this one.

Propped up against the toilet wall, renewed by the sun, Norm is content.

A young lad with creases ironed into his jeans is approaching. He has the designer casual look of a

North Shore boy. Judge not that you be not judged, Norm is reminding himself.

'Excuse me, sir, can I have a word with you?'

'I think I can fit you in before my next appointment, lad. Take a pew.'

This teenager's skin is unblemished. He's keen to get on with his spiel, before he loses his nerve and wets his Levi 901s.

'My name's Andrew. I'm with a team of people moving through this area to speak to people about the purpose of life.'

'Norm. Good to meet you, son.'

The well-travelled hand held out to the boy causes consternation. This is not in the script. He handles it like a packet of three-day-old fish.

'Norm, I'm wondering if you've given much thought to your eternal destiny?'

'Well, it's funny you should say that — I was just reading something about that when you turned up.'

Andrew is hearing the voice of his instructor. *Your conversation is on the railroad to salvation. Whatever happens, don't let it become sidetracked.*

'The Bible tells us that all have sinned and fall short of the glory of God. Do you believe that, Norm?'

'Romans 3:23 if I'm not mistaken. Do I believe that I'm a sinner? Well, I wake up most mornings surrounded by empty bottles. They're my witnesses. Every day they line up and say to me, "Norm, no matter how much you con yourself or others, you're an alkie arsehole." But then there's another voice I hear as well. You know what that says?'

'Could we put that question to one side and deal with it . . .?'

'Look, you asked the question, son. The other voice I hear comes from the second part of that verse you started to quote. I think it says something like *since all have sinned and fall short of the glory of God, they're put right by his grace as a gift.* I wake up and I breathe the air and I see my bottles, and then I hear this voice: "Norm, I've put you right by my grace as a gift." And then I turn to the bottles and say, "Hear that? Now piss off." And they all keep quiet.'

'Scripture says that unless you are born again, you cannot enter the kingdom of God. I'm sure you wouldn't want to miss out on the kingdom of God?'

'Depends who else is there, to tell you the truth. Like I said, I was reading something interesting about heaven when you arrived.'

The incongruity of this broken old man producing a Bible has Andrew flummoxed.

'Yeah. It's about some rich guy who lives in a bloody great mansion. Only this beggar by the name of Lazarus turns up at his gate, see? Anyway, Lazarus carks it, and gets carried straight to heaven by the angels. And the rich geezer, he dies as well; only he ends up in the fire. He figures there must have been some mistake. And being an important bloke, he kicks up merry hell about it, so to speak. He spots Lazarus up in heaven, and he wants him to come down and look after him, cool him down a bit. But he gets a funny answer. Where is it now? Yeah, that's it. "Son, remember that you in your lifetime received your good things, and Lazarus in like manner evil things; but now he is comforted here, and you are in anguish." Now what do you make of that?'

'I don't know . . . I . . . Jesus says that no man comes to the father but by me.'

'Yeah, well, Arthur would have a few things to say about that.'

'I'm sorry?'

'Never mind. Listen, Andrew, you couldn't spare us a few bob, could you?'

'Uh, no, I don't think that I should. I better be going. Nice talking to you, and I'll be praying for you.'

'Good on you, sport. I need all the help I can get.'

He's not quite running, but it's the sort of walking they do in the Olympics. Norm isn't the only one laughing.

In a city park a couple are sitting, holding hands. He's a big rough Maori man with wild hair and holed sneakers. She's a well-dressed blonde woman with classic features. She has tears on her cheeks,

55

but is calm. They're holding hands.

'This is crazy. I don't know why I'm telling you all this.'

'I'm crazy too, so it's all right.'

She's giggling despite herself.

'I have to go soon, Arthur. The children will be home. It's been so good talking to you; I feel like I've been washed on the inside. But I want to hear about you as well.'

'Give me your phone number.'

After another searching look into his eyes, she extracts a pen from her bag and scribbles on a scrap of paper.

'Go now, Margaret my Queen, and I'll tell you some more next time.'

He strokes her cheek, the gentlest of strokes. White doves explode into flight from the centre of her stomach. She stands to find that someone has wound down the gravity.

He watches her until she's out of sight. As an afterthought, he puts in an order for angels to watch over his love.

'There was a guy looking for you earlier on.'

'Yeah, who?'

'Some preacher bloke from the church. Said he was supposed to pick you up for a meeting at three o'clock. Something about a TV programme.'

'That's right — thanks, Pete. I wonder what the time is now?'

'Couldn't tell you, mate. Have a look at the clock in the kitchen.'

Arthur winds through the corridors, following the smell of boiled cabbage. *Quarter past. Not too bad. Ten minutes to walk there. Clocks are just a distraction when you've got eternity to look after. No-one appreciates that. Still, better get a move on.*

They're sitting in the manse lounge. She was ten minutes late herself. But there's been another ten gone by since then. She can't stand waiting on other people. She has an uneasy feeling that the vicar's looking up her skirt.

One of the angels is rearranging her robes. The other's sitting on the stereo unit, with a slightly brighter whiteness than usual.

'Another cup of coffee, Karen?'

'No thanks. Look, if he's not going to show, I better arrange a few other things.'

She waves the cellphone like an armed grenade.

'I'm sure he'll be here — let's give him another five minutes. How's the programme coming together so far?'

'Looking good. We've got great one-liners from the social workers, most of who'll be out of jobs when it screens. And a super interview with this naff guy from some health agency or other — by the time we edit that up he'll look like Nixon defending his honour. But we need the human face, personal anguish, something for people to relate to.'

That sounds interesting. But the only thing that's interesting him is that the black net stockings are attached to a suspender belt.

She crosses her legs the other way, and pretends to be interested in the religious books on the book shelf next to her chair. Beats me how people can write so much about all that bullshit.

Steps on the veranda presage the knocking at the door. Kevin ushers Arthur in as if he were parading a stud bull.

'Karen, this is Arthur; Arthur, Karen.'

Mutual kia ora, one having more syllables than the other. Cushions sighing.

'Now, Arthur, I'm just doing the initial research for a television programme we're producing. Kevin has told me a little about you: I understand you live in a boarding house.'

'Yeah, down Shelly Beach Road.'

'How many of you living there, Arthur?'

'Hooh, I'm not sure — twenty-five or so I'd say.'

'My God, twenty-five? How many bedrooms?'

'Six. But there's the garage out the back where old Taffy and Jim sleep.'

'Yes, good, good. So you have to share your rooms?'

'Yeah, but I've got one of the good ones, with just Pete and John.'

'It must be a depressing place to live?'

'Depressing? Nah, it's great. It's the best place I lived in for a long time. They're all good guys there. Anyhow, where do you live?'

'Excuse me?'

'Where do you live? You're asking me all this stuff and I don't know anything about you.'

'Ponsonby, but . . .'

'How many bedrooms have you got?'

'Three, but . . .'

'And how many people?'

'I'm there on my own at the moment, though . . .'

'Wooo, that must be pretty depressing, eh?'

He may just have winked at the angels.

'Not at all. Look, Arthur, do you mind if we get this back on track? I understand you came to the boarding house from hospital.'

'Yeah. They were clearing the ward out for some reason or other.'

'So you were thrown out.'

'No, I arranged it all with the social worker. She was a real hard-case woman, Gina. It was her that jacked me up with the boarding house.'

This isn't going the way that Karen hoped. She throws an accusing glare at Kevin, who responds with a practised look of concern. It's one of a repertoire.

'Tell me, Arthur, what was it like coming out of hospital? Adjusting back into the community? Did you find you'd become institutionalized?'

'I'd been waiting to get out for a long time. They drug you up in there so much that your piss would keep a pack of dogs stoned for a week. I had trouble remembering who I was.'

'You lost your cultural identity?'

'No, my godhood. Sometimes I'd go a whole week without remembering that I was the second son of God.'

'I see. Did you ever feel . . . suicidal?'

He's hanging his head at the memory. It was in the Oakley days of padded cells. He came back from ECT with a black hole in his brain. Everything was sucked into the vacuum, even his father. The stomach pump was bad, but it brought everything back. He thanked them for it afterwards.

'Once, maybe. You ever been in a psych hospital?'

'Well, only on the administrative side, I must confess. But living in the community must create problems of its own, I imagine.'

'Lady, I hear that the Jews had trouble adjusting to life outside the concentration camps. But none of them asked to go back.'

Her angle is a write-off. *But there could be another way of tackling this, by God . . .*

'Tell me some more about being the son of God.'

Arthur knows that this is the opportunity his father has created for him. He will communicate his true identity to the world, and then the drama can unfold. He's leaning forward, his face shining.

Something stirs within Kevin, and he follows the conversation more closely. Something that came to him in the night.

As soon as she closes the car door and fastens her seat belt, the whole house of cards comes tumbling down. It's very much like wakening from a dream, changing realities. She simply cannot believe what has just happened.

I gave him my phone number!

She starts to shake all over, and grips the steering wheel for support. It's a mixture of fear and anger; mostly anger. She's angry at herself.

Now she's driving down the motorway, going faster than usual. She's desperate to make the shelter of harbour before the storm hits. Ponsonby is at her heels, and all that it contains.

In point of fact Ponsonby is very mellow, taking the evening air. It scratches its back on the indigo sky and opens its legs to the world.

Digby is shouting Roslyn to a sit-down drink in a pub, playing the gentleman with what's left of his $50.

John is scrabbling through a rubbish bin on Jervois Road. Not before he's given it his blessing.

Pete is rolling a smoke for Sandy on the veranda.

'You know, Sandy,' he says, 'it's not such a bad life after all.'

Karen is shrieking with laughter, recounting her day to some media buddies at a new and trendy café.

'There was I,' she chortles, 'with a randy priest on one side and the son of God on the other! How divine.'

The two angels are writing a report. There's the odd bit they leave out.

Kevin is shouting at his youngest son to stop speaking with his mouth full. He isn't feeling very good about himself.

Arthur is walking back down the hill towards the boarding house, singing. It's perhaps the best day he's ever created. He celebrates by hanging out the evening star early.

Norm is very nicely done. He bends his legs and lets rip a juicy fart, inhaling its rich alcoholic vapours. Life has its simple pleasures.

The buttocks in Howick are clenched.

3

The radio's simpering and bitching over some civic outrage. There's nobody here who gives a shit. She turns it off.

In her harbour the water's calm, but the skies are moody. The children are keeping their distance, suckling up to the technical tit, eager for the lotus. Even the cat's watching her warily.

I can do this. I can hold on to my sanity. I can put him out of my mind and he will cease to exist. My husband's name is Brian. He is a moderately successful banker. He loves me as much as he knows how to. Mark and Stephanie are my children. They are beautiful, everyone tells me. I look after them. I am their mother. I am lucky. I am very lucky. If I feel empty it's because . . .

No. Fold in the beaten egg white. Fold, don't beat. Slowly and calmly. I can do this.

Not once has the telephone returned her interest.

The manager of the boarding house is Bob. He's young for the job; lean, fit, blond-bearded — a failed hippie. He loves the old buggers, in a funny sort of

63

way. No bullshit, though. *I'm here to make a living, not play their fairy bloody godmother.*

Bob's pissed off. The TV crew have just blown the fuses for the second time with their lights. The television in the lounge has died, and now he's got seven grumpy men muttering and stomping about.

'Look, the wiring's pretty rooted, eh. Run an extension off the stove in the kitchen and you should be right.'

Fair go; ya'd think these technical jokers would have the odd brain between them. I dunno why I agreed to let them in in the first place. Five minutes of fame. Bloody Arthur, mad as a meataxe. What the hell do they want with him, anyway? He'll be in his element, right enough.

The reporter's a bit of orright, though. Karen how's-yer-father. Wouldn't mind a penetrating interview with her. Not that she's shown any signs of interest. Probably a lesby leg-licker. Here she is now.

'Bob, isn't it? OK if I ask you a few background questions? Seeing I'm here? Good. How long have you been running this place?'

'Yeah, well, it must be round seven years now. 'Course me old man had it before then. He got into it in the fifties. We used to live upstairs, the family that is. I came back from overseas when the old boy shuffled on, and I just sort of took over running the show.'

'And most of the men you've got here are ex-psychiatric patients?'

'Well, there's a bit of a mix really. They're all bloody bonkers in one way or another, not too good at looking after themselves. Used to be mostly alkies in the old days, but since they started turfing people out of the psych wards we've picked up a fair few of them.'

'And you make your living from these people?'

'Yeah, that's all I do for a crust. There's not a helluva lot in it after you pay yer overheads and bad debts, but I get by. Why's that camera on me? You never said anything about filming.'

'It just helps me to remember what you've said afterwards. Excuse me for saying it, but the conditions here are not that wonderful.'

'The old guys like it that way — it's sort of comfortable, ya know? Ya can't run something like this as if it was a hotel, for Christ's sake. They're forever pissing their beds or throwing up in the dining room. I'd like to do the place up a bit, but I've got no money for it. I look after the old buggers, though. I don't chuck them out if they miss a few weeks' board, not like some places. Two or three of them are still here from my father's time. I grew up with them.'

'Some of these men are sleeping four to a bedroom.'

'It's company. Most of them are used to being in

wards of one sort or another. I've got to make a living, don't I? The more guys we've got in, the better the operation runs, the better they eat.'

Sanctimonious bitch that she is. Already got me pegged as a money-grubbing bastard. Like to see her scrubbing the dried-up shit off someone's hairy arse. That'd put a wrinkle in her perfect bloody complexion.

I could have done a degree in anything I wanted. Mathematics, law, marketing even. Anything except this piss-useless theology.

Kevin's reading the Situations Vacant. It's a form of sulking with God. Not that it makes any difference. This afternoon at 3.00 people will arrive at the church and expect him to say something, make sense of the ugly ditch of death.

They'll be sitting there and the bloody awful music will stop. And I'll look at their faces. I'll see the fear, and it'll be like looking in the mirror. The words will all be there in front of me, the scripture verses. In my father's house there are many mansions. But next to me, mocking every platitude, the mahogany box. In my father's house there are many coffins. Enough for one each. Just the right size, with a choice of handles.

So we'll agree to get it out of the way as quickly as possible. Give it back to the smiling undertaker from whom it came. Burn it, bury it, drop it in the sea. Just get rid of it. So that we can cleanse ourselves with sausage

rolls and small talk, smother ourselves in the comforting
ordinariness of life. Purge the black bitch who's lifted her
skirt in our faces.

My job is to make it all flow smoothly. To oil the
conveyor belt for its path to the furnace. To comfort the
afflicted without afflicting the comfortable. To be calm
and confident and reasonable, even a little humorous.
Not to shout or groan or beat on the lid of the coffin.

The maître d' of the mysteries of death. I don't want
the job. Every word of faith made false in the speaking.
Better to keep silent. Better to dig ditches than try to
cover them. Better to do anything but this.

Arthur is in the centre, with the white lights burning. It is as he has always known it will be, the world watching and waiting. Beyond the world there are other spectators he cannot speak of.

Karen has finished arranging herself. The all-seeing eye is awake.

'Arthur, why were you committed to a psychiatric institution?'

'Because I started telling people who I was.'

'And who is that?'

'The second son of Almighty God. I am the one who is to come, the . . .'

'How long ago did you first go to a mental hospital?'

'Years ago now. I was in Oakley first of all, 'cos I punched this guy when he put a needle in my arm.

So they put me in M3. Then after about five years they shifted me over to Carrington, Ward 5. You get a much better class of patient there.'

'You still believe yourself to be the son of God?'

'The second son of God. I'm not trying to replace Jesus. But he had his job to do, and I've got my job to do. My father has sent me to bring a message to the world.'

'What message?'

'That the time is up. The world is going to end. Everything you see here will be gone. My job is to round up the ones who are ready to listen, look after them. And a few other things that I'm not allowed to talk about.'

Karen can't prevent a minor smirk. This is just the sort of crap she's hoping for. Show people what sort of nutter is out there on the street in the name of community care.

'So we're all under threat from the end of the world?'

'Everyone will be sifted and shaken. Even people like you: rich people, old people, children — you'll be glad you had an abortion.'

The smirk is snap-frozen.

'I beg your pardon?'

'I said you'll be glad you had an abortion, 'cos you wouldn't want your kid . . .'

'What's going on here? Stop the fucking camera!

68

What do you know about me, you loony bastard? My private life has nothing to do with you. How did you . . .? Have you been snooping around, you bloody sicko? Christ, no wonder they locked you up! Donny, get him out of here!'

'Ah, it's his place, Karen.'

'Well, get me out of here then. Stop bloody staring. If I hear a word of this outside of here you'll all be down the road so fast you won't know what's hit you. Now pack up and let's go.'

Around Arthur everything is spinning. Something has happened, but he can't quite get hold of what it is. *Was it something I said?*

Pete's laughing fit to bust. He never knew TV could be so entertaining. He's gone out on to the veranda to try to stop, but he can't.

Karen walks the length of the drive with his laughter chasing her. You'd think it was the devil up her bum.

Bob comes up beside Pete, puts an arm round his shoulder, shares the laughter.

'Good bloody riddance, eh? Smart-arsed bitch. Here, look out, yer spilling my cup of tea, ya stupid old bastard. Have to give ya an extra pill tonight or we'll never get ya to sleep.'

But his eyes are almost tender.

The old house is sighing and wheezing, joining in the mood. The floorboards have an extra spring in them. There's a light in the place that wasn't there before.

On a high branch of the young kauri tree out the front a bird is singing opera.

In the lounge the fuse blows again for no good reason and the television pops into silence.

'What the fuck,' says Bob, 'let's have something good to eat tonight.'

Arthur sucks on his failure. There it was, the big chance, and it all went wrong. There's a heaviness on him, like the weight of a wet jacket.

How can I make them listen? You ask too much of me, father.

I ask nothing but your love and availability.

Bollocks.

I love you, car. I love you, meter. I love you, rubbish bin . . .

John stops rigid, starts scratching behind his ear.

Over by the shop door a young girl, four maybe, in a sun frock. She hauls at its side seams, then lifts it up altogether so that she can straighten her knickers properly.

He feels the swelling in his pants, helpless to stop it. A thin, high-pitched squeal comes from the back

of his throat, like the sound of a Zip boiling. He
starts banging his head with his hand. He turns,
hurries away. There are tears on his cheeks. He
touches nothing.

'Mummy, a funny man was looking at me.'

After waiting so long, the ringing of the phone
frightens her when it comes. Her ears are ringing
with adrenaline.

'Hello? Oh . . . Penny. No, of course I'm not dis-
appointed. No-one; don't be silly.'

'Nothing much — getting tea organized. How
about you?'

'Good on you — I love lavender. We're thinking
of putting some around the side, next to the steps.'

'Oh, he's fine, busy as usual. He's hoping to go up a
grade in the salary round next month, so he's working
a lot of extra hours.'

'Yes, that'd be lovely. How about you come out
here, just for a change?'

'No, I just don't want to go to Ponsonby at the
moment.'

'Great. Make it around twelve-thirty, and we can
eat out on the deck. Bye.'

Why does she stare off into the distance after
hanging up the phone? There's nothing to be seen
there.

The walking lifts his spirits. Out with the people and the sun, the sweet warm breeze of summer. Arthur's heart expands to take in all that he has made.

Skywash of cerulean blue. Creamy white buildings glowing in reflected glory. The seats on the pavement. A busker ladling music over the street.

The people. He tangata, he tangata, he tangata. Faces forged in the fires of life, each full of stories and sufferings. Each one with a hungry heart lurking in the forgotten depths.

Arthur would hold them all, comfort them, stroke their hair, sing softly till they slept and dreamt. He would love them and forgive them and cherish them. If they would have him. If they would receive him as the son of God.

He sits on the low wall on the corner, where the Gluepot once stood. He likes to sit there on the edge of the great waterfall, listening to the rush of traffic falling down College Hill. He looks across to the city towers. Not a stone will be left standing in that terribly silent dawn.

One door was already locked, and he was about to bolt the other when he noticed her still sitting in a pew.

The agony was over. The singing and the praying and the grieving. 'Thank you, vicar, a lovely service.' 'You made a good job of that, young man.' 'He would

72

have liked what you had to say, vicar.' 'I appreciate your prayers.' His face muscles are aching.

So why is this behatted old woman still sitting in the church?

'Do you think you'll be much longer? Only I was just starting to lock up . . .'

'Sit down, young man. I want to talk to you and I don't want to get a crick in my neck while I'm doing it. That's better. Now, there's some things we need to sort out. You don't know me and I don't know you, but I did know Tom. A lot better than you did and a good deal more than his late wife would have appreciated.

'Now don't look at me like that; I haven't come here for confession. The good Lord understands love and the mistakes it leads to. I made my peace with God a long time before you were born.

'No, don't say anything — you had your chance at speaking up there, and now it's my turn. In fact that's what I want to talk to you about. You were being cynical when you addressed us. Oh, you can look as wounded as you like, but you know it's true.

'I'm a stupid old woman with more dead friends than live ones, but I can spot insincerity when I see it. Now I don't think you're a fraud or I wouldn't be sitting here talking to you. So I can only imagine that you're having some crisis of faith, or whatever the fashionable term is for it these days.

'You're not really convinced that there's anything on the other side of death, are you? That's why you were so supercilious today. There's two things I want to do for you. The first is to tell you that you're wrong.

'Do you think that was Tom that went off in that casket? Wild, funny, dear Tom? The man I loved, do you think he can come to an end as easily as that, like switching off a light? That was his body, all right, and parts of it I'll miss dearly, but it wasn't *him*, for goodness' sake. You're right to be frightened by death, but recognize it for what it is, boy.

'And now the second thing I want to do is pray for you. So kneel down. Go on, don't look so offended.'

The little woman is standing over him, with her hand on his shoulder, praying. And light is bucketing down from above, filling him, flooding him, pouring down the aisles.

Two angels are diving in and out of it like dolphins. They just knew this assignment was going to be good.

The nameless woman stops abruptly and leaves, closing the door gently behind her.

There, in the church, is a man weeping.

Brian has a rare break for a cup of tea. He sits at his desk while drinking it, surveying his little kingdom at the bank. If things work out well he may go a few steps further up the ladder. They remember his name now, and he knows he's being watched.

The dull ache in his back reminds him of last night. Margaret was at him like never before. Midweek sex is rare enough, and nothing like that for a hell of a lot of years. He was astonished, gave way before the juggernaut of passion. Finished up exhausted, ravished. Frightened, if the truth be told. And then she turned over without a word.

Is something up with her? I should take her out for dinner one of these days, get a baby-sitter in. Once this promotion round's over. Maybe we can celebrate.

It has a strange barrenness, this small cul-de-sac in the eastern suburbs. No power or telephone lines to be seen. Perfect lawns with straight edges. Mock tile roofs. Shrubs. Penny decides not to park up the drive. Perhaps the car drips oil, and then where would we be?

She notices the superb regularity of the mortar between the bricks — you could almost mistake it for veneer. And the aluminium windows. So much less maintenance. So much less charm. Even the doorbell is one which plays an electronic tune. And the door can hardly open for the depth of the carpet.

They make their way out onto the deck, which mercifully has no view. The food is prepared, arranged, delicious. It isn't until coffee and cheese that Margaret will be drawn beyond superficiality.

'How are you doing, Marg? I mean underneath all of this?'

She's silent for some time. Successive emotions are trying themselves for size. None of them is sufficient.

Penny reaches across the table and holds her hand. The touch recalls that other holding of hands in a park in another country, and the tears come.

She tells the story of another person, her strange encounter with a man she doesn't know. As she hears it once removed, she knows it's the story of a madwoman, that the thin ice of sanity has already cracked and fallen beneath her.

This other woman who has always been there is holding her shoulders, kissing her forehead. Then stroking her hair, kissing her lips. The fondling is so familiar, the old pathways never closed even while neglected. Margaret would have received her, welcomed her to the soft centre, but Penny would not.

It might have been an hour later when she awoke on the couch where Penny had laid her, stroking her hand until she slept. They talked then of the options, quietly and calmly. Penny's great sensible peace descended over them.

As Margaret is watching her go, the waves are less threatening than they were. But there's sure as hell a breach in the sea wall.

She wants to wash her hands of the whole project. 'Dump it, it's a load of shit.' But the producer insists on re-editing it as a news item.

'Be reasonable, Karen, the story's still there. We'll run it tomorrow night. What the hell's got you so rattled?'

She's experiencing a panache deficiency. For the first time for years, she wants a smoke. *How could he possibly know? It was a lifetime ago, done in Australia. A week's holiday. Not even the father knew, slimy little bastard that he was. I've forgotten it, put it behind me. It was just a clinical procedure, that's all. My decision.*

The paper she was holding in her hands has somehow been torn into little pieces. She's not even sure what it was.

He's singing as he comes in the door. Unusual. Especially after a funeral. She's eyeing him suspiciously, the spousal Geiger counter. There's a strange light about him. Extra warmth in his kiss. *He needn't think it'll lead to anything.*

'I take it the service went well then?'

'No, it was bloody awful actually.'

She was right, that tough old chook of a woman. He'd been posturing and posing, playing the religious game. Needed a boot up the bum. And he'd got it, thanks to her and God.

A cloud crosses the sun, perhaps. Whatever the cause, a shadow falls across Ponsonby. Arthur notices it, shudders.

In a park, John is shuffling along, almost running. He's seeing terrible things, playing the forbidden memory tapes.

There's a demon nipping at his heels.

Arthur rings the bell. A bald man, still distracted by 25 across, emerges from the back room. His eyes narrow and his brow creases at the sight of this prospective customer.

'How can I help you, sport?'

'Ah, this is a motel, isn't it?'

'Well, it's not a convent, mate. What can I do for you?'

'I was wondering, ah, what it would cost to stay here for one night?'

'Eighty bucks the night, this time of the year.'

'Yeah? Just for one night?'

'Standard rates. Plus another twenty-five for each extra adult, twelve for kids under thirteen.'

'Hooo. That much, eh? How long do I get to stay for all that?'

'In from noon on, out by eleven the next morning. You want to book?'

'No, no, I'm just finding out the cost. So I can save up for it. I don't suppose you do any discounts?'

'Discounts? For what?'

'Religious groups, that sort of thing.'

'Nah, charge them extra, mate, if it was up to me. Here, you want to take our card. I'll write the room rate on the back. Give us a ring; you'll need to book.'

Strange joker, that one, he's thinking. *Doubt we'll see him again. Why couldn't I be running a motel in the Bay of Islands?*

'Too many Maoris,' says Arthur, closing the door, smiling.

There's thunder in the streets on this late evening. Not from the sky, but from deep in the ground. It's a slow rumble.

A mongrel dog pricks up its ears, sniffs the breeze, whimpers. The traffic snarls up Ponsonby Road. The sky hangs, not doing one thing or the other. A child is tossing and turning in bed.

The old villas hang their heads, dwell on memories of Irishmen beating their wives, with the blood running down the walls.

The air prickles.

Roast lamb. Well, it's mutton actually, but there are roast potatoes and peas and gravy. You'd think it was Christmas again. Bob is presiding, carving the meat.

'C'mon, Arthur, you better take the first helping. Yer the star of the bloody show, after all.'

Like feeding time at the zoo. Old Wal has a silver strand of saliva hanging from his bottom lip. Taffy's rubbing his hands, rubbing his hands. No-one's talking. You might miss something, the food might run out, anything could happen. No medical procedure was ever watched as closely as the slicing of this roast.

'Keep yer mitts off, Sandy, there's plenty to go round. Bill, get yer hand outta yer pants, ya filthy old prick. Now there's two beers each and that's it, orright? I catch anyone rifling the fridge and they're dead meat. For God's sake, Pete, the gravy's going all over the fucken table!'

They're all happy, belching and farting and dropping scraps of food all over the place. A couple of the men are missing, but that's not unusual. Probably sleeping upstairs.

'Well, Arthur, me old mate, yer going to be a TV hero. I rung them up this avvo and it's gonna be on the news tomorrer night. What d'ya think of that?'

'No good, Bob. I never got the chance to say what I wanted to.'

'Never mind, mate. That's showbiz. Ya stuck a flea up that bimbo's fanny anyway. She won't forget ya for a while.'

Arthur is tuning out. There is trouble in some distant galaxy. He is combing the universe, searching for the source of it. The unbearable sensitivity of godhood.

He walks through the lamp-laced street corridors, making his way back to the church. He leaves behind a bemused wife, idly eating peanuts. She's washed in different colours by the flickering screen.

Prayer isn't something he indulges in, by and large. Tonight he's hungry for it. *Is it possible to have a prayer habit? What sort of group would I have to join to get off it?*

Ahead of him the angels are swooping on. Turning to look back like impatient children. They're calling to him, urgent and anxious.

The church is benignly empty when he arrives. He doesn't turn on any lights. The street lights make an ethereal atmosphere. Peace hangs in the air like incense. Walls soaked and dripping with the meditations of the generations. Did he decide to kneel at the front, or did it just happen? Some gravitational whirlpool perhaps.

Here he is now. A poor, insignificant man at the junction of two worlds.

The side gate was unlocked. John is creeping down the side of the house, silent as a shroud. He is careful to watch where he puts his feet. Every few steps he stops, turns, scratches his head. His eyes are wide with terror.

Past the bathroom window he is sneaking. His breathing is ragged. He is licking his lips.

He knows before he looks that this is the child's room. An instinct for it. He is bobbing his head up above the window sill and peering in.

A small blonde head protrudes from the quilt. Soft innocence, like a child in a manger. A boy or a girl? Impossible to tell.

John's heart is beating wildly, no rhythm to it at all. His loins are hot and hard and painful.

The double-hung window is open a little at the bottom. To let the air in.

He is poised there, looking.

In the church Kevin is wrestling with a great darkness which has come upon him. A chill blade has slid up into his heart.

He is aware of an awful panic and terror some-where. Sweat breaks out on his top lip. His prayer has no words. It is all effort. Like trying to lift a great weight which is too heavy for him. It keeps falling back.

John has touched the window with his fingertips. He is in two places at once. He is doing it, and he is watching himself doing it. He wants to scream, to cry out. He is so very very scared.

Kevin wails with a terrible groan. He cannot hold it. The dark weight is slipping, crushing. The angels are holding each other, waiting.

In his bed Arthur lurches into consciousness. He has been dreaming of a dry stick, bent to breaking point between two powerful arms. If the stick breaks, there will be no way of putting it back together again.

He is taking the weight of the window on his fore-arms. It is sliding up, imperceptibly, silently. The blonde head is breathing deeply, evenly. There is a teddy bear next to it. John had a teddy bear once, centuries ago.

A mother snores gently in front of the television set.

Arthur takes it all in at once, seeing everything. He raises his hands above his head and shouts into the darkness. 'No!'
   Pete jumps in his bed.

Now it moves up easily. As if someone has lent a hand, bent their back to the task. It is shifting, shifting.

John pulls his hands away as if he's had a shock. He turns and runs, crying again, clattering back through the gate.

She's awake, woken by some noise. She's lumbering through to check on the children before going to bed. All is well. *Kevin's late*, she's thinking. *What on earth can he be up to?*

It's as if he can't hear Pete swearing at him. All he's aware of is John's empty bed, and the darkness of the night.

Looking at his watch, Kevin can't believe how much time has gone by. Must have fallen asleep. But he's feeling exhilarated, as if his team had just kicked the winning goal. His breathing is clear and clean and fresh.

The angels are back in the church. Their hands are shaking so much they can hardly get the joint together.

Arthur calls down blessing on the earth. He is in bed again, but not sleeping. He is worrying that this might not yet be finished.

He picks the teddy bear off the floor and places it back on the bed. Kevin is in his daughter's room. He bends over her, kisses her hair. Notices a cool breeze, lowers the window.

It is one of those dreams that is brighter than reality. Brian is woken by her murmuring. Wonders what she's dreaming of.

She is in a large empty room. There are wooden floorboards. As she walks around, the footsteps echo. She squats in the centre, draws her knees up. Lonely. She notices a window on the far wall, with the curtains drawn. Seems to be some sort of light shining through.

Gripping the curtains, pulling them back with a flourish. Falling to the floor. Huge, immense, filling the whole of the window frame; the moon. Light that you can feel hitting your skin. Surging waves of gravity buffeting.

And then she is falling, falling in the moonlight. Into the blackness. There are faces in windows which she passes on the way. Brian. Penny. Her mother. An old headmaster. Staring through the glass, watching her fall.

Landing ever so gently, light as a feather. Sinking into miles and miles of white lacy softness. Absorbed, embraced, cosseted. Somewhere there is a soft breathing. She can feel the spicy freshness of it on her face.

Even before she turns, she knows it is him. Both

of them naked. His beautiful warm brown against the white. His eyes know everything. She smiles, and warm treacle flows from her centre.

She is still smiling when she wakes.

Ponsonby shakes itself free of the night. Morning nudges the darkness over the Waitakeres and into the cold depths of the Tasman. The bakery is already spreading its yeasty breath along the ridge. The sun finally hauls itself from somewhere behind Rangitoto.

In an upstairs apartment bed springs are squeaking. A dribble of reluctant starters is waiting at a bus stop. A transvestite is stumbling across the road near Norfolk Street, wig askew and make-up smudged.

The post office clock notes the hour, but no-one is interested. At a money machine a man with dark eyes is trying PIN numbers on the card he stole. Dave from the Busy Bee is whistling as he arranges produce on the footpath. The air is thick with radio waves, and their premature jocularity.

In a park, a pohutukawa branch is swaying as it catches the first breeze.

Norm has bitten the bullet of the day. *Could be time for a shave*, he's thinking, scraping his hand across the stubble. *Just because a man sleeps rough doesn't mean he has to let himself go to the pack. 'Course it's not so good with cold water, but thoughtful of the council to provide a basin and tap and mirror.*

There's a bad smell in the air today, he's thinking. I don't like the looks of things. Watch your step today, boy, watch your step.

Even the morning dose of scripture doesn't quite hit the mark. *Something's happening today, Lord, but I'll be damned if I know what it is. Likely be damned anyway,* he chuckles.

A walk to clear my head. Tour of the estate. Check on the serfs. Never know what I might find.

Boarding house Bob is suffering. Paying the price for finishing off those beers after they'd all gone to bed. Mouth like a cow's arse. Eyes hanging out like a monkey's vulva.

He's stumbling around the kitchen, trying to put together a cup of coffee. Things keep falling over in front of him. Inconsiderate.

Arthur coming in, frowning.

'You seen John?'

'John? Can't even see the bloody table yet. Too early. Why?'

'He didn't come in last night.'

'Aw, shit! He hasn't been at it again, has he? Arthur? Has he? I thought they said they'd bloody well cured him.'

'I don't think he's done anything wrong. I just want to find him.'

Arthur leaves Bob to his cursing and continues the search.

Tired this morning. Bone weary. Kevin sits at his desk and commands the phone not to ring.

He picks up the prayer book, flicks through it idly. One catches his attention. He turns back to it: the prayer of absolution. For some reason — who knows why? — he reads it out loud:

All things have been reconciled to God the creator
through the life, death and resurrection
of God's Son Jesus Christ,
and the Holy Spirit has been sent among us
for the forgiveness of sins.
By the authority of Christ given to the Church
I absolve you from your sins
in the name of God, Father, Son and Holy Spirit.
May God give you peace.

Almost feels like I'm saying that for someone in particular. Well, whoever you are, my friend, may you find the peace you need.

Towards the back of the reserve is his favourite pohutukawa. *Must be a hundred years old, I reckon.*

Norm loves the way the gnarly old roots burrow themselves into impossible crevices, holding the tree to the cliff face. *Reminds me of meself.*

Even from a distance, with peripheral vision, he knows something is wrong. The way the branches are moving.

Then he's seeing it clearly. He's seen it before, in another place, but the sight still reams him. A man on a string, swaying in the breeze. Little fellow, hardly anything of him. Tongue.

John.

Oh Christ no.

John.

You poor broken little bastard. Hang on while I get you down.

It takes some time.

Not so young as I was once. This is the part they never show you in the movies. Just as well he's not heavy. There you go. Easy, easy.

There's a note in John's clenched fist. Norm tugs it out, unravels it. It's done in crayon, capitals.

Doesn't mean much to me.

I LOVE YOU CHILD

Arthur sees Norm coming across the reserve, cradling the body in his arms. Like he was carrying a child or something.

He knows. He knows.

He's taking the rag bundle from Norm. So tenderly. As if there was anything more that could get broken.

They're carrying him back to the boarding house, neither daring to break the silence.

They're laying John down on the couch. Stroking his hair, his face.

The men are standing around, dumb to know what's expected of them.

Bob's cursing everything that ever lived, trying to find a phone number for the Ponsonby police station.

Arthur wept.

4

Arthur, with his delusions of a special mission to the world, is one of a number of psychiatric patients who have been released from institutions in the name of community care. What this means in reality is living in an overcrowded and substandard boarding house, with inadequate supervision from the health authorities.

'Fortunately, Arthur has no violent tendencies and does not pose a threat to the community at large. But can the same be said of all psychiatric patients who are walking the streets today? It is apparent that many former patients have fallen through the cracks since leaving hospital and are now unaccounted for.

'The winners in this restructuring seem to be the entrepreneurs who operate accommodation services at the bottom end of the scale. The dirty and unhygienic conditions that we have shown you tonight are typical of the living situations of many ex-psychiatric patients.'

Bob's face appears on screen.

'The old guys like it that way — it's sort of comfortable, you know?'

A harshly lit shot of a bedroom, which picks out the mould on the walls. Bill lies on one of the four beds with his hand down the front of his pants.

Back to Bob.

'I've got to make a living, don't I?'

'And in a late-breaking story, we have just learned that one of the residents of this very boarding house, a former child molester, has committed suicide. He hung himself in Point Erin Reserve in the early hours of the morning. His is not the first tragic death resulting from the new regime, and it is unlikely to be the last.

'This is Karen Bligh-Farnsworth for *Nightly News*, Auckland.'

'They should never have let the nutters out in the first place.'

Brian confirms this with a rattle of the newspaper he's holding. Not that he's reading it. Just something to watch television over the top of.

Margaret in the other chair is unquestionably silent. You would have to look very hard to see that her fingernails have turned white where they meet the arms of the chair.

The news has skittered on, but Margaret can

only see Arthur's face. Here in her lounge. He has come to her, as he promised.

She's done a real hatchet job, Kevin's thinking. *What a hard-nosed bitch.*

'Isn't that the place you went down to? Where they want you to take another funeral? Is it that poor man who's killed himself?'

'John Roberts, his name is. I used to see him wandering up and down the streets, touching things. Seemed a harmless enough little chap.'

'Why'd they ask you to do it?'

'No family to speak of. I've got friendly with one of the men at the boarding house, and he told the manager to ring me.'

Arthur, he's thinking. *Can't seem to get him out of my life.*

The empty bed doesn't help. Bob still hasn't decided who can take it. Just lies there flaunting itself. Uncaring of its former occupant. Ready to receive the next one, to give its warmth to whoever might come along.

And Pete's saying nothing. Pointedly. Lying with his face against the wall.

The night straps itself around Arthur, buckles itself in. The pain has coagulated, shifting now in thick lazy lumps through the chambers of his heart. A morepork cries in the distance, because something has to.

I should have known. I should have known. You should have told me.

From the ceiling there's an uncompromising silence. And beyond it, black, impenetrable night. Even the stars are frugal, withholding more than they give. The moon, of course, is unperturbed.

I'm not sure that I can bear this. I don't know if I'm strong enough.

Nothing. Not a whisper.

The rooftops of Ponsonby sail across the valley. They're graceful and orderly, in a chaotic sort of way. They have weathered unimaginable storms, but here today they slide quietly through the green and bask in the late-morning sun. She's watching them from her kitchen window as she dials the number, is finally ushered through to his extension.

'Brian? Penny here. Penny Preston. Yes, good thanks. Listen, I'm sorry to ring you at work, but there's something I wanted to talk to you about. Are you able to talk privately? Good.

'It's about Margaret.'

And now the Chihuahuas of guilt are yapping their heads off, dancing and nipping. *To go behind her back? To Brian? What are you doing? A friend?*

'I'm a little worried about her. It's nothing serious, but I suspect she's not too emotionally stable at the moment. There's been a couple of occasions lately

94

where she hasn't been handling things too well.'

Booting the beastly little canines out of the way, amidst much yelping and whimpering.

'Nothing that I feel free to talk about without breaking confidence. I just feel concerned for her, in case things get out of hand. I thought I should tell you, make you aware of the situation. I've suggested she get some help, but she's not keen to at the moment.'

'No, I wouldn't put any pressure on her right now. I think she just needs lots of love and attention, and a bit of extra rest. Perhaps even a holiday without the children?'

'Yes, I see. Well, that's your decision anyway.'

'And there's one thing I want to ask of you, Brian. Please don't let on to Margaret that I've rung, will you? Thanks. Let me know if there's anything I can do to help out, take the children or something.'

God, I hate that man, she's thinking as she hangs up. *Such an arrogant prat.* But sharp little teeth are already sinking into the fleshy part of her conscience.

'C'mon, ya hopeless pack of pricks, get a move on! We only got ten minutes to get up there. Taffy, put yer bloody shoes back on, ya daft old bastard. Ya can't go to church in bare feet. Where the hell's Sandy?'

'In the van, in the van,' Digby's chanting, running his fingers through his hair for a bit of a tidy-up.

Some of the men have found their own way up to the church. Others are staring vacantly at an early soap opera, immobile even for death. Bob's doing his best to get the remainder under way.

'Shit, Wal, is that the cleanest shirt ya've got? Ah well, never mind. John wouldn't have noticed. Bill, do yer flies up. No-one wants to see yer ugly bloody donger waving at the crowds. Aw Christ, Pete, where's yer teeth? Well, go and get them and put them in yer mouth! That's the one under yer nose. Right, then, let's start getting in the van. Gidday, Norm. Where'd ya get that outfit from? Fair go, look like a bookie.'

Norm is standing somewhat stiffly, as if all his clothes were wet. Took his stash and bought a suit from the Sally Army shop. Even shoes and a tie. His eyes are red. He has a little on board, to see him through.

'Any chance of a ride up the road?'

'Yeah, 'course there is. Ya better sit up front with me, or some mad bugger'll dribble on yer fancy suit. Do us a favour, will ya? Go and get Pete — and make sure he's got his fucken teeth in.'

'Where's Arthur?'

'He went up early. Said he didn't want John to be alone in the church. Been hangin' on the coffin like it was gonna take off somewhere, every chance he's got. Funeral director's getting pissed off with him.

Jeez, Sandy, ya can't take that bloody bottle with ya — give us a break.'

Finally they're all stumbling into the back of the van. Norm up front like a bodyguard. Bob counting heads before slamming the door.

'Let's get outta here.'

Kevin is having real problems with his part of the service. *Two funerals in the same week — who'd have this ratshit job?*

Looking over his shoulder, it seems, is that little old lady with her lecture and her prayer. *None of your nonsense this time*, she's saying.

One angel looks at the other.

She was one of ours, you think?

Without a doubt.

The church is womblike, embracing. Arthur hears the murmuring voices, prayers of a generation. *Like a wharenui*, he is thinking. But not as warm.

A soft gloom hangs in the building, tangy with incense. Up the front the coffin, on its ridiculous silver trolley. Candles burning in the background.

An ancient organist steadies herself before the controls. Survivor of a thousand dirges, giving thanks that it's not yet her own. She's a little nervous of that big man muttering over the casket. *I wish he'd sit down.*

'Oh come on, Tim, you've got to be joking. We've done that piece to death if you'll pardon the expression — let's get on with something else.'

'It's part of the original story, Karen. Who could've guessed that one of them would top themselves? Christ, if only you'd had him on tape before he died . . . But anyway, this suicide is part of the whole deal. We can repackage the thing, put it back as a doco. It'll rate through the roof, guarantee it. Death, sex, crime; what more could you ask for? So be a good little reporter and go along to the funeral, see what happens. Only take you an hour, and you might get some good background.'

'No bloody crew, all right? I don't want cameras crawling all over the place.'

In some remote vault of her psyche, somebody is feeling bad about the way she packaged the story.

'Don't worry, Karen, we do know how to be discreet. The cameras will be parked across the road, just long shots of the coffin coming out, that sort of thing. Naturally, if anything develops, you can give them a call . . .'

'Wonderful. Absolutely bloody marvellous. When do I pick up the award?'

He's wearing a grey pinstripe suit. And a solemn but caring face. *Looks like a bloody great dick to me*, Bob's thinking while he shakes his hand. By which he's being gently guided away from the door.

'A word in your ear, if I may.'

The perfumed breath of the undertaker. *Wonder if he's tippling his own bloody embalming fluid?*

'Now everything's fine; just as we arranged. You need to be aware that there's a shortfall between the funeral benefit available and the total cost, to the tune of around twelve hundred dollars. As Mr Roberts doesn't seem to have any relatives forthcoming, I presume that you will, ah . . .?'

'Pay the bill? 'Course I'll pay the bloody bill. I told ya that yesterday, dint I?'

'Quite. Well, perhaps you'd be good enough to just put your signature here?'

'Ah, shit. Great sense of timing, mate. Where they train you jokers — Transylvania? What ya gonna do if I don't sign it, then? Take his bleedin' body back and hold it till I pay? Here, give us it. And then just keep outta me way.'

The grey vulture head is pulled back in distaste. *It's the living I have problems with.*

In the cafés and restaurants there is no prospect of death. There are lattes and cappuccinos, tortes and muffins, green salads and vegetarian quiches. There are sparkling conversations, wicked jokes, witticisms and cynicism and gossip of the intellectual variety. Not a sign of death in the whole lively street.

Only the streetware has doffed its cap. The lamp-posts are dull, the rubbish bins crabby, the traffic lights sluggish. They miss the touch of a friend, the daily anointing with love.

Across the road from the church, a woman with waxed legs has noticed the hearse. It reminds her of a stunning joke about a bisexual gravedigger. *You'll love this one . . .*

Bob's pulling them out of the back seats and making them sit down the front. 'Put that fucken cigarette away,' he hisses. There are perhaps forty people in the church, most of them street people. How does the word get round?

Kevin surveys them as he rises to begin. A fat man is investigating the contents of his nose. The organ is wheezing its last.

'My friends, we are here today because of John Roberts. Because of his life and because of his death. In some way he has crossed each of our paths, and we are different for having met him. We have three jobs to do today. The first is to remember John and his life, the second to give thanks for him to God, and finally to pray for him as we commit him into the grace of God.

'We are not going to be dishonest about John. We cannot ignore either the dark spots in his life or the manner of his death. We feel the loss even more because he chose death over life, elected to leave us on the outside of his pain. At times like this we do well to be honest both with ourselves and God, and to tread carefully. We need to call on the mercy of God, not only for our own lives, but for that of John.

'I'm going to read some verses of scripture shortly, which speak of the love of God. But I want to call on your help when we come to remember John. I'd like to make space in the service for any of you to share your personal memories of John, tell a story about him, perhaps say some last word of farewell to him. When we come to that time, I'll invite you to come up to the front and speak to us. You might like to think now of what you would like to say.'

A well-dressed woman slips quietly into the back pews of the church, leaving her sunglasses on.

'Listen now to the word of God . . .'

The ringing tone repeats itself untiringly. There's no-one home, he finally deduces. *Did she say she was going out anywhere? I really should start listening when she prattles on in the morning. Too much on my plate, that's the trouble. Damn that Preston woman. She's got me all stirred up for no good reason. Nothing wrong with Margaret. Probably just a bad case of PMT. Still, where the hell is she? Ah well, try again after three; she'll have to be home for the kids.*

'Lisa, bring me the Mitsuki file, would you?'

In the front row, close as he can be to his old friend, Arthur pricks up his ears. Norm alongside him like a tailor's dummy, breathing sherry.

> You are full of compassion and mercy:
>   slow to anger and rich in kindness.
> You will not always be chiding:
>   nor do you keep your anger for ever.
> You have not dealt with us according to our sins:
>   nor punished us according to our wickedness.
> For as the heavens are high above the earth:
>   so great is your mercy over those who respect
>   you.
> As far as the east is from the west:
>   so far have you put away our sins from us.
> As parents have compassion on their children:
>   so do you Lord have compassion on those who
>   respect you.
> For you know what we are made of:
>   you remember that we are but dust.
> Our days are like the grass:
>   we flourish like a flower of the field.
> But as soon as the wind goes over it, it is gone:
>   and its place shall know it no more.

'Hoo, that's good,' whispers Arthur, nudging Norm.

'Where d'that come from?'
   'Psalms. I think.'
   'Yeah? In the Bible? Not bad.'

Kevin notes another well-dressed woman entering quietly, this one blonde. She's looking rather nervous and out of place, like maybe she got the wrong funeral. Deciding to stay, she too opts for the back row.

As the organist nears the end of the hymn she produces a definitive flourish, rather pleased with herself. She looks in her little rear-view mirror. Sees rows of untidy men standing, not even holding hymn books, let alone singing. Staring into the distance, half of them with their mouths gaping.
   Cretins.
   But there's one rather dapper gent in the front row, next to that big Maori chap, singing his heart out. Pity he can't hold a tune.

'So I'd like any of you who have anything to share to come up the front here now, as a sort of tribute to John. Please use the microphone so we can all hear.'
   And he sits down. This is the nerve-racking part. The long silence when you wonder if you're going to have to abort the whole thing.
   Wal farts; a short crisp fart. None of the men

103

smiles. Norm wonders if that was Wal's contribution to the occasion. Sandy starts rocking his leg up and down, makes the pew throb.

Finally Bob can't stand it any longer. Swaggers reluctantly to the front.

'Look, I'm not used to this sorta thing, eh. But old John was orright. Never said much of anything to anyone, but he didn't cause any trouble, either. Most of yas won't know this, but John came from the South Island, down Christchurch way somewhere. Grew up on a farm. My old man knew his old man, going back a few years now. He reckoned John was a bright little bugger — sorry, vicar — clever little boy, till one day he fell off a ladder, hit his head on the ground. Never said anything much from then till now. Used to live in some sort of special home, but when his father died, me old man arranged for him to come up here and live in the boarding house, like. Meant he could get out a bit more.

'Anyway the thing I remember about John was, one time after he got into a spot of trouble and spent some time away, he came back to the house. Wanted his old room back. Kept throwing his stuff on the bed, even though I told him he couldn't have it. We was pretty full, see, and old Billy — some of yas will remember old Billy — he was sleeping there. So I take John downstairs and show him his new bed, but he didn't look too happy about it. Anyway, I thought that was the end of that. And for a while it looked like we'd sorted it out.

'Then about a week later, old Billy comes down sheep-faced and tells me he's pissed his bed — sorry — wet his bed. First time ever. But from then on, every morning, Billy wakes up and finds he's wet his bed. We tried cutting down his drinks before bed, but nothing worked. So in the end it was no good, see. I had to jack up a rest home for him, where they're set up to cope with it. So he moves out, and John gets his bed. Looks like the cat that got the cream.

'A fortnight or so after that, I get a ring from the matron at the rest home. That bloke ya sent to us, she said, he's never wet his bed since he's been here. Funny thing, I thought, maybe just the change of place or something. Wasn't till a month or so later I found out what was really going on. I got it outta Tom one night when he was having a few beers. Seems every night in the early hours of the morning, John was creeping into their bedroom. He'd lift the blankets on the bed, and tip a whole milk bottle full of pi. . . . urine on Billy's sheet.

'I had to laugh — crafty little fella. Never thought he had it in him.'

The men are rumbling with laughter, though most of them have heard the story before. Even the organist has trouble keeping a smile off her face.

'So there ya go. But I dunno why he had to go and do this for. Why d'ya do it for, John?'

Bob has clamped his lips together to stop anything else getting out. But his Adam's apple is doing strange things.

'John was orright, I'll tell you that. I'll miss ya, mate. I'll miss ya.'

Kevin has developed a bad case of itchy eyebrows.

A wild-eyed woman struts her way up the aisle. Bridget, a psych woman from one of the rehabilitation houses. She has a long face with rather scrubby black hair, and the gait of an ostrich.

'Morning, vicar.'

With an exaggerated bow.

Kevin knows from the shine in her eyes that she's quite crazy today. Anything could happen.

'My name's Bridget; hello everyone.'

A chorus of muttered echoes.

'I just want to say that since they cut my benefit, the rent's gone up. So I can't hardly afford my Tampax any more. What are you laughing at, Digby? This is a church we're in, not a fucking movie theatre. Now where was I? That's right, and I can't afford my smokes either.'

She pauses for dramatic effect, enjoying the power of holding the floor. Kevin's wondering if he's going to have to salvage the situation.

'But John, see, he sometimes gave me a smoke, you know? Sometimes even some money. And he didn't expect any favours for it. Not like you, Digby.

'So I can't say much about John, but I want to leave him something.'

She strolls across to the coffin, and with an exaggerated flourish places a cigarette on the lid.

'And that's a bloody tailor-made as well!'

Daring anyone to contradict.

'That's all. I'm going to sit down now.'

Karen in the back row is biting the inside of her lip. She's having trouble staying resentful. Even with Arthur's big head up the front.

Behind her the angels are preparing something.

Next up is Colin. Star of the Psychiatric Survivors Christmas party. Banned from karaoke bars all over central Auckland.

He's leaning over the microphone, threatening to swallow it live and whole.

'I'd like to sing a song for John.'

A groan from the punters recognizes the inevitable.

Looking over at the organist. Giving her a wink.

'Don't suppose you know any Elvis tunes, do you, darling? Well, never mind, I'll sing on my own. This one's for John. Did I say that? Right.

Amazing grace, how sweet the sound . . .

His voice is bouncing in and out of tune before striking some middle ground and settling on it. The crooning is strangely evocative.

Was blind, but now I see . . .

Slow tears are struggling to find a path between the pits on Wal's face. A fat bead of snot glistens from one nostril.

Sporadic applause as Colin finishes.

'Thank you, thank you. You know John, he was a good fella, he'd come round my place sometimes, have a cup of coffee and a smoke. I'd sing him a few songs, he never said he didn't like them. Ha ha. I liked him a lot; I wrote this poem for him.

There was an old man called John,
Who liked to walk hither and yon;
He couldn't get free,
So he climbed up a tree,
And now the poor bastard has gone.

'I wrote that myself. Ha ha. But you know John, I wonder what will happen to him? He was a very naughty boy at times. Not that we want to talk about that. I suppose I could sing you another . . .'

'Siddown, Colin.'

'Yeah, right, sorry Bob. I'll sit down then. But you know John, we had a few laughs together. Ha ha.'

It takes the two of them to lift the heavy jug and begin to pour it, ever so slowly, over the top of her head. A thick shining liquid is oozing out.

A certain seraph is hoping he gave them the right formula. *Must be a couple of centuries since I tried this particular one. What a night that was.*

Karen is beginning to feel rather strange.

The most elegant drunk in the city balances carefully on her high heels as she makes her way to the podium. Roslyn's thin face is radiant, but the glow is not entirely natural. She flicks her long grey hair away from her face.

'John was a gentleman. Always a gentleman.'

She can't say any more, but as she's returning to her seat, her shoulders are shaking.

There is a period of silence. Pain cannot be digested quickly.

The undertaker at the rear of the church is trying to catch the vicar's eye. Tapping his watch with portent.

Kevin rises briefly.

'Please feel free to speak if there are others of you who wish to. We have plenty of time.'

There is a deliciously warm sensation gathering in the pit of her stomach. She uncrosses her legs, puts both feet on the floor. The liquid honey is spreading, coursing upwards with relentless pleasure.

The same seraph is relaxing, remembering.

A weary woman; a study in brown. Carrying her burden to the front.

'I'm a visitor here. I don't know any of you. I . . .'

And now she's clutching both sides of the podium, racked with heaving, dry sobs. Kevin is drifting up beside her, settling his arm around her shoulder. The greeting subsides. She wrenches herself under control. Cold fury arranges her features.

'I never knew this man.'

Jerking at the coffin.

'Except for on the other side of the courtroom. He . . .'

A titanic pause.

'He molested my daughter. She was six, my beautiful little girl. It broke something within her. She was never the same again.'

Now her voice is calm and mechanical.

'They gave her all sorts of counselling. But by the time she'd finished giving evidence to the court, she was like an empty doll. At eighteen she killed herself. Jumped off a bridge. I couldn't even see her body, because they couldn't fix her up properly.'

She turns to address the coffin.

'I'm glad you died the way you did, you rotten

little bastard. May you rot in hell.'

Surfing back to her seat on a wave of rage. Shaking and shaking.

Shit, Kevin's thinking. *Serves me right for taking a risk. How do we ever get the thing back from here? God help us.*

Not, this once, a fatuous petition.

Karen's losing it. The back of her head is blowing off. A wonderful breeze is blowing right through her, ripe with fresh apricots and sliced capsicum. There's music playing like she's never heard before.

A sense of peace as gentle as a silk shroud, as deep as a silent rock pool.

Full of the honour of a friend, Norm is on his feet.

'Lady, that's not fair. That was a long time ago. Like you said, you didn't know him. I did. I knew him. I knew John. He did wrong, no question about that. It was what killed him in the end. He hated himself, you see, for what he'd done. He was always trying to make up for it, only he couldn't. You have to understand, lady, he wasn't a bad man, even if he did bad things. It's not fair to come here to his funeral and . . .'

That's another one crying, unable to go on. Holding both sides of his head as if it threatened

111

to fall apart, howling like a little boy.

It's Arthur now who comes to his rescue. Enveloping him in a hug of gigantic proportions. Holding him. Absorbing it all, soaking it up. Guiding Norm back to his seat, before turning to face the congregation.

Margaret! And the reporter from the TV, locked in a beam of light.

He turns to the woman in brown, still shaking in her pew.

'What was your little girl's name? Alice? I want to karakia, pray for her.

'Father. Alice was the girl you made. You saw her and loved her. She was always special, and she remains special for ever despite what was done to her. Take her to yourself and hold her until all the pain has gone. Heal her from the sins of others. And look here on her mother. She has the grief you know about, Father. The grief of losing your heart. So you need to take care of her, you hear? Amen.'

He is wandering over to the coffin, touching it, stroking it.

'John, you see what you've done, e hoa? You can hear it all now. You did wrong, man, and you're going to have to carry that for a long time. I looked into your heart, little brother, and I saw all the bad that you'd done. But I saw your love too. It got twisted so that it caused a lot of damage, but you had so much love and no-one to give it to.'

Arthur stands now beside the coffin, one hand resting on it. He speaks to the people, riveted all by some compelling quietness to his voice.

'God didn't make us for this. Not to snarl and bite at each other, to twist each other's lives up and throw them away like bits of paper. It wasn't meant to be like this. It's all got out of hand, all this hurt . . . People suffering and starving, children dying with no-one to love them, old people stuck away in homes like old books that nobody reads any more.

'Everyone living like there's no such thing as right or wrong, like it doesn't matter how you treat people. Snuffling and grunting after money like a herd of pigs, climbing all over each other. We're worth more than that, all of us.

'See old John here, shut up in his coffin. His life's come to an end. Not much more he can do; all his rights and wrongs are over. But he's got to face up to it. Got to front up to his Father, get his life laid out in front of him like a whole heap of rubbish on a trestle table, so's they can rummage through it together. And it's no different for any of you.

'But the whole thing's gone too far. It's got to come to an end. So the Father sent me here to tell you that he's going to wind it all up. Call it all in. Pretty soon now. So you better sort yourselves out while you got the chance.

'John can't do much more.

'Father, look on this man that you made and have mercy on him. I don't want you to overlook what he's done, but look too at that love that he had. He was a broken child as well. Let my word stand for him, and take him into the place of healing. Amen.'

Through the glorious haze of light Karen sees him up there, his face chiselled out of rock. Each word he speaks punches into her heart with awful impact. It is a time-free zone; nothing but truth, its speaker and a hearer.

There's white silk shimmering around her, a thousand choirs descanting their purity in song, wave upon wave of sweet, buffeting freshness echoing out into the universe.

'Well, fuck me gently,' she says.

Which is precisely what's happening.

In the wake of silence which follows Arthur, Kevin folds the notes of his concluding remarks and puts them back in his pocket. Reluctantly stands to speak.

Notices the woman from the television shaking like a leaf.

'I was going to pronounce the committal at this stage of the service; commend John's body into the hands of the Lord. But I wouldn't want to add or take away from anything that Arthur has just said.'

Sees that the well-dressed blonde down the back is quietly weeping.

'Many of us have been moved in one way or another by this service. I might even suggest that God has been with us. I am a priest of the church. Some of you might think I have a special relationship with God, but it's not true. In fact just this week I have been discovering how very little I know of God. I feel like something of a fraud, especially in the presence of the overwhelming honesty which you have all contributed today.

'But I know enough of God to recognize his presence. For whatever reason, there is the reek of the Spirit about what has happened here today.

'The world may not notice the passing of John. There will be no school prizes offered in his name; no John Roberts Drive designated by the city council. But we know something of immense value. That for all the tragic consequences of his life, for all the twisted nature of his love, John is important enough to God to be present at his funeral. That gives us all hope that perhaps even our own tragic and twisted lives may be of some interest to God. I suspect that is John's gift to us.

'One more thing before I close. Those who know Arthur, I think you should listen to what he has to say.'

Wal belches, and sighs.

They're taking the coffin on their shoulders, with the undertaker fussing and finicking. There's Norm and Arthur on one side, Colin and Bob on the other.

Unaccountably, unforgivably, unforgettably, the organist is playing the wedding march as they process out. Kevin looks at her in wonder, but her state of shock is profound.

They slip the mortal remains of John into the back of the hungry black hearse. The last journey.

'Haere ra, e hoa. Kia kaha.'

Arthur's cheeks are wet again.

Margaret stumbles out behind them all to see the hearse sailing into the mainstream. She's confused, embarrassed, inclined simply to duck away to her car.

Arthur sees her, threads his way to her.

He is wrapping his arms around her and drawing her to his great chest. It is like coming out of a cold wind into the lee of a hill. As if this is what all her life has been leading to, this one embrace of warmth and homecoming.

He is lifting her head to look at her, and she is spontaneously kissing him, long and full and deep.

In the far, cold reaches of the universe a new galaxy flares into existence, spewing forth stars like fish eggs.

A bunch of old men are laughing and clapping, wondering if it might be their turn next.

Kevin is noticing the wedding ring on the woman's hand.

Karen is scared to breathe, let alone move. Her head is humming with several megavolts of pure power. She has been hollowed out like an old kumara, and then filled up with some impossible ambrosia.

He finds her there as he comes to lock up.

'Ah, shit,' he says. 'Not again.'

'Yeah, orright, knock it off, you two. Now listen up. Everyone's invited down the boarding house for a few beers and a bit of a feed. Don't get too excited, it's nothing flash. Yer all welcome; I'll see yas down there. All you jokers get back in the van, hurry up.'

Arthur looks at her, the question in his eyes. She consults her watch, considers, smiles. *Why not?*

'So what happened, d'you think?'

'I imagine God picked you up like a tambourine, and gave you a bit of a shake.'

'I'm really losing it here. You mean it was some sort of religious experience? I can't believe it. I just don't go in for that sort of thing. You can't begin to know how bad this is for my image.'

'Are you telling me you regret it?'

'Are you kidding? Every orgasm will be an anti-climax from now on. Oh, I'm sorry . . .'

'Don't be. I'm married, so I know what you mean from both ends of the spectrum.'

'Shit. This is so confusing. Will I be allowed to swear still? I'm not going to become a wretched Bible-banger, am I?'

'It hasn't stopped me, and no, not if you don't want to be. All that's happened so far is that God's decided to let you know that he's about the place. What you do about it is up to you.'

'What about this Arthur? I mean, while I was out of it there it seemed like he was God's gift to the earth; like there was something special about him. Is he mad or the only sane one among us?'

'That, Karen, is the sixty-four-thousand-dollar question.'

The old girl is revelling in the crowd, throwing her windows open to the breeze. Spreading her halls to the guests, allowing the happy chatter to soak into her grubby walls. Remembering former glory days of balls and garden parties, when the paint was still fresh on her timbers.

Margaret has kicked her shoes off. She loves the noise, the laughter, the lack of pretension. Already she's made brief forays from Arthur's side, got to know some of the men.

Pete showing her a secret photo of his wife. Wal showing her a boil on the back of his leg. Digby offering to show her his bedroom. All of them stuffing sausage rolls and cream cakes into their mouths, sprinkling their conversation with crumbs and spittle.

She is joyous, full of impish fun like a schoolgirl. Giggling and teasing with them all. Always glancing back to those brown eyes of approval, feeling her heart stall like a bird on the wing.

When Colin begins to sing, she nuzzles into Arthur, quiet and contented.

It's some time before she looks at her watch again.

The television van is still sitting there, with the two crew looking entirely pissed off.

'Where the hell have you been? Tim's been on the phone threatening blue murder. We thought you must have ascended into bloody heaven!'

Brian replaces the phone once more. This time he's worried.

5

It is one of those indeterminate days. Summer poised at the top of the Ferris wheel. Autumn like gravity, waiting to have its day.

But for the moment the air remains syrupy and satiated. It is still possible to hope, to believe, to be gloriously irresponsible in the lingering evenings. Winter will never come to Ponsonby, reclining languidly along the ridge, absorbing the libations of the sun.

There will always be people walking the street in shirts cut from Polynesia, children laughing on the tarseal cricket pitches, sauvignon blanc flowing from the taps.

Even in Howick, amidst walk socks and bowling hats, cicadas are tuning their orchestra. Hibiscus flowers wave their blatant sexuality in the most orderly of gardens, daring the citizens to disapprove. The atmosphere exudes salty smoke from a thousand gas-fired barbecues on a thousand hardwood decks.

Margaret is exultant. She's sucking fingerfuls of

ice cream gouged from the packet. Slicing celery to the accompaniment of Vivaldi. Raising her voice in nonsensical trills which alarm the budgie. The children are frightened and delighted at the same time. Caught up in her sudden playfulness despite themselves. Who can resist fresh strawberries with unlimited cream?

Her harbour is not so much calm as luxuriant. The waters slurp and gurgle, the shores sighing under the raking of their soft fingers. And there in the middle, a magnificent tall ship in full sail, proud with wind. The gap has been navigated, the harbour entered. Perhaps the ship will dock.

'Don't play the prima donna with me, Karen. We're already running late — let's just get the bloody thing in the can so we can start shooting this fraud story. OK?'

'No, I'm sorry, Tim. I won't do it the way it's cut at the moment. You either change the angle or get someone else to do it.'

'Why, for God's sake? The other day you want to roast them slowly with salt on, and now you're worried about hurting their feelings? It's a revelation to me that you acknowledge the existence of feelings, let alone care about them. It's just a story, Karen; loony child molester loose on the streets in unsupervised accommodation, exits sideways.

Bread and jam, lovey, bread and jam.'

'I'm not even going to discuss it. We chop it, change it, or someone else does it. That's the bottom line.'

'Right. Have it your way, then. Bill can do it. I'm not losing a good story just because you decide to find moral scruples. But your conscience better not get too tender, darling, or you may find this is the wrong industry for you.'

In the silent vaults of prayer, Arthur knows that things are moving. Events are hauling themselves into line. It is all so clear and obvious, the mundaneness of the present beginning to shine under the brush of the future.

He is seeing things again, spread out before him in brilliant technicolour. Looking on from a great height as the tides of history part and roll back. And there, between them, the path which he must follow.

You are my chosen one, to lead my people to the other side.

Your will be done through me. I will do that which you ask.

The sermon is refusing to emerge. He can feel it brooding down there, sliding among the dark waters of the imagination. But no amount of coaxing will persuade it to rise to the bait.

The knock on the door is a welcome distraction. *Shit*, he thinks, *is it that time already?* A 10 o'clock appointment with the mysterious Mr Jorgensen. Who asked to see him without indicating what for. Doesn't pay to be unavailable to well-off parishioners.

David Jorgensen, squat, stolid, thoughtful-looking chap, irregular member of the congregation who closes his eyes during the sermon. Whether for rest or reflection, who can say?

'Come in, Mr Jorgensen. Have a seat.'

'David, please.'

'A little sticky today, isn't it? Still, better not complain about the heat.'

'No, I suppose not. Look, Kevin — you don't mind if I call you Kevin? — I'm a fairly direct sort of person, so I'd like to get right to the point. I have something of an ethical dilemma, and I thought I might run it past you, get your reflections on it.'

'Certainly. Though I can't guarantee to be much help.'

'I'm not looking for an answer, I just want to talk it through with someone. It concerns my work, so I'd like to be certain that what I discuss here is completely confidential.'

'Absolutely. I understand you're a doctor?'

'Yes, well, I'm a psychiatrist really. Working at Auckland Hospital. The situation is that I've got myself into something of a tangle. I'm afraid I've fallen rather head over heels for a woman at work.'

'A patient?'

'Good heavens, no. A nurse, Gwenda.'

'You're not married, are you?'

'No, my divorce came through last October. But that's not the point. Not only is it someone on my ward, but she's on the nursing staff and I'm a doctor. It does raise certain complications.'

'What are they?'

'Oh, respecting professional boundaries, confusing roles, that sort of thing. I wouldn't tolerate it in a colleague of mine.'

'You're in love with Gwenda?'

'Totally. Ridiculously, for a man of my age.'

'How far have things progressed?'

'We're sleeping together, if that's what you mean. Last week I found myself interfering in the rosters so that she could be on the same shift as me. We've been eating lunch together across in the Domain on odd days. I think some of the other staff are beginning to twig that there's something going on.'

'And Gwenda is a free agent?'

'Not exactly. This is where things get even more messy. She's actually just at the tail end of another relationship, but with, ah, another woman. She's still living with this woman, even though the relationship has cooled off. Can't bring herself to tell her that she's gone hetero. I've been putting a bit of pressure on Gwenda to move out and live with me. But I'm not sure it's such a good idea. So, vicar, what do you think?'

'I sense that you're feeling uncomfortable about the whole thing.'

'Look, cut the crap, Kevin. If I wanted touchy-feely counselling I would have gone somewhere else.'

'OK. You want my opinion, I'll give it to you. You're paddling downstream towards Niagara Falls. Not only are you crossing boundaries and messing in your own nest, but the relationship sounds like it has some basic flaws. It's possible that you've had time to readjust from your marriage, but Gwenda is certainly on the rebound. And just to make it harder, there's the whole question of sexual orientation for her to sort out.'

'You think I should end it?'

'I think you have a responsibility to. At least create some space in both of your lives to be able to see things more clearly. If it proves to be an enduring relationship, perhaps sometime further down the track you can alter your working situations to make it easier.'

'Yes. That's the sort of advice I would give too. But I'm not going to take any notice of it. I find myself incapable of even thinking of withdrawing from Gwenda. I just needed to hear someone say it. Confirm my own stupidity. You know, I pride myself on understanding what makes people tick, on the subtle neuroses which cloud perspective and judgment. I know the tenuous subjectivity of emotion, the dysfunctional havoc it can wreak in a person's life. And yet here I am like a schoolboy, unable to do what I know is right because of some mooning love. We're pathetic creatures, aren't we? Hellbent on self-destruction.'

'Human, David, human.'

And beautiful with it, an angel is thinking.

'Where were you this afternoon? I was trying to get you.'

'I went in to Ponsonby, to see Penny and do a bit of shopping. I was late leaving so I got caught up in the traffic. Mark and Stephanie let themselves in — they were fine.'

'You know I don't like them coming home to an empty house. For goodness' sake, Margaret, you've got little enough to do in a day. I would have thought being home after school wasn't too much to ask. One of the reasons I work so hard is so that you can be free to look after the children.'

'Is it? Or is it to keep out of the house? At least I'm home in time to spend some time with them, eat a meal together.'

'That's unfair. You know why I'm working late at the moment.'

126

Brian is distracted by the television. He reaches for the remote and restores the volume. It seems to be a follow-up on the mental health item.

There's a long shot of a church, people emerging from its doors. Margaret watching in dumb terror. Seeing herself, not liking the hairstyle. The shot moving relentlessly closer. She cannot hear the voice-over. But Arthur is there, walking towards her. *No, no, no!*

Brian sitting up, alert, peering at the screen in disbelief.

Arthur approaching Margaret, his arms beginning to move. The camera panning past them to focus on the coffin. *Thank God!*

'Margaret, that's you! What on earth were you doing there?'

'I saw the television cameras there and popped into the church to see what was happening. It was the funeral for that chap who committed suicide. The cameras must have caught me as I came out.'

Brian staring. Uncertain now. *Is she lying to me? Margaret? Unthinkable. But . . .* The thin fence between trust and paranoia reduced to so much matchwood.

So easy to lie. So natural on the lips. And now some deep instinct causes her to rise and offer a cup of tea. *I'm cheating on my husband*, she thinks. And almost giggles.

Pete and Sandy keeping guard on the veranda. Arthur, keen now for company, joining them. For some time they're sitting in silence together, sharing what? Acceptance, perhaps.

A mangy black cat perches on the veranda rail. Rascal. Resident of the house for longer than most of the men can remember. Scarred from a life of sexual conquest and common assault. Cat ears dog-eared. A mobile flea farm. Glowering at Arthur with something approaching respect.

Arthur chuckling. Pete perplexed.

'What you laughing at?'

'That cat. He doesn't like competition. Thinks he runs the world.'

'He doesn't?'

'Not while I'm around. Though I might just give him a small kingdom to run in the next life. With a harem.'

'What about me?'

'You, Sandy? Let's see; for you I'll find a hut high up in the mountains, with a track that takes two days to walk. It'll be rough; plain old rough-sawn timber with a veranda out the front. There's a soft bed inside, and a table and two chairs. Bread and cheese on the table. It's surrounded by bush. Lots of tree ferns, and down in the valley totara and kauri and rimu. Birds singing everywhere. From the veranda you can look out to the sea, where the sun sets in the evening. And you sleep every night without dreams.'

Arthur is seeing it; and being seen, it exists.

'What d'you reckon, Sandy?'

But there are tears in Sandy's eyes, and he can't frame any words.

The table is glowing with the honeyed warmth of ancient kauri. Six hundred years standing sentinel over a green land freshly tossed up by the sea. A hundred years as wallboards in the Criterion pub, witness to the strangled desires of generations. And four years as Penny's dining-room table, cherished and polished.

At one side of which she is sitting, watching the sunlight strike the vapour rising from her cup of tea. Summoning emotional reserves not troubled for some time.

On the other side of which, Gwenda.

Gwenda of the red hair and flashing temper. Gwenda of bad jokes and huge appetite and stubby fingers. Gwenda of vivacious laughter, generous heart and soft body. Gwenda with the quick fuse to explosive passion. Penny's Gwenda.

No longer.

'So when are you moving out?'

It all comes down to this in the end. The practical details. The sorting out of possessions and working out of finances. Perhaps Armageddon will be accomplished by accountants.

'Saturday, I thought. No sense in prolonging it. I've got a truck coming round.'

'I'll give you a hand. You have to watch these moving people; they're so clumsy.'

'Penny! Stop being so bloody sensible! I wish you'd scream and yell, or throw things at me. Tell me you hate me, that I'm a stupid blind bitch. Anything but practi-bloody-cality.'

'Sorry, Gwen. It's my way of coping.'

A way of coping. A defence mechanism forged over the years in situations much the same as this one. A method of reducing the chaos; of sorting things into practical issues which can be dealt with one at a time. After which the worst of the hurt has passed, and only the dull, grey hollowness remains. *How many times have I held the handle of a cup of tea while my world collapses around my ears?*

Of course the relationship died months ago. Smothered to death by my own predictability. Hacked down by hundreds of small decisions which I made in our best interests. I always destroy what I love best. Can't help it. And each time it gets harder.

But for a man?

'Brian, you've been handling this Mitsuki file, haven't you?'

'I certainly have. A lot of hard work for the last three months, but it's finally all completed.'

'I think you better come into my office.'

Cityside Motel. Your hosts: Sally and Bernard Freeman. Competitive rates. Conference facilities.

Arthur is turning the card, inspecting it from different angles.

Considering one of his own. Heaven's Mansion. Your host: Arthur, Second Son of God. Divine setting.

Instead he's painstakingly pushing the buttons on the phone in the right sequence, racing against the tone which will tell him he has been too slow.

'Cityside Motel. Bernie speaking.'

'Yeah, it's Arthur here. I came to see you a while back to check up about a room. You gave me your card.'

'Yes . . .'

The sound of cogs whirring. *That big Maori bastard. Never forget a voice.*

'I want to get a room next week. Friday night. For two people.'

'Now that will be one hundred and five dollars for the night. I'm afraid I'll have to ask you to pay that sum on arrival; is that all right?'

'Yeah, yeah. Just make sure the room's booked. I want to get there just after twelve.'

'Certainly, sir. And what name shall I put the booking in? Mr and Mrs . . .?'

'Just Arthur will do. Arthur.'

The streets have so many memories. Irish labourers, singing and shouting and taking the tops off bottles with their black and broken fingernails. Clinging to Catholicism to keep them upright in a land too voluptuous to be believed. Getting an education for their kids in between beating them senseless.

Michael Joseph Savage, prime minister and boarder with a local family. Eventually opening his own home on a Sunday afternoon to the poor of Ponsonby. Arranging jobs and houses, sometimes dipping into his own pocket for bread or smokes. Now then, now then, what can be done?

Pacific Islanders, consuming shiploads of taro in a single fortnight. Digging up the back yard for an umu. With raw fish and chop suey. Piling on clothes for the winters. Singing the opposition churches down in harmonies imported straight from the studios of heaven. Young ones growing sullenly angry, forming a gang with the name of a snake.

Students, knocking holes in walls and lighting fires on the road during their wild weekend-long parties. Staining bed sheets and various items of furniture with the secretions of their lithe and raging bodies. Organizing demonstrations. Stereos exploring the outer limits of speaker technology. In rooms fuggy with sweet mary jane.

Artists, painting and sculpting and writing and composing. Hoisting antennae for the sporadic emissions of the muses. Feeling the humming vitality of the ridge rising through the very soles of their feet until it erupted wet and hot in the heart. Forgetting to eat in their wild, ecstatic episodes of pulling things out of darkness and into the light.

And then the yuppies. Porsches and BMWs abandoned on roads which never thought to have off-street parking. A new breed, so intent on renovating the villas that they inadvertently ripped the spirit out of them and sent it away in a wastetaker. Spreading money and charm like the thin slick of oil a boat leaves in its wake. Poisoning the water.

All of these held by the narrow streets, with their resplendent memories. And in the evening time they steam back into the air like fragrance from wet flowers. When couples stroll up the middle of the asphalt, leaving the footpaths to the cars, they breathe it in and grow unaccountably nostalgic. Children dancing and yelping squelch it between their bare toes. Dogs sniffing at lampposts have to filter the residues of more than a century.

Such is Ponsonby.

It accounts for the peaceful melancholy which Penny wears like a cloak as she strolls in the dusk. Is it possible to be contented and broken at the same time? It must be.

The options are dropping away. At the age of 39 relationships are not as accessible as they once were.

I feel my breasts drooping, my womb shrinking, my skin hardening. I have made my choices, and my choices have brought me here.

Alone.

Which is not quite the same as lonely. *I will grow old alone, die alone. But not without dignity.*

Not without regret, either. For what might have been. For what was and then was lost. For what will never be.

In the centre there is an ache whose name is Margaret. *It will die with me.*

And in this same spectral evening Karen sits alone in a small restaurant. She has chosen a table in the window to observe the Ponsonby nocturne.

Disjointed thoughts are circling through her cerebral atmosphere like gulls anticipating a storm. But in the centre there is a calm like none other she has known. Something has been opened which will never close again.

She is contemplating the candle on the table. Its simple purity. The stillness and brightness of it.

Light shining in the darkness, washing everything it touches with softness and beauty. Such a small thing, bringing so much pleasure. For a few moments she is losing her sense of boundaries; uncertain whether the candle is on the outside or inside of her.

And then another light draws her attention. The edge of the moon, rising over the cityscape. It creeps higher as she watches, peering into her window. Looming huge and menacing, swelling into dominance.

Almost full, she is thinking. *How long till it makes the perfect circle?*

A day is as treacherous as thin ice. You start out on it full of confidence. Thinking only of where you're heading; hardly even considering what's under your feet. And then with one resounding crack it betrays you, opening up so that you slide into the dark icy waters.

'So the whole thing was a scam, right from the start?'

'I'm afraid so, Brian. A very sophisticated one, to say the least. But the upshot of it is that we've advanced one-and-a-half million dollars to a corporation which only exists on paper.'

Brian is sweating despite the chill. He has to remind himself to breathe. The pallor of death is upon his face.

'Of course any one of us could have been taken in by the quality of the documents. Unfortunately it was you. Bad luck, really. But someone will have to carry the can, and your name's at the bottom of the approval.'

'What's going to happen?'

'Too early to say, really. Of course the Fraud Squad is involved. They're wanting to meet with you as soon as possible. And the media seem to have got hold of it, though goodness knows how. No interviews without approval — we need to manage the situation carefully. Apart from that, I thought you might like to take a few days off, get out of the place until things are resolved.'

'Yes, thanks.'

The bastard's suspending me. If only there was something to take hold of, to get a grip on.

This time it's cool, deliberate, planned. Margaret is taking pleasure in the subterfuge.

She chooses her clothes without inhibition. Whatever has the smell of summer about it. Standing naked before the mirror, evaluating. Trying the profile. Satisfied. Smiling as she absently runs her fingers through the golden pubic hairs.

In the end deciding against the bra. An expression of the freedom coursing through her veins like caffeine.

I am alive, and doesn't it feel damn good? He has brought me to life.

The woman behind the cosmetic mask is keeping an eye on him. Watching from behind the counter, monitoring the surveillance mirror. Here's a likely candidate if ever I saw one.

Arthur's picking up boxes and tubes, turning them in puzzlement. The problem is he can't read, and is a little shy to ask. The only times he's been in chemists' shops before have been to hand over a prescription to be filled.

The hard part of the will of God is the detail. No problem with the visions and prophecies; easy enough to accomplish the big miracles. But there are times when preparing for the new age seems rather mundane and mechanical, even for the second son of God.

Embarrassed, having no choice, he ambles over to the painted lady. Entering the tent of her perfume. She pulls back ever so slightly. *My aura again*, Arthur is thinking.

'Excuse me, lady; I need some help.'

'Certainly, sir; what are you looking for exactly?'

'Well, I need a whole bunch of stuff, really. I want some massage oil, something that's got a spicy sort of smell to it. And some of that, ah, what do you call it? A bit like Vaseline only flasher and better smelling.'

'Lubricating jelly, perhaps?'

There's the beginnings of a wry smile making its way among the lipstick and foundation.

'Yeah, yeah, that's the stuff. And let's see now, some candles, scented ones if you've got them. Then some of that men's stuff that you stick on after a shave. And, oh yeah, a box of tissues. That should do it.'

'Condoms?' She asks the question with all the sophistication and panache of a pharmacy assistant, trained never to register judgment.

Arthur's looking at her as if she's pronounced the unforgivable blasphemy. To his ears it's not far off it.

'No. No condoms.'

The timing may be ordained, but Norm doesn't appreciate it. Running into the vicar. Trying to be nonchalant about the bottle he's just purchased, now sheathed in its paper bag.

'Hello, there. I met you at the funeral; you're a friend of Arthur's, aren't you?'

'Yeah, Norm. How's it going, vicar?'

'Kevin. Fine, thanks. Are you heading off down the hill?'

'Yep. On my way home, such as it is.'

'Mind if I walk with you? I was going to call into the boarding house.'

'Suit yourself. It's a good enough day.'

Norm keeping his reserve. Partly from suspicion of clergy. Partly because of the bottle under his arm. They're setting off together, an unlikely couple. Kevin slowing his pace to fall in with Norm, who has more time and less energy.

'How long have you known Arthur?'

'Arthur? Let me see now. Must be three years, anyway.'

Norm's thinking of that day when he discovered an intruder on his patch. Sleeping on a park bench. Great brown head protruding from under an old coat. Snoring with the resonance of a minor earthquake.

'What d'you think of him?'

The answer is some time in coming. Norm stops, looks hard into ecclesiastical eyes. Living on the streets for a while makes you a little cynical. No casting of pearls before swine. Especially religious swine.

'I think he's very special. He's either the second son of God like he says he is or else he's mad as a hatter. I haven't made up my mind which yet. But regardless of that, he's probably the best bloke I've ever met in my life.'

'He wanted me to spread the word to my congregation about his secret identity.'

'He's been round a lot of the churches asking them to do that. Hasn't got anywhere with them.'

'I told him I couldn't. For obvious reasons. But

there's been times lately when I've seriously wondered if he might not be what he says he is. And then I think I'm the one who's off his rocker.'

'Arthur has that effect on a lot of people. He's a real mystery package.'

As they part ways, Kevin is no less confused.

Asking an alcoholic for a judgment call on a wannabe Messiah; I must be in a bad way.

The angels are relaxing in a spa. Giving each other mutual foot massages. Which may lead to other things, given time and space.

Interrupted, however, by a seraph wearing a cobalt-blue robe and sipping a pink gin through a long straw. With magnificent flashing rings. Heaven not being quite socialist.

'Well, my lovelies, how did it go?'

'Just like you said it would. She'll be lucky if she comes down before judgment day. Where in hell do you get that stuff? We could sure use some.'

'I didn't get it from that dreadful place, dearies. It's actually an old recipe from the days of the prophets, but wild cherubim couldn't tease it out of me. Well, not without a bit of effort anyway. So, my pretty white doves, what are we going to do with you next?'

'We're quite enjoying what we're into at the moment.'

'I'm quite sure you are, precious, and I'm sorry

for intruding; but of course, you're speaking of your assignment, aren't you? How naughty of me to misunderstand. Well, all right. Call me easy, but I'm happy for you to stay on the case, so to speak. I think you might find there's developments approaching which will intrigue even your limited imaginations. But enough of this absorbing tittle-tattle, my celestial beauties. I must fly; a little something of cosmic proportions awaits me.'

There's a burst of magnesium white as the seraph leaves.

Bloody divas, they're so precious. A little bit higher up would be nice.

She's sore, blood-gorged and replete. Missing the generosity and gentility of Penny, but excited by the novelty of pumping penetration.

He's happily exhausted; spent like a cartridge case. Heart rate gradually easing back. They lie side by side in that no-man's-land of post-coital rumination.

'What will become of us, Gwenda? I still have moments of panic, thinking it's too good to be true.'

'Can't things be good and true at the same time? I don't want to think too much about the future, or the past. There's just the two of us hidden away in this room, where no-one can touch us. We only have the present. Let's not lose it.'

He can't help himself. His analytical mind

is already testing possibilities, assessing odds, contemplating strategies.

'You've told her?'

'Yes.'

There's a long silence occupied by Penny. Gwenda is inhaling her mustiness. David is regretting her pain. Imperceptibly, the temperature has changed.

Sitting on the bar stool, seeing his own image in the mirror. A man in shock. A man forlorn. A man losing his job. He nurses the whisky as if it were a breast.

He can't think when he might have last been in a pub on a weekday afternoon. But for now it's a fallout shelter. A safe place to sit and mull on the random indecencies of fate. With the slow anaesthetic of the alcohol shifting the pain sideways.

How does one tell one's friends? One's wife? Is it possible to drop chaos into casual conversation? *By the way, dear, I think I might be losing my job.*

Other possibilities have registered on the options board. There's the insurance. A hose on the exhaust pipe. A swerve into the path of an oncoming truck. Would the shame be worse than this? *At least I wouldn't be around to experience it.*

His glass has emptied itself.

'Another one, thanks.'

It's the same park in which they first talked, so many

years ago. Arthur arriving early, not being too sure of the time. Lowering his large frame onto a park bench.

A harried mother watching him with anxiety. Finally gathering her rumbustious brood about her and leading them out of this apparent danger zone.

The sun warming his body. Arthur leaning his head back, catching it on the vast expanse of his forehead. He can smell the grass drying.

A monarch butterfly settling on his knee. Coaxing it on to his finger, lifting its beauty for closer inspection. *Ah, yes, my friend. You are on the other side. But do you remember where you came from? The fetid darkness from which you sprang?* He blows gently; the butterfly steps onto a current of air and is gone.

Arthur surveys the glass cathedrals, stretching on tiptoe to outreach each other. An oversized flag drooping at the top on one shining monolith. *Tombstones for an age*, he's thinking. An age which soon will draw to a close.

He summons the languishing afternoon into focus. Deepens the blue of the sky, lowers the pitch of the cicadas, freshens the breeze by a knot. Calling the trees to draw nearer. Sprinkling birds through the branches for garnish. *And now, may my queen arrive.*

It's not her footsteps that announce her presence, for she's walking on grass. It's not her perfume, for she isn't wearing any. It's not her voice, for she's silent.

Yet Arthur knows her coming from the first eager step off the footpath. It's her spirit, her presence, her being.

She sees the shock of tangled black hair immediately. Adrenaline pumping. Joy rising. Deciding to sneak up on him, attack him from behind. She makes it to within three paces of him before he speaks.

'Your eyes are beautiful, Margaret.'

'How would you know? You can't even see them, you big hairy spoilsport.'

Throwing her arm around his neck from behind and holding him in a headlock.

'Now I've got you, and you're all mine.'

Tilting his head back with the other hand, and brushing her lips teasingly across his.

'I've been sitting here for a couple of days waiting for you. I was just starting to get a bit hungry — thought I might trade you for a mince pie. Wondered if you'd run off with Digby.'

'I might do, too, if you keep telling me lies like that. I thought the son of God would at least tell the truth once in a while.'

'Only when it's needed. The rest of the time I'll tell you that you're ugly. Jeez, you're ugly. I'll have to get me some shades to save my eyes from that white face.'

She's round the front, punching his chest. With

all the impact of rain on the ocean. Tumbling into his arms, falling across his lap, kissing now with passion.

'Hey, steady on. I need those lips for eating. Anyone'd think you hadn't had a feed for a month. And they reckon Maoris were cannibals!'

But he holds her there on his lap, arms encircling, foreheads pressed together. Eyes joined in a *fête-de-deux*. Some time is passing. The secrets of cold fusion there for the taking.

She manoeuvres her chest in close against his. Making sure he can feel the unencumbered flesh beneath the cotton dress. Whispering in his ear.

'Arthur, I want you.'

He's lifting her casually, lowering her gently to the seat beside him. *Have I said something wrong?* All the insecurities rushing back in to occupy their home ground. But then she's held by those eyes, and it's all right again.

'Margaret, I want to make love with you too. But it has to be done right. The right time and the right place. This is not something just for us. Our father has put us together.'

'Oh, Arthur. I get so confused when you talk about all this. I don't know anything about God; why would God be interested in me?'

'If you know me, you know God. If you give yourself to me, you'll be giving yourself to God. Whether you understand it or not, you've been chosen, the same as I have. There's nothing you can do about it — no use hiding and pretending it's not true.'

'But why? What for? What's the purpose of it all?'

'You trust me, Margaret?'

'Of course I do, but . . .'

'We're to have a baby together.'

Stunned, shattered, shocked silence. His eyes all encompassing.

'Arthur! I'm married. You know that. It's bad enough this, but . . . a baby! It's just not possible.'

Be a bloody miracle seeing I've had my tubes tied. But this doesn't seem to be the time to mention such a peccadillo.

'Margaret? Trust me. Look at me. That's right. Trust me.'

And he's holding her, enfolding her. For the moment his warmth and strength are all the answer that she needs. She's content to let the rest drift in the air like so much smoke. When you've leapt from the diving board, it's too late to hold reservations. As Arthur is stroking her hair and telling her of a motel booked for next week.

Perhaps madness is contagious.

'Aw shit, vicar, ya caught us a bit unprepared. We don't get too many visitors down here.'

Bob's stubbing out his cigarette on the dinner

plate, clearing some of the stuff off the table so that there's room for Kevin to sit down.

'Wal, take that filthy bloody magazine up to yer bedroom, will ya? The vicar doesn't want big tits up his nose, does he now? Tell ya what, vic, how about a cuppa tea?'

'Call me Kevin, and yes, I'd love a cup of tea.'

'Right. We just made one for the boys. Only thing is it's got sugar in. We put the sugar in the pot when we make it, see? Saves pissing around with teaspoons and that. So what brings you down to this neck of the woods?'

'I just thought I'd call in and see how you're all doing. Sometimes it takes people a while to adjust to a death, especially a suicide.'

'Suppose it does, sometimes. Though the blokes here are pretty much used it, eh. Always some poor prick topping himself. It's the messy ones I don't like — hacking through their veins with blunt razor blades and bleedin' all over the soddin' carpet. Sorry, Kev, I'll be putting ya off yer cuppa in a minute. Yeah, so ya sorta get used to it, much as ya can. I reckon about half the guys I've had in the house over the years have ended up offing themselves. Nothing much ya can do about it except give 'em a good sendoff and then get on with things.'

'I was impressed with the honesty of what people said at the funeral.'

'It's just the way things are in this part of the world. When ya live with alkies and murderers and maniacs of one sort or another, there's not much room for the usual bullshit that passes for politeness.'

From the lounge there comes the sound of raised voices, arguing over what channel they're going to watch. Suddenly the volume on the TV shoots up to maximum.

'Turn that fucken thing down or I'll knock yer stupid bloody heads together! Sorry, Kev. Tend to shoot off me mouth a bit; ya probably noticed. I'm afraid it ain't very religious down here most of the time. 'Cept for Arthur, of course. He raises the tone of the place.'

'What d'you think of Arthur's claims — to be the second son of God?'

'Christ, he's as mad as the day's long, mate. Don't tell me he's got you going as well? We get all sorts in here. If they don't think they're the devil, then it's Elvis or the Pope. Come to think of it, no-one's wanted to be the Pope for a while — must be going out of fashion. One loony we had thought he was the Virgin Mary. If his name had've been Mary he would've been a bloody virgin orright — ugly as sin he was. So Arthur's just one of a crowd. Nice bloke, though; got a lot of time for him.'

'Quite.'

The moon pulls and the waters rise. Its yellow light scans the streets, filters through slatted windows. There is gravity in the air, and tides are turning.

The growing orb is reflected in dogs' mournful eyes. In beds across Ponsonby people find themselves starkly awake, itching in some untouchable place. Here and there a menstruating woman is cramped with pain.

Pete wakes screaming, and Arthur holds him in the brightness of the night.

Margaret fakes sleep, drained of comfort, while Brian weeps quietly beside her.

6

Arthur is holding the key like it opens the future. The door to the room is already ajar. Pretty flash. A TV and all. Most important, a bloody great bed. *Long time since you were in a bed like that, boy.* He's shutting the blinds and closing the door. Work to be done.

The time is ripe, ready to be picked.

This is the hour of your work, my son. Now go and perform all that I have told you.

'I arranged it with Penny ages ago. I can't believe that you've forgotten about it.'

'Did you? You might have done. I just can't quite think straight at the moment. What's it about?'

'We're just going out for dinner, that's all. A girls' night out. I thought it would be better to stay there overnight than drive home after drinking wine. Look, it's here on the calendar.'

Where I just wrote it, but Brian never looks at the calendar anyway. Quite handy that he's so distracted at the moment.

'Yeah, OK, Marg. I suppose I must have agreed to it, though God knows why. What are we supposed to do for dinner?'

'It's all there — lasagne. Just heat it up in the microwave — there's a salad in the fridge. Mark'll show you how to use the microwave if you're having trouble.'

'Marg?'

'What?'

'I've been all right, haven't I? I mean we've never wanted for anything, have we? The house and everything. I've always tried to do what's right, what's expected of me. I know I should've spent more time with you and the kids, but I've had to do my job as well. I'm not a great father, but I'm as good as anyone else I know. It's not like there's been a lot of choices. Things seem to have slipped away from me somehow. But we've never wanted for anything, you and I.'

Is it duty or sympathy that makes her hold him?

'No, Brian, we've never wanted.'

Certainly it is not love. Now she knows that.

Bob was reluctant to give him so many sheets at first.

'What the bloody hell are ya gonna to do with ten sheets? Have a friggin' toga party?'

'I can't tell you. It has to be kept secret until everything becomes plain.'

'Yer a fruitcake, Arthur. Yer madder than a chook

with its head cut off, and half as good-looking. I'm even nuttier for going along with all yer bloody harebrained plans. Orright then, ya can have ten sheets, but ya look after them or I'll cut yer balls off and serve them to ya with spaghetti. And make sure they're back here by Tuesday when the laundry truck comes.'

'Ka pai, Bob. You're a good man.'

'Yeah, and Roslyn's never been kissed. Get outta here, ya big Maori maniac.'

He worried that ten sheets might not even be enough when he saw the size of the motel room. But now, standing back and admiring the work of his hands, he is well pleased. It is as he has seen it.

And now for the candles.

It's nearly 5.00 p.m. That explains why there's so much traffic on the highway, leaving work and heading for the sanctuary of home and weekend. A shiny metal ant trail. But she's heading the other way, against the flow. She's going in a different direction.

In the back seat is her travel bag. What do you pack for this sort of thing? What items are necessary to have an affair? To sleep with a man who isn't your husband? To spend a night in a motel with a psychiatric patient? Not very much, she decided the third time she packed the bag.

She notices that she's speeding, and relaxes her

foot on the accelerator. *That's not like me. To go over the limit.*

Everything is in place. It has taken most of the afternoon. Soon she will be here.

The angel sitting on the coffee table looks across to her colleague, lounging on the sofa. But there are no answers there. He's preening himself, wishing that mortal mirrors could carry his reflection.

Arthur is removing his clothes and getting into the shower. It takes him a while to figure it out, seeing there's only one tap-thing. For one of the few times in his life, he's enjoying the feel of soap and water on his skin. It's part of the preparation. A cleansing for what must begin.

He allows the water to stream over him, washing, washing. Then he's throwing his great head back and releasing a torrent of sound into the heavens.

Adesh dada kadeesh tama ladabas tadama nis kadaka mush karaka bos tadeeshta ramata dini olo ba disdini gos tada demeesh lala badis mara nas bara kadis toi.

The angels are instantly alert and looking at each other. There's a hole torn in eternity and time is seeping into it. So much is for the first time clear. They exchange a very high five.

She parks the car and gets out of it quickly, before

there's a chance to reconsider. He's seen the car coming and is out there to meet her. He stands there grinning.

'Haere mai, Margaret, Queen of Heaven.'

She drops her bag and enters the shelter of his arms. He holds her.

'Come inside and see.'

He's leading her by the hand. Then he's scooping her up into his arms as he carries her into the motel unit.

'Arthur, you idiot. Put me down.'

In the open-plan living area there's a table. Arthur's covered it with a sheet, set places, put flowers and candlesticks in the centre. There are wineglasses there, which he found in the cupboard.

'It's lovely, Arthur, just lovely.'

And she's kissing him, with intent.

'Let me just put my things in the bedroom.'

'No! I'll put your bag in there. You're not allowed to see until later.'

'Mmm. Mystery. I suppose I'll have to wait then, won't I? Though I'm not very patient, I can tell you now.'

While he's gone, she spins around in a girlish circle. She smells the flowers — roses — rebuking herself for noticing that the stems are rough-cut, taken from somebody's garden. *I suppose I should be feeling guilty. But I'm not.*

He returns and fetches a bottle of cheap bubbly from the fridge. He's rattling around in the cutlery drawer, looking for something.

'You don't need anything to open that. Give it here. You're not very experienced in this game of seduction, are you? Just as well, too.'

She pours two glasses, with care. Handing him one.

'To us, Arthur, and our night together.'

'To God, who brought us together.'

From the fridge he produces food. There's cold cooked chicken and some potato salad. It came from the kitchen of the boarding house, and no doubt Bob will already be noticing it missing.

They sit down to eat, with an odd formality.

'I want us to pray,' he says.

'Fine by me.'

'Father, the earth is yours and everything in it. You have given us life and put us here to share it with you. This is our kai which we have by your grace. It is a good kai. Bless our eating; bless our drinking; bless our talking; bless our sex. Amen.'

She's blushing. She tries to hide it by having a long drink. But Arthur's watching her.

'You shouldn't hide your face. It's good to have a face which doesn't keep secrets.'

'This whole thing is so impossible, Arthur. And

yet I'm so happy. I haven't felt so free and alive for yonks. I want it to last for ever, but I know it won't.'

'Every time lasts for ever if you use it right. When I was just a boy, up north, my grandfather used to take me out fishing. He always knew where to go, eh. We'd just catch enough for what we needed, and then pull our lines in. And he'd lean back in the boat and light him a smoke and talk to me. Man, he had some stories to tell. I wanted him to go on and on for ever, and never stop. I said to him one day, I wish we didn't have to go back. I still remember him looking at me with his one cloudy eye. "Arthur," he said, "you see the way we pull those fish in. Then we're going to take them back home and make a big kai and eat them. Isn't that right?" Yeah, old man, that's what we're going to do. "Well," he says, "that's the way to live. When something good's happening, you got to pull it in on a line and take it on board. And then you've got to take it home and eat it. That way no-one can ever take it away from you again." He taught me a lot of stuff, my grandfather.'

'You know that's the most you've ever told me about your family.'

'Three years ago I went back up for my grandfather's tangi. It was good to be back up there. I was having a few drinks and a yarn with one of my uncles. I told him about me being the second son of God. Next thing you know there's a big argument. One of my cousins is a Christian, and he started telling me I was wrong, that I had a demon. I must've hit him, I suppose, 'cos there he was lying on the ground. There was a big korero, and they decided I was porangi, crazy. They wanted to call in a doctor. So I took off and haven't heard from any of them since.'

She's standing behind him now. Massaging his shoulders. Running her fingers through his woolly hair. Bending down and brushing his face with her own.

'What's wrong with this food, you skinny white thing? C'mon, help me finish it, eh?'

'There's something I want you to see, Margaret.'

He's leading her out the front door. There's a small porch area at the front of the unit with two chairs. They sit there. Spread out before them is the cityscape, shining in the evening light.

'What?'

'Sit here and shut up, woman. And look.'

What is there to see? The jagged horizon, the Sky Tower giving the finger to God, china-blue sky bleeding into purple. Traffic grunt and birdsong somehow in partnership to make a weighty peace. And then there is a movement. A bending of the air, a flattened light which pops into vision and begins climbing.

The moon.

Impossibly huge against the toy buildings. Massive and mellow, gliding into the sky. Dominating, demanding. If you sit still you can feel the gravitational whirlpool, sense your mind tracking into orbit.

Full as it ever was, rising and mysterious.

He's whispering something.

'On the night of the second full moon of the year, when the air is still and the morepork cries; then she will give herself to you and all will begin.'

'Sorry?'

'We can't stop this thing now, Margaret, even if we wanted to.'

'I'm ready. I was just thinking, watching that moon, how easy it must be to travel that far above the earth. To be free to sail through the heavens like that. I have this vague memory of something within me that is free and majestic, like the moon. I can feel it rising, Arthur. It's strange, seeing the moon like this; I almost feel like I'm looking into a mirror which can see inside of me. When I was little I always had the sense that I was special in some way, you know? Like there was some sort of purpose, some sort of meaning to my life. Then somewhere on the way through it all got tangled up with shabby little things — important enough at the time, but unworthy somehow. I thought that the rest of my life was going to be like that. Duty, politeness, doing the right thing, being a good wife and mother, dying quietly with the minimum of fuss. But now I can see something different. I'm going to follow the moon, Arthur. I'm going to just break free of the horizon and float into the night. I'm ready.'

'OK. Just give me a few minutes to arrange some things. I'll come and get you in a minute.'

While he's gone she hears a bird calling its lament over the city. *What is that? A morepork?*

There's a shock of adjustment as he opens the bedroom door, leading her in by the hand. It takes some moments for her brain to unscramble the signals, to make a pattern from them. She gasps.

The walls have disappeared. Instead there's a cocoon of whiteness. Everything is covered with white sheets — the walls, the floor, even the bed is stripped back to its white sheets. On either side of the bed and at other points of the room there are candles burning, the only light. The air is thick with fragrance. It is like a shrine.

'It's beautiful. It's just beautiful. When did you do all this?'

'C'mon into the other room. We should take our clothes off out there, bring nothing in with us.'

He leads her out again. Her hand goes to the button of the blouse, to start undoing it.

'No. You just stand there. Be still.'

'Yes, master.'

She giggles.

He is undoing the buttons, one by one. The tail of the blouse is pulled out from the top of her skirt, very slowly. It hangs loosely, the front open a little and revealing a slice of flesh. Broken by the white of her bra. She has her eyes closed, head slightly back, an edge of apprehension. Now kneeling down in front of her, running his tongue around the outside of her belly button. She rests her hands on his great head and sighs.

Standing, he slides the blouse back off one shoulder. He notices the freckles on her skin, smiles. Brushes the bareness with his fingertips, so gently. And kisses the inside of her neck. Then it is the turn of the other shoulder. When he kisses her neck on the other side, she murmurs and makes as if to reach down with her own lips.

'Be still, I said.'

The blouse is hanging off her upper arms, gaping widely so that the fullness of her breasts pushes through. Moving behind her, he slips it down and off completely. He draws her arms back behind her, cradling her upturned palms in his. Bending to run his tongue around the inside of each palm. Then popping her fingers into his mouth and sucking them one by one. Still holding her hands out behind her, he runs his tongue along each inside arm, from the wrist up to her newly shaved armpits.

Her inner world is a maelstrom of pleasure. There is a firestorm in her synapses. Sensations crowding in on top of each other. Her skin has become unbearably sensitive, magnifying every touch. The warmth in her groin is creeping outward. There is a gentle throbbing in the whole of her body as her heart responds to the demand.

He lifts her hands and places them on top of her head, leaving them there. Those light fingers down the length of her back. Kisses under each armpit. Then the fingers are under the back of the bra strap. He pulls it outward slightly. She feels the pressure on each breast, and strains against it. Reaching around the front of her from behind, he strokes the top of her breasts where they are exposed and lifted by the bra. Slides his palms down to the slight bulge of her tummy that she feels so self-conscious about.

His hands are behind her again, and she feels the hooks being undone one by one. The anticipation is glorious and painful. The last one pops the tension of the bra, and the cool air finds its way to her nipples. He leaves the bra hanging there, but eases his hands up from underneath until he is cupping each breast; a living bra. The nipples are straining for attention, but he simply brushes a finger over each of them before turning his attention elsewhere.

Her skirt has a side zip. He lowers it slowly, so that

she can hear and feel each of the metal teeth popping apart. The skirt slips to the floor with a minimum of encouragement. She slips her bare feet out of it and kicks it to one side. Arthur seems to tolerate this minor transgression of standing orders. He kneels down behind her and applies his tongue to the crease of flesh behind her knees.

He is standing again, running his fingers just inside the waistband of her bikini briefs. He grips the side seams and pulls gently upwards. The pressure on her pubic mound is exquisite. Then, with his thumbs tucked into the top of the knickers, he draws them down with agonising slowness. There is a prickly sensation as the air mixes with the moisture of her vulva. Again she disposes of the clothing with a flick of her toes.

Arthur is standing behind her. He cups two hands to her buttocks and squeezes ever so gently. Then he walks to the front of her. Takes her hands from her head and lowers them to her side. Slips the bra straps from her shoulders and lowers it, discards it. He takes a couple of steps back to regard her.

She is naked.

She is aware that her breath has shortened; almost a panting. He is looking at her, observing her, admiring her. But more than that; loving her. His eyes are full of encouragement and tenderness. He has a slight smile on his face. She has never felt so safe in all her life.

The angels are spellbound. They dare not move or speak, for fear they may break the atmosphere. They are feeding on the love, as only angels can.

It is her turn now. With her eyes she lets him know that the same rules apply. She begins by kissing him softly on the lips. Then with her fingers she touches his face. Closing her eyes, she explores it as a blind person would. Feeling the cracks and crevices, the character and the mana. She brushes his eyelids with her thumbs, kisses him on the lips again.

Kneeling down, she removes his socks. She takes each foot in turn, massaging it firmly between her fingers. Each toe gets individual treatment. The belt is next. She is undoing it. Sliding it out through the belt loops. It takes all her strength to get the top button of his jeans undone. The zip is an easier project. Lowering it, she repays the slowness. The jeans fall under their own weight. He steps out of them. She remains kneeling in front of him for a few moments, grinning at his hardness straining against the underpants.

He can feel the warmth of her breath through the cotton underpants. He is tempted to act quickly, to begin, to rush. He summons his strength, remembers what this is about, brings himself under control. His muscles are snapping into hardness, his mind clear. The air is thick with wairua and aroha, and something else as well. He cannot help himself shuddering.

Margaret stands, begins unbuttoning his shirt. With each button she is stroking a little more of his chest, running her fingers through the thick curls of hair. When they are all undone, she pushes her hands gently against his stomach. Slides them up to the shoulders and pushes the shirt back off them. It falls to the ground. Touching him with no other part of her body, she grazes his chest with her nipples. Back and forwards, back and forwards.

One hand down the front of his underpants, gripping the thick stake which pulses in her hand. There is a rumble from the back of Arthur's throat. She draws the last garment down by its sides, holding while he steps away from it. The great horn jerks upward in celebration of its new freedom. Kneeling in front of him, she holds it with one hand while the other fondles his scrotum.

The male angel is staring in astonishment. His partner looks at him with a new disdain. Nevertheless, the atmosphere is, well, arousing. She floats behind him, and reaches into his robes until she finds what she knew would be there. Hard and hot. It breaks his concentration.

Arthur reaches down and lifts her to her feet. He kisses her at length and with enthusiasm.

'Now we can enter.'

She finds it hard to move, but he leads her into the whiteness once again. The candles produce a light of serenity and softness. The musky scent goes right to the back of her head.

It's like a religious experience, she is thinking.

He guides her to lie down on the bed, face down. From somewhere he has produced massage oil, spreading it onto his hands. And then he is beginning on her back.

It is as if each of his fingers has been individually trained to provoke pleasure. They stroke, they caress, they prod, they press, they squeeze, they knead, they explore. As he massages her shoulders she can feel the tension leaving and the flesh luxuriating. The oil produces a delicious, creamy sensation.

He is continuing to work his way down her body, applying massage oil as he goes. Her lower back becomes a playground of pain and pleasure as he digs his fingers deep into the muscles and manipulates them. When he begins on her buttocks she begins to make a noise, unable to stand it any more without some form of expression. It is a cross between a sigh and a groan. His thumbs work some sort of magic which threatens to throw her whole body into spasm.

Then it is the turn of her legs. He works his way down without any attempt to hurry. Any stiffness in her calf muscles dissolves ahead of his agile fingers. When he reaches her feet he gives them special attention. He presses into the soles until it hurts, but each time as she is about to cry out the sensation becomes one of numbing enjoyment.

The way he handles each foot, as if it were an item of great value and fragility.

A naked angel is a sight to behold. Here they are, the two of them, shining in full radiance as they dance their own special steps of ecstasy. Not that they've forgotten their mission of observation. More like they're taking their research to new levels. Mortals can be so inspiring, given the right circumstances.

With a hand on her shoulder he turns her. Now he is applying the massage oil to her front, smoothing the path of his hands. They are gentler now, searching and soothing. He works on her breasts until her nipples seem ready to pop their corks. And then he cools them with his tongue. Drawing the rough texture of it across the very tips.

She thrusts upwards until he is forced to take her

into his mouth. At first it is just the nipple which he is chewing with his lips. But then he sucks and draws the front half of her breast into his mouth, drawing it away from her with the suction. She gasps and reaches out for the sides of the bed with her hands. Then it is the turn of the other breast.

It is building up within her like a volcano. Some lid has been wrenched off, and there is a rush of molten substances towards the surface. There is no space for thought, no distance for evaluation. There is just sensation; unrestrained, pulsating pleasure.

He places his hands underneath her knees, draws them upward. Spreads them apart with the minimum of movement. He kneels between them, applies the oil to her inner thighs. His hands are moving up and down, up and down on the inside of her legs. The fingers adding their contribution.

As well to try and stop a natal contraction, or resist gravity. It is rising within her, picking up a rhythm and compulsion of its own. Onward and upward and outward, gripping gut and bowel alike in a relentless surge.

It is the stopping of the motion on her thighs which gives the only faint clue. He bends down, parts the lips of her vulva with his thumbs, and inserts the tip of his tongue.

It is as if he has pushed the plunger to detonate a truck full of explosives. She rears up, arches her back, gives a muffled scream. Arthur watches in wonder the rhythmic contractions of her vulva, clearly visible.

It erupts within her in one gigantic, cataclysmic surge. From the soft centre between her legs there begins a convulsion that bucks her into the air. She has become one great living throb which consumes body, soul and spirit. Again and again it courses through her, ravaging her, driving out sense and perception. Liquid colours sweep across the chamber of her being. Finally it begins to subside. She struggles to breathe again.

'My God, Arthur. What was that?'

He allows her to fall back on the bed, resting for a few moments. He strokes her forehead and murmurs her name as she struggles for a sense of control.

And then he is back there again with that tongue, probing and flicking and teasing.

'No, Arthur, I can't . . .'

But here are the spasms again, over and over and over. Mauling her, crushing her, ripping apart the constraints of rationality.

At the same moment there is an angelic climax in the air above them. The high-pitched, ululating scream that is the signature of seraphic orgasm is unheard by Margaret and Arthur. Though not by all. The cosmic pair notice all too late. There is the sound of slow hand-clapping and much laughter.

Around them is what we commonly call a host of angels. Watching with interest.

Might as well get your robes on, you two. We enjoyed the show, but it's not really on your account that we're here.

She wants him inside her now. The last two orgasms have reamed her, made her loose and wet.

He lowers himself between her legs. The glans of his penis is burning against the mouth of her vagina. She is finding it hard to breathe again. She wants to throw herself towards him, be impaled on the spike which is pulsing against her moistness. But she somehow holds back, sensing his restraint and great patience. Choosing the excruciating tension over the quick release.

They lie there like that for what, two minutes? She would swear in a court of law that it was an hour.

And then, and then. Slowly, steadily, surely. He begins to move within. The vaginal walls stretch and tremble. The terror and the joy are inseparable. He is filling every crevice. And still it comes, on and on, deeper and deeper. And when she feels that she cannot possibly contain him, there is one more push and he is chocka block within her, consuming and consumed.

She groans as the convulsions are triggered again, squeezing and squeezing. Exhausting her.

He feels every one of the spasms as if it were his own. It is getting difficult to know where Margaret stops and Arthur begins.

The universe is in constant flux. Space and time never cease the ballet of creation. There is no downtime in the foundry of life.

Occasionally there are alignments of certain types, which have consequences not always apparent.

One such alignment is about to take place.

When her climax has subsided, he begins, slowly, to move inside her.

She feels every move in the ocean depths of her psyche. There are giant undersea tremors, shaking the very floors and walls of the main.

Her hands move up and down his arms, as he is sliding so carefully between her thighs. She feels the muscles there, the bridled strength. Then she grips his back and groans in delight.

He bends down, clamping the nearest breast with his mouth. He lifts it, swallows it, flicks at the nipple with his tongue. And then for equity's sake, the other. And all the time, the gentle penetrating movement, in and out in perfect rhythm.

The waves are growing mountainous again, wallowing against each other. She can feel it welling up again, expanding from the depths.

She clamps Arthur's buttocks with her hands, urging him to stop. Too much at the moment and something will give way. For a dangerous moment she hovers on the brink, with muscles in tremor and threatening to clamp. Ever so gradually it fades, and she rides the wave downwards in relief.

For a time she lies there, holding him still. He is nuzzling her neck. The oil and sweat and candle scent are all mixed together with a hint of eternity. She is scared to inhale deeply in case it causes movement and sets her off again. The candles burn with an unnatural purity, glowing in the whiteness of the room. The film of moisture on her eyes causes the candles to glisten in a kaleidoscope of patterns and colours. Is heaven different from this?

Time to find some control.

Margaret uses her legs to roll him over on to his back. She is determined not to lose him out of her in the process. Once she has him below her she laughs, and he laughs back. Looking down into that genial face with all its strength and grace, she is struck by an unfamiliar sensation. Awe.

She puts her hands on his shoulders and pushes herself up, riding to the very tip of his penis. There she holds herself, contracting the muscles in her vagina to squeeze his glans. His face contorts with pleasure, and she watches it, gratified.

She drops suddenly, unexpectedly, from this perch; like a hawk on its prey. The resulting thrust causes Arthur to cry out, and sends paroxysms of pleasure shooting up her spine. Again she feels her muscles clamping, and has to ride out another wave which threatens to overcome her.

Easy how you go.

Leaning forward, gently and slowly, she lowers her breasts until they touch his chest. She sweeps them back and forward against him, luxuriating in the sensation. She presents her nipples, one at a time, for him to nibble and suck on.

Then, straightening her back, she reaches behind and underneath her to take a handful of testicle. An exploratory squeeze causes Arthur to buck and pulse within her in a not unpleasant fashion. For a short while she controls their pleasure with this hand.

Recovering some poise and energy, she starts to rise and fall upon him, riding that penis as if it were some wild unbroken stallion that needed calming. With each stroke it seems that the beast swells inside her. The sensation is liquid honey, oozing.

The assembled throngs are beaming and applauding, taking credit for it all like good spectators.

Michael has joined them. Something important must be going down.

He calls them together to sing. It is the song which inspired the *Hallelujah Chorus*. These mortals will take credit for anything.

Arthur can hear it. It's not the first time he's heard the angels singing. But he's always reduced to tears by the beauty of it.

She sees him crying, whether from pleasure or pain she knows not.

She leans right back now, placing her hands behind her on Arthur's knees. Dangling her head back to its farthest extremity. Her grip on the intruder tightens. She can feel the throbbing of his pulse. The legacy of his beating heart transmitted to her through the walls of her vagina.

If there was one moment to hold, this would be it. Leaning back like that, she is open to the universe, open to life. And it feels for all the world as if the universe is hard up inside her. Each ragged breath causes ecstasy through the movement and friction it brings. There is a type of madness of passion which has flooded her. It's almost as if she can hear singing somewhere, a majestic, swelling chorus.

He reaches up and tweaks her nipples. They are

so swollen that they are painful, but even the pain is received as pleasure by this stage. She luxuriates in it, wanting to give more and take more, wanting to screw the brains out of reality.

His fingers trace their way down her stomach, stopping to explore again the delicate belly button. Then he is playing with her pubic hair, stretching it and teasing it.

All of this time neither of them has moved the vital muscles.

They are camped on the slopes of chaos.

Everything is sliding into place.

The silent orbs drifting on the tides of gravity. Somewhere in the foothills of eternity a nova flaring. Unseen forces contending.

It is beginning.

She leans forward, pivoting on the fulcrum which impales her. Forward she goes, degree by delicious degree. Now she is stretched out full length against him, her breasts flattened against him, her legs matching his. She is kissing him on the lips. Teasing, then hard. Biting.

Together they roll and he is on top. Immediately his weight adds depth to the penetration. There is no more room for anything. He is filling her from the inside.

She is murmuring now. A mixture of words and noises. Primal stuff rising from the very core, pouring over the sandbanks of her consciousness.

And then he is moving again, and everything with him.

Every toehold has given way, and there is a falling, falling.

The floor of the sea is rocking under a vast earthquake. Wave after undulating wave is pumping the rock as if it were a rubber diaphragm. Above there are cubic miles of cold, black ocean compressing into rhythmic striations.

Heaving into swells.

In and out, he moves, up and down. There is no restraint any more, no discipline, no measure. They are beyond their own limits. Normality lies riven.

She opens her legs to Arthur and to God. Her feet are in the air. She holds to his buttocks and wills him to move harder. She cares not whether she should die.

He is humping and thrusting. Driving strokes, over and over. Pounding and grinding. Pushing his full length to the very hilt and wishing it would go further. Gripping her shoulders to pierce her more fully.

It could be anger. Hatred. It might be the dance of

death. An act of murder, this relentless stabbing of flesh. The frenzy and the lust. This primitive wailing.

The mighty, flexing rock-skin tears under the pressure. The undersea strata rip like a sheet. From the molten centre there pours forth magma. It rises in great globules into the sea. The glowing redness of it shrugs aside the icy mass, begins the journey to the surface.

She can feel it coming.

In Arthur's psychic galaxy there is a firestorm. A hundred stars have released their formative energy. Tongues of fire flame out across the cosmos. As they touch new star clusters, these too are loosed and burn.

There is a silent rumble moving through the unimaginable spaces.

He stops at the end of an upstroke. She screams. Claws at his back, raking with her nails. Her head is thrashing from side to side in desperation.

Poised above her, he throws his head back and calls out.

And then he falls. The final stroke. Long and deep and hard.

She screams louder. Thrashes in death throes.

He is whimpering and crying.

'Kua mutu,' he gasps. 'Kua mutu.'

The magma bursts through the surface in a terrifying explosion. There is fire and steam and columns of black smoke. The sea parts and is vaporized. Waves rush back from the centre, towering, and then fall back on themselves. It is apocalyptic, appalling.

The fire in the heavens begins to feed on itself. Chain reaction. White-hot nuclear tempest, sweeping all before it. Searing, sundering heat; consuming matter in its path. Outward, outward, outward. All is burning.

The angels have reached a crescendo which even Michael has heard only twice before. Their song is liquid glory, spinning gossamer strands into existence as it arcs out into the receptacle of being.

For this teardrop of time, the alignment is perfect.

A great hum of energy radiates outward as the corridor is opened.

The fire from below meets the fire from above.

Hot sperm sluicing down the passage. Erupting into the canal. Pumping, thumping, kicking. With each ejaculation he shudders from head to toe.

With a cunning all of its own, her vagina picks up

the rhythm and works in harmony. The contractions are strong and hard, squeezing every drop of life-bearing fluid from the stem of his penis. Banging and bucking and clenching.

Each pulsation rolls through her like thunder, causing her to tremble and moan. On and on and on it goes. Multiple meltdown of the cerebrum. Pleasure so thick and real that it oozes and seeps.

Fire in the hole.

Arthur is standing under a tree. It is on the top of a small knoll, which stretches down to the sea. Along the shore there are pohutukawa trees. The ocean glistens under the sun.

There is a voice speaking. He knows the voice without turning.

Arthur, my son. I have chosen you from the dawn of creation, and set my seal upon you. You have been sent for a purpose which is yet to unfold. Because you have been faithful to what I have asked of you, the wheel is in motion. You are the son that I love, and from you there will flow blessing upon blessing.

There is a chanting from below. Arthur looks out and sees a waka bearing down on the shore. In it are his ancestors, chanting a waiata as they paddle. He hears in it his own name.

Margaret is standing at Muriwai. She is at the top of

the cliff, watching the huge breakers roll in and crash on the rocks below. The air is crystal clear, rinsed by a storm. She can see far out to sea, deep into the blue-green water.

The sea calls to her. It is pleading for her. She feels herself drawn to the lure.

She steps out from the top of the cliff, into the air. She is sailing downwards, gliding like a gull. Then the sea has her. She is enfolded by it. Drawn down to its depths. A mighty wave picks her up and flings her onto the rocks.

She is shattered, splintered, crushed. In her bed of pain and blood she lies, while wave after wave pounds over her, into her, through her.

Wave after wave, as if it would never stop. She cups her hands around his shoulders and squeezes into him.

He collapses on top of her, no strength left in his body.

They lie there, incapable of speech.

Through the window there is light beaming.

Outside, the moon.

7

Ponsonby wakes early. The morning air is still damp with the caress of night, but already shafts of sunlight are feeling their way up the ridge. Dave is whistling as he arranges the fruit on the footpath. It's some tune he heard at the market this morning and now can't get out of his head. The street is quiet. The occasional religious jogger, sweating in ecstasy. A dog barking. Across the road there is Digby.

'What's the matter, Digby? Wet your bed?'

'Morning, Dave. Got a smoke for me?'

'Got as many as you care to buy, my friend.'

'See you later, Dave.'

Those tendrils of sun sneak across the white walls of her apartment. There's an interesting pattern where light from the holes in the blinds falls across the Pamela Wolfe original. Karen wakes alone and at peace. There's no traffic noise yet.

She finds herself smiling for no particular reason. Well, all right then, there is reason. It's Saturday. It's morning. There's sunlight on the wall and birdsong in the air. The apartment is still and friendly. The matai floorboards are glowing in a self-congratulatory fashion. Down at the bakery the croissants will still be warm. Fresh coffee in the kitchen.

And inside of me, what? Delight. Cynical bitch that I am, I'm glad to be alive. There's a freshness about everything, as though I've never seen any of it before.

Shit.

She staggers from the bed while the phone is screeching at her. Catches her foot in the sheets and stumbles to her knees. *Fuck fuck fuck.*

'Hello?'

'Oh, hello, Penny, Brian here. Not too bright and early for you Ponsonby types, am I?'

'Marginally. What do you want, Brian?'

'I just wanted to talk to Margaret, if I may.'

'What? Margaret?'

'That's right. She did stay the night, didn't she?'

'Ummm . . . Yeah. Of course she did. Sorry, I'm still half asleep. I'll just go and look for her.'

Fuck. What am I going to do now? She spends a minute rubbing the knee she fell on and blinking hard, trying to wake up.

'Hello, Brian? It looks like she's got up and gone already. There's a note on the table to say that if you ring, to tell you she's doing some shopping before she goes home.'

181

'Blast. I wanted her to pick up some bagels for us on the way. Never mind. I'll wander out and get some myself.'

'Brian, how are you? Marg told me about the trouble at work.'

'I'll be OK. I just wish they'd hurry up and sort it all out so I know where I stand. It was a bit rough when I first found out, but Margaret's been wonderful. I don't know what I'd do without her.'

You may find out soon enough, you poor bastard.

In a motel room, a woman wakes in a sea of light. The rising sun bounces around the room, reflected by the white sheets. She is naked, sore, replete.

Around her she sees the stubs of the candles, inhales the scent of sweat and sex. In a kitchen chair which he's brought into the room, Arthur. Naked. Smiling.

He's been up most of the night, watching her, praying.

'I've been waiting for you, Te Kare. You're very beautiful in the morning light.'

She stretches herself, feels the satisfied tiredness of every muscle. 'What time is it?'

'Morning time. That's why it's not dark any more.'

Margaret launches herself across the room, sitting astride him on the chair. She grabs two handfuls of hair and uses them to pull his forehead against hers. Looks into his sparkling eyes.

'Don't get smart with me, little boy. Otherwise I'll break this off.'

Reaching down to grab his flaccid penis.

'You tried last night, but it's still there. Must have nine lives, eh?'

'I could try again?'

Already the thing is growing in her hand.

'No, Te Kare; we have to pack up and go. Last night was special — we don't want to take anything away from it.'

'Hmm, a sadist, huh? Well, you can't stop me having a little breakfast.'

She's kissing him with a passion.

The day has done up its buttons and made it onto the street. On the corner a young girl is playing the flute, busking. She has a sign which reads 'Help support my school trip to Fiji'. A pair of skaters bounce along the pavement, in regalia. Sniffing for reward, a well-known springer spaniel is walking his beat. The cars have begun their Ponsonby promenade, to see and be seen.

David absorbs the sights over his eggs Benedict. Eating breakfast at a sidewalk table with Gwenda, he's wishing he'd discovered all this twenty years ago. Perhaps it wasn't there then. Now there seems to be so little time left, and so much still to do.

'What d'you say we take a winter holiday?'

'Winter? How can you be thinking of winter on a morning like this?'

'Just planning ahead, you know me. It's good to go somewhere warm in the middle of winter.'

'Where to?'

'Oh, I don't know. Rarotonga? An island somewhere, with crystal-clear water and coconuts. What d'you think?'

'Fine. It'd be wonderful.'

She's smiling deeply, looking at him.

'What?'

'D'you plan everything?'

'Not everything. I just like to think ahead, that's all. I suppose I like to be in control. Why?'

'I was just wondering; what we did last night. In bed. Did you plan that? Only it bore a remarkable resemblance to a scene I saw in a movie last year.'

'*Saigon Secret*? I'm sorry — I'm not a very inventive person, not naturally spontaneous. I wish I was different, but that's just who I am. It's probably hard for you to understand, Gwenda, being so creative. But I'm afraid I'm just a boring little psychiatrist, reduced to re-enacting scenes from the movies.'

'David, there was nothing about last night that was boring. Please, I'm not trying to make fun of you. I just find you so interesting, and, well, quirky. We're so different, you and I. Perhaps that's why I love you so much.'

But David is burying his head in the menu to avoid being seen by a former patient of his, walking towards them.

Margaret has left, reluctantly. Arthur hands the key to the man behind the counter. Who winks at him.

'Seems like you two had a good time last night, eh? Had complaints about the noise from the unit next to you, but I couldn't bring myself to break it up. How's your back, then? Bit sore, is it?'

Arthur's staring at him. The man takes a step back.

'No offence, mate, no offence. Well, you're all paid up so that's it then. Got everything out of your room?'

Arthur fills the door frame as he leaves.

From the comfort of a park bench, Norm surveys his domain. The trees lift and fall in the breeze. The grass is cropped, newly mowed; the warm smell of it drifting across the park. The cicadas have begun their canticle to the sun.

All that my eye surveys, and the cattle on a thousand hills. Not bad for a poor man.

He throws his head back and peers into the sky, one hand shielding the sun. The blue is a rich azure, unblemished and endless. It soars mile-high above him, a seamless gateway to the universe.

Did anyone ever see such a sky as this one? Under

this sort of sky anything is possible. Anything at all could happen. The possibilities are boundless, unlimited. Norm, you old bastard, you're a lucky bugger to be born under a sky as big as this one.

From the corner of his eye he notices the brown hawk. High up and almost motionless, resting on the currents, waiting.

He lowers his head and reaches for the bottle in his pocket.

'Dr Jorgensen? It is, isn't it? I couldn't see you properly behind that menu thing.'

'Hello, Colin. Keeping well, are we?'

'As well as any other lunatic. Ha ha. Who's this, then? Your latest girlfriend?'

'This is Gwenda. Gwenda, Colin.'

He takes her hand, and with an exaggerated bow, kisses it.

'I used to be a count, luv, though some people call me different. Not many people believed me, but good old Dr Jorgensen here, he believed me all right. Colin, he used to say, you're such a count. Ha ha.'

Gwenda grins inanely, uncertain how to react.

'Good to see you've been out of hospital for a while, Colin. Things working out OK?'

'You know me, Doc. In and out like a ram in a ewe paddock. Ha ha. But I'd rather be out than in, if you know what I mean. Oh, don't mind me, luv.

I'm all talk. Harmless as a dog with no balls. It's the medication, see — it won't stand up when it's told. Isn't that right, Doc?'

'Look, we're just about to have some breakfast, so if you don't mind . . .'

'Breakfast out here, eh? Well, good on you, Doc. The job must be paying all right. Nice to meet you, Gwenda. You're a bit of all right, luv, you are. Better than that hard-faced old bint I saw you with last time, Doc.'

'That was my wife, Colin.'

'Yeah? Well, she looked like it too. You're doing well for yourself now, Doc. You keep it up, if you know what I mean. Ha ha. Enjoy your breakfast. And luv, just a word of wisdom from old Colin — you make sure you take your pills as often as I take mine. Ha ha.'

Arthur tightens the day where it threatens to grow loose. Takes the slack out if it as skilfully as any plastic surgeon. It's the first day of the new era, so it needs to look presentable. He stands back to admire his handiwork.

Where did that hawk come from? I don't remember putting it there.

Regardless, the day is humming with everything required. The hard sun baking the last drop of moisture from the earth. Drawing the scent from every flower until the air is filled with sweetness and fecundity. Blooms of all kinds unfolding themselves, waving their pollen-laden organs in the slow heat. Posturing and posing, outdoing one another in shameless sexual soliciting. Bees overcome with opportunity, dragging themselves homeward with baggy legs.

His heart is full of song, and the world is singing it.

'So, was it a good night last night?'

She's alert, filtering for any sarcasm. Grinning from ear to ear, but not on her face. She can still feel the ache in her groin.

'Yes, it was very good. We had a wonderful time.'

'Where did you go?'

'A new place, it's only just opened. Shangri-la, it's called. The food was delicious. We did the whole menu.'

'I tried to ring you at Penny's this morning, but I missed you.'

Lurch.

'She said you'd already left to go shopping. Doesn't look like you bought much.'

'No, I couldn't find anything in my size that I liked. Were you all right with the children last night?'

'Oh, we managed. Thanks for the lasagne — it was good.'

'Brian?'

'Hmm?'

'Did you see the moon last night?'

'No; we were watching TV. Why? Was there something special about it?'

'Oh no, I don't suppose so. It was full; I thought everyone would have noticed.'

The heat makes him restless. He's prowling round the kitchen, wanting someone to blame. Pete sits there reading the paper. Indifferent to moods.

A blowfly drones around Bob's head. He swats at it ineffectually.

'Fucken flies. If you bastards would clean up properly we wouldn't have flies. But ya spray yer dinner round like fountains in a shit farm. Dirty plates left all over the bench. No wonder we get flies around the bloody place. Pete? Did ya hear me?'

'Huh?'

'Flies. Dirty little bastards spewing and shitting all over the place. We got to get rid of them.'

'Right.'

Pete rolls up a discarded section of newspaper and holds it in his hand. Without looking, still reading the paper, he strikes out so suddenly that Bob jumps. The blowfly drops to the table like a stone.

Bob is open-mouthed with amazement. It takes him some time to get a sentence together.

'Yeah, right. So yer just gonna leave that dead fly

there, are ya? So it can find its way into the food. Never mind, we might have currant buns so's no-one will notice. I don't know why I bother with you lot. Must have stood on a sacred ant in a previous life.'

But Pete isn't listening.

Once a month, Kevin meets with his spiritual director. A rather grandiose title for the wizened old man sitting across from him. Father Patrick is a Catholic priest without parish, as he's officially designated. The truer story is that the Bishop can't stand him, and refuses to let him loose on a congregation of the faithful. Not since he gave a homily on the Whore of Babylon, describing the ecclesiastical hierarchy as the longest standing brothel-keepers in history. These days he potters about doing a little bit of spiritual direction and attending the odd demonstration.

On this fine Saturday morning, Kevin is troubled.

'Would it be blasphemy, do you think, to imagine that God would send someone else after Christ?'

'I don't have a very good nose for blasphemy, Kevin. What do you think?'

'I imagine it probably is. After all, we confess Jesus to be the full and final offering of salvation. So, technically, there's nothing left to add, is there? To claim anyone else as having a similar sort of role would only subtract from Christ; steal some of his glory. So it would have to be blasphemy.'

'Is that what you believe? Or is that just the echo of some theology professor you admired?'

Kevin smiled. You could never underestimate Father Patrick. Sharp as a razor.

'All right. The truth is I don't know what I believe. My allegiance is to Jesus, I'm clear about that. Everything I know about God I know because of him. But there's been a couple of times lately when I've had, well, experiences. Like God was pointing me to this particular person, and telling me to listen to him. That he was sent from God.'

'Tell me about this person.'

'He's . . . Well, he came to see me. And then he was at a funeral I was taking, and he spoke. He, uh, he spoke very well. He lives here in Ponsonby. Down Shelly Beach Road, actually. I, uh, don't know much about his background . . .'

'Kevin, I haven't seen this much smoke since Father O'Leary set the Presbytery on fire by falling asleep with a fag in his mouth. Let's be honest with each other, shall we?'

'Sorry. The fact is that he's a psychiatric patient, living in a boarding house. His name's Arthur. He claims to be the second son of God, and wants me to tell people about it. He's quite mad, of course. I don't know what this is all about, why I'm tempted to believe him. Must be some sort of midlife crisis or something.'

'Leave the psychoanalysing to me, yes? That's what you pay me for. How do you know he's mad?'

'Well, he's a psychiatric patient, for goodness' sake. He's been in Oakley and Carrington, on medication. And this claim to be the son of God, well, it's preposterous, isn't it? They all believe they're Genghis Khan or the Queen of Sheba or something.'

'Who are you trying to convince?'

'Myself, dammit, I know that. But what's the alternative? If he's not mad? To believe that he really is the son of God?'

'What is it that's so shocking about that?'

'It's that borderline, isn't it? Between sanity and insanity? Religion blurs the edges. Arthur believes he's the second son of God. Some other chap believes he's Satan or Napoleon or someone. We can't believe them all, can we? We have to say at some point, this is sane and this isn't. Otherwise we're pushing Christianity into the same basket.'

'That's what's really bothering you, isn't it?'

'Well, frankly, yes. It worries me that I start to believe what Arthur, a psychiatric patient, says. But it worries me even more if we work back the other way, and ask if Jesus was really sane.'

'Would he have been any more believable? There's a story in the gospels, isn't there? Mark 3:21, I think, about Jesus' family coming to take him back home because they thought he was mad. How's that different from your friend Arthur?'

'That's it; that's the trouble exactly. Would I have felt any different about Jesus than I do about Arthur? I doubt it. But then what am I saying? Either that Arthur may be genuine or Jesus was mad as a hatter. It's blasphemy whichever way I go.'

'Could God send a psychiatric patient?'

'I want to say no, that would be bloody stupid. Why complicate things? I mean, who would listen? Everything would be stacked against them from the start. But . . .'

'Yes?'

'Well, if Jesus came back into our world today with the sort of claims he was making, might we not lock him up as a nutter? And if that's true, who's to say that Arthur couldn't be the second son of God?'

'Exactly. Perhaps you need to broaden your horizon about where God will turn up in life.'

'Hmm, yes. Maybe that's what I need to be working on. That's good, that's good, Father.'

'And Kevin?'

'Yes?'

'Arthur probably is mad. I wouldn't want you to be chasing rainbows.'

'Well, at least I haven't starting seeing angels yet.'

In the laughter which follows, our two angels are feeling somewhat belittled by the turn of conversation.

It's sometime after eleven when they finish their breakfast, lingering over the lattes. They stroll back along Ponsonby Road, hand in hand. Grazing the shops, with more curiosity than intent. It's in Magazzino that they come face to face with Penny.

The greetings jump and stutter. Emotion and emphasis come at all the wrong places in their sentences. David tries to avert his eyes, tries not to evaluate Penny as a competitor. Penny isn't so reserved. She stares long and hard, the sadness indelible in her eyes.

Gwenda is unnaturally interested in the magazine she's holding. She studies it even while exchanging the cruel inanities of social intercourse. It's Penny who offers the excuse and leaves, to universal relief.

Only then does Gwenda recognize the rag in her hands as a copy of *Penthouse*.

In the afternoon Brian plays cricket on the back lawn with Mark and Stephanie. It's never happened before, and the children are cautious until they begin to enjoy it. Margaret watches from the deck.

'Watch me, Mummy, watch this.'

It's like looking through binoculars the wrong way. She can see them all right, but they're so very far away. She's an observer looking in on somebody else's life. Disguised as a member of the family, but playing someone else's part.

Brian is smiling. He allows himself to be bowled out, so that Stephanie can have a turn at batting. The sunshine, the grass, the endless chatter and giggling of the children. Where did all this come from?

A pity I can't persuade Margaret to join in.

It's something she doesn't do a lot of, walking. But on a day like this it seems inevitable.

Along Franklin Road the plane trees are strutting their green magnificence. The sunlight filtering through them dapples the street. The villas lounge back from the road front, hoping for a tan. Karen bends to pick a flowering head of lavender, examining its purple grace before raising it to her nose.

A monarch butterfly stumbles through the air and alights on the fence beside her. She bends down to observe it more closely. The butterfly regards her, folding the bright sails to meet each other.

As a girl she'd gather the chrysalises from the swan plants and bring them inside. Her father would help her to arrange them in a glass case in her bedroom. Every day when she came home from school she'd inspect them, looking for signs that something was about to happen. When one emerged there was always great excitement. The best part for her was when she'd take the fresh butterfly outside and release it in the air.

So much beauty, borne for a time in something so ordinary. But such a short life. A moment of splendour before the end.

Must beauty always be so tragic? Tragedy so beautiful?

The butterfly steps onto the air and ascends, oblivious to mortality.

There is still much to be done. The important things are done in secret. It is only their outworkings that people see and admire.

Arthur is on his knees in the bedroom. He is unnaturally still, his gaze fixed on nothing finite. His breathing is slow and even.

He is travelling through the heavens. The purple-black is liquid and cold. Movement is so strange when there is no air to brush past your face. It is only the waxing and waning of stars which marks the progress of his travel. So very slowly his destination is drifting closer.

As he enters the gravity field of the nebula there is a sense of relief. Inward and onward he soars, heading to a familiar cluster.

He prepares himself as he reaches the outer eddies of the corridor. It is always so sudden. The force which grips your innards and tries to expel them. The sudden rush of acceleration. The loss of all senses. The speeding through total blackness.

And then, so welcoming, the flame-blossoms. Giant, gaseous eruptions of colour, pulsating around him. A million different hues spilling into each other, dancing for joy. The strengthening of gold as he moves further in. Until it is thick molten gold, coursing around him and through him.

The light. For which eyes cannot serve. The retina-scorching, nucleic-white light. Impenetrable.

The singing. Surging into the endless vaults, raking the soul with its beauty. Spiralling into the billowing light.

'Here, move yer arse, will ya, Arthur? Only I want to change the blankets on this bed, see?'

It's gone.

'I'll get it!'

'Hello. Oh, hi, Penny, just a minute. I'll take it through to the bedroom.'

'That's better. Listen, I owe you forever, Pen. Thanks for covering for me this morning. I never thought he'd ring — I'd have been dead in the water.'

'Where do you think? With Arthur.'

'Better than that. God, Penny, it was unreal. I'll tell you about it sometime, if I can.'

'You bet I'm smiling. I haven't stopped since. I had to powder my cheeks when I came home to try to stop them glowing.'

'No, of course I don't know what I'm doing. If I

knew what I was doing I wouldn't be doing it. But I am doing it, Penny, and it's so good.'

'I know, I know. I can't help it. I try to tell myself how stupid I'm being, and before I know where I am I'm thinking of him again. I can't expect you to understand, Penny, but be happy because I'm happy. Please.'

'No, not a thing. Or at least I don't think so. You must have been pretty convincing this morning.'

'He's OK. It might be the shock or something, but he's actually seemed happier the last couple of days. As if a burden had been lifted off him.'

'I guess. But I can't survive on pity any more. Not now. I don't know what I'm going to do, Pen. I've got no plans, I haven't thought anything through. I'm just going with the flow. Riding it out to see where it leads.'

'How's Gwenda?'

'Why didn't you tell me, you bloody martyr? Oh, you poor thing. I'm so sorry. Who is he?'

'No-one I know, thank God. Look, sometime next week I'll come in and see you, take you out for lunch or something, OK?'

'All right then. Love you. Bye.'

It's an exercise book with a hard cover. A picture of some mountain next to a lake somewhere. Norm got it cheap off the bloke at the stationery shop after they'd swapped stories about the Korean War. The pen's clipped onto the back of it, so that he won't lose it.

He doesn't write in it every day. Just when he has something to say.

It's now two weeks since I had a dry day. I'm beginning to lose the hope of hoping. Every morning I think this might be the one I stop, but I'm never much past breakfast before I'm into it again.

I had a dream last night that I thought I should write down. I was travelling down a rough track in a sort of stagecoach. There was no-one else in the cabin with me, and I remember wondering who the driver was. I could hear the beat of the horses' hooves. All of a sudden it stopped, and everything was quiet. I climbed out to see what the trouble was, but there was no-one in the driver's seat.

The horses were very still. I went over to them and touched one, and it was wooden. I looked around me, and I was in the middle of a big flat plain which stretched as far as the eye could see. When I looked back, the stagecoach and horses had disappeared, and I was alone. The moon was beating down on me. Not hot like the sun, but with a strange sort of light.

There was a flash of lightning, and thunder which shook the ground. A bush just in front of me burst into flames. There was a voice coming from the bush, and I went closer to see what it was saying. 'Norm,' the voice called,

'Norm. Help me, Norm.' I recognized it straightaway. It was Arthur. I stepped into the burning bush, and there he was inside. We were in the middle of the fire, but not burning up.

He was strapped to a big table in a white room. There was an axe buried in the top of his head, and blood everywhere. The life was draining out of him. 'Help me, Norm, help me,' he kept saying. I reached out to touch him, but there was some sort of barrier between us that I couldn't cross. Where his blood was dripping on the floor, flowers were springing up and blooming.

Then everything went still, and there was the roaring of a great lion. Somehow the roar made sense to me, I could understand what it meant. 'This blood will drench the furrows of the earth, but behold what issues from it.'

I woke up with that terrible roaring still in my head. I was frightened. I still am. I worry about Arthur, about what will become of him. I don't know how to be a friend to him.

God, I don't understand the way you work. I don't know what you want of a burnt-out alkie with no brain cells left. I'm an old donkey who stinks up the air and brays in the night. I'm good for eating thistles and farting, but not much else. But if you have something for me to carry, then I'll do it as best I can.

Nothing good ever came in an envelope with a window in it. Bob hates the business side of things.

His sister Bonnie does all the accounts for him. He just has to remember to write in those bloody cheque butts for her. But he opens the mail, and culls out the rubbish.

He can't make head nor tail of this letter at first.

Another local authority of some sort; pedantic pricks that they are with all their regulations and compliance orders. Couldn't organize a booze-up in a brewery, these sad little broken-arse bureaucrats.

It's the words 'revoke your licence to operate' which jump out from the margin-to-margin bullshit. Only then does he twig who it's from. He remembers the inspection, months ago. A woman with a clipboard and a voice from Remuera. *Toffee-nosed bitch with a stick up her bum.* He might have got a bit smart with her, but he was having a bad day. Wal had pissed himself and was wandering around with no pants on.

He sits there like a stunned mullet, reading the letter over and over again. *What the fuck does it mean, revoke your licence to operate? Close us down? They can't bloody do that. Can they?*

The effect is dramatic. There's a long, thunderous roll, a short trumpet blast, an eruption of purple smoke and there he is in the midst of it, nicely set off in his cobalt blue. Seraphs can get away with outlandish entrances.

The angels are instantly alert and business-like. They're in enough trouble as it is.

'Well, my white-winged watchers, what have we been up to? Taking the concept of partnership a little overenthusiastically, have we? And in front of quite a distinguished audience as well. Tut tut. I do so hate show-offs, don't you? Although I do hear that the spectators had a fabulous time. Next time you're performing, you must invite me along. Unless of course it's a private showing. Now what have you got to report, you libidinous lovelies?'

They glance at each other, sheepishly. The female angel is the first to overcome her embarrassment.

'We're sorry, Shacinda, we got too involved in our mission, and, well, one thing led to another. Forgive us, please.'

'Oh, nonsense. Forgiveness is not an issue. You've been spending too long with humans. What I want, Geranne, if it's not too much trouble, is a report on Arthur.'

'Everything went very well, just as you'd suggested. He hasn't contacted her again, yet, but I don't suppose that matters much. He seems to be clear about the next task, but we'll keep an eye on him just in case. A while ago he was trying to make contact, but he got disturbed.'

'And the other chap, Kevin, is it?'

'Yes, he's coming along nicely as well. He's a bit

slow, but I think he'll be ready in time.'

'Good, good. And how about you, Burlain? Have you had any, shall we say, penetrating insights?'

'Only that Arthur is going to need all the help he can get. The mortal world is so hard and cynical.'

'Quite. You can be assured that our protégé is getting support from the very highest quarter. So I don't think we need trouble ourselves about his welfare. You two just keep up the loose surveillance. Don't interfere unless it's absolutely necessary. We don't want to frighten the horses. And just be a little cautious about how involved you get in this assignment. Mortals can become very attractive. Try to remember that you have a job to do.'

'Shacinda?'

'Yes, my sweet?'

'You know that ointment which we used on whatshername, Karen?'

'Yeeees?'

'I don't suppose you'd have a teeny bit spare, would you? Just for recreational use?'

'I'm sorry. I'm afraid I gave the last of it to a very dear friend of mine. You'll just have to find some more wholesome means of entertaining yourselves. I'm sure that won't stretch you too far.'

'Yeah, can I speak to Barbara Harmon, please. Yeah, OK. I'll hold.'

He drums his fingers on the table, making galloping noises. There's a sheen of sweat on his upper brow. Bob hates poxy classical music, especially when it comes down the phone line at you and you can't turn it off.

'Hello? Yeah, look, it's Bob Davies here from the boarding house in Shelly Beach Road.'

'That's right, yeah. I just got this letter from you, and I'm having trouble understanding what it means. What's this stuff about revoking my licence? I didn't even know I had a licence.'

'So what does that mean in plain English? That I'm not allowed to run the place?'

'You've gotta be joking, lady. What d'you expect me to do? Turf these old geezers out on the street because you think they're overcrowded?'

'Oh yeah, two months; that's real big of ya. Listen, even if I had the money to do the alterations, which I don't, the place wouldn't work with fewer guys per room. The numbers just don't stack up.'

'Well, what is yer problem, then? Ya think ya can sit there in yer fancy bloody office nibbling on biscuits and tell me how to run my business? How'd ya like to swap jobs for a few weeks, eh? Maybe I'll bring a few of the poor old bastards round to your place, and ya can put them up for a while? No? I guess we'll just have to chuck them out on the street, then, won't we? I'm sure they'll have a lot more personal space to sleep in then.'

'Objectionable? Ya haven't seen objectionable yet, lady. Shit, I'm not even in a bad mood yet. But I'll tell ya what: I'm sick of stuck-up charity queens like you trying to interfere with my work. Where the hell are you at three o'clock in the morning when someone's gone troppo and trying to set the place on fire? I haven't seen you round when a bloke's slashed his wrists in the bath and painted the walls with his blood. There ya are, hiding away in some mirror-glass building, sucking pineapples up yer arse and telling me how to run my home. Well, I'll tell ya. This pineapple's got a fuse in it, and if ya fuck with it ya'll have nothing left to hang yer knickers on. So you just pull yer finger out of whatever dyke you've got it in and go and find something useful to do. Have a nice day.'

He sits there still trembling with rage, the sound of the phone slamming into the table still echoing around the room.

Shit. Ya've really crapped in your own nest now, boy. I don't think that's gonna help a helluva lot.

Things have shifted. Not just what has gone out of him, but something else. Arthur worries away at it, but can't quite draw it out of the distance. He rubs his palms together and sniffs.

Pete sucks away at his smoke, periodically breaking

into a hacking cough. Sandy's snoozing in the late evening sun, his methylated breath heavy in his nostrils. The chair where John sat is empty. No-one has been keen to claim it.

There, through the gap in the trees, is the Waitemata. It sparkles and shines for them. Arthur's proud of the particular shade of blue.

Inside, they can hear Bob thumping and slamming and cursing. Something's got him wound up, and they all know to stay out of his way. Dinner could be a bit rough tonight.

'When you going to bring Margaret round to the place again, Arthur? She adds a bit of class to the joint, that one does. She should come round and see us.'

'Yeah, I don't know, Pete. She said she wants to come over sometime and see you all. She's a good lady, eh?'

'A cracker, Arthur, a real cracker. I wasn't too sure when you were talking about the Queen of Heaven and all that, you know? But she's a beauty, that one, a real queen. You're a lucky man, Arthur. You make sure you treat her right, you hear?'

'I've been pretty careful so far. You live in this place long enough, you forget how to treat a woman. Isn't that right?'

'Forget how to treat one? Jeez, Arthur, I'd forgotten what one looks like till you brought Margaret round.

Apart from Roslyn, that is, but she doesn't hardly count. A man needs to have a woman round now and again.'

'What happened to your wife, Pete? Is she still alive?'

'I dunno — I should think so. Take a bloody strong poison to kill off a reptile like her. She left me, the first time I got sick. She used to come and see me in hospital, every week when I first went in. Then it was once a fortnight, and even then she'd miss some. When I got out, I found out she was shacked up with this guy I used to work with. She'd even given him my car. I was still a bit fragile, so I just let things be. I haven't heard from her for years now. Last I knew she was living down country in Taranaki, with some other bloke ten years younger than her.'

'You miss her?'

'Nah, I don't miss her. She was a hard woman; crush your balls and put 'em in the stew, she would. But I miss women, the smell of them, the way they laugh, that sort of thing.'

There's a huge crash and a curse as Wal bursts through the door, missing the handle in his urgency. His mouth is working and there's a long bead of saliva hanging from one side of it.

'What's up, Wal? You look like the cat pinched your dinner.'

'I was just talking to Bob, and he says they're trying to make him close the place down. For good, like.'

'Who's they?'

'I don't know. Somebody. They can't do that, can they, Arthur? They can't make us shift out of our home, can they? I don't want to go anywhere else. I like it here. Apart from that arsehole Frank. But I don't want to shift.'

'Hey, don't worry, Wal. It'll be all right. Everything'll be all right. We won't have to move out, I'll make sure of that.'

So that's what it was, he's thinking. *Another opportunity for me to prove myself.*

The darkness, when it comes, is soft and gentle. There again, in the distance, is the call of the morepork.

8

'So, Karen, what have we got on the Mitsuki thing?'
'Not enough yet. All there is so far is the sniff of fraud. Jap businessman flies in, looks at investment possibilities, talks to lawyers and banks, flies out. I got Robin to do a bit of digging around. Turns out he's wanted in Germany for shooting through on a development project, taking most of the money with him. So Robin leans on a few sources, and comes up with a rumour that Global's already given him a credit line for more than a million.'

'Solid?'

'A good source, but we've got nothing substantial yet. Global's closed down tighter than a frostbitten scrotum. But I've got a nose for this one. He's got the money and run, you can count on it. That's why they're into damage control.'

'We'll need something good before we can go with this, Karen. You need to find someone who'll talk. Even then we'll have to legal it before we go to air. I'm not taking any more chances after that Boland fiasco.'

'I've got Robin working on it. We know the Fraud Squad are sniffing around, but it's wall-to-wall no comments from them. I think we've got to find a way in through the bank.'

'Well, that's your job. You find a way in, darling, and get this broken open before anyone else gets hold of it. Let's aim for play-time next week. Can do?'

'I'll try. And Tim?'

'Yo?'

'I'm not your darling.'

There's a worm of anxiety burrowing into the centre of her calm. She's ignoring it for the most part, aware only of a faint slithering in the distance.

Still and all, three days with no contact. And after . . . after . . . Margaret's drifting again. She has a smile on her face. She toys with a strand of hair hanging next to her face, looping it round and round her finger. The faintest blush would be noticeable on her cheeks if anyone were looking.

She sighs and goes back to folding the washing. The clean smell of it is satisfying. The telephone maintains its silence, indifferent.

'This is going to be difficult for all of us, Brian.'

Fuck. I'm going to be chopped.

'The board has met and discussed the issue from beginning to end. We recognize the realities of banking, that we're always vulnerable to this sort of thing. That's why we have regulations, systems to try and protect ourselves. One of those is the quality of our staff. We provide training, we elevate them gradually to positions of trust, and then we rely on them to do the job we pay them for. As Loans Officer, it was your responsibility to evaluate the risk involved. You've let us down, Brian.'

Dawson is arranging the papers on his desk as he's talking. He picks up a sheaf of loose ones and taps them until they all line up. He puts them down again as if there were some importance to placing them in exactly the right spot.

Brian is empty and numb. He wants to leave the room. He wants to sink his fist into the loose flesh of Dawson's face. He wants to rewind the tape and start again. Instead he straightens the creases on his trousers.

'I went through all the proper procedures, as far as I'm aware. The documentation was very thorough. You'll remember that I discussed it with you, owing to the size of the advance. You were very keen to establish a Japanese client base, as I recall.'

'Yes, yes, that's all in the past now, and I don't think it's going to help any of us to go over the ground again. The fact of the matter is that you were the Loans Officer, and you gave the approval. Responsibility brings consequences, and I'm afraid we're at one of those points where the consequences are painfully apparent.'

'You're sacking me?'

'Don't be ridiculous, Brian. Sacking is what we do to some junior teller with three months' experience. What we're doing with you is negotiating a redundancy deal; a package which will let you move out with some dignity and a bit of financial backing to see you through. I think the board's been pretty generous, all things considered.'

He moves the papers to the other side of his desk. It's a sign that another task has been completed; an item moved from the in-basket to the out-basket. He looks up at Brian and smiles, half expecting some answering sign of appreciation.

This is another connection. One more strand in the design of the web. Arthur knows it, feels it deep in his gut. Things are *happening*. It's all part of the plan, part of his task to accomplish.

I am becoming who I am. As I move from one step to the next, my father shows me the way I must go.

'What is hidden must come out in the open. What I have given to you in secret must be declared in the street. What has been appointed must be performed. What will come must be announced. In you my will is enacted.'

He knows the story of the children of Israel when they were in slavery. How God appointed Moses to lead them out of their oppression. How Moses fronted up to the Pharaoh and demanded the freedom of his people. How there was miracle after miracle. How finally the sea parted and Moses led them through. How the Egyptians drowned as they followed. Deliverance!

And it needs a deliverer.

'Don't worry, Bob. It'll all get sorted out.'

The morning sun catches the wafer as he hoists it aloft. For a moment it becomes a moon, shining with reflected glory, full and round and white. He studies it for a moment before snapping it in half. A clean, crisp break.

'The body of Christ, for you.'

How casually one handles the mysteries. It becomes routine, like setting the table. He does it all with efficiency and confidence. The breaking, the pouring, the motions and the words.

What does it achieve, this early Eucharist of a Wednesday morning? Two parishioners, sometimes three. Why do they come, to go through the motions over and over again? The security of repetition? The endurance of ritual?

But Kevin knows why they come.

Here they are, the two of them. Shuffling to the front to kneel at the rail. Opening their mouths like goldfish to cannibalize their God. It's the eating

213

and the drinking, the tasting and smelling. God's so bloody ephemeral, so wispy, so hard to get hold of amidst tangibles like cancer and divorce. Too big or too small, it doesn't matter which. God in the pure sense is untouchable, and so useless.

Here you have him in a form you can grapple with. Fit him in your mouth, swallow him, digest him in your stomach. The physical taste of God — it's something you can get a liking for.

Kevin sculls the cup, and feels the warmth in the pit of his stomach, radiating outward. It's not such a bad metaphor, he's thinking, if you have to have one.

'I'm worried about Peter. He went AWOL last night, and they had to sedate him.'

'Edwards? I thought we had him stabilized. Let's have a look at his file.'

David rummages in the Rotafile to extract the right document. As he turns back he notices her thigh where her uniform has ridden up. He studies the file intensely.

'Hmm, it all looks OK. First committal. Provisional diagnosis of schizophrenia, though God knows that's a house called Legion. These episodes of psychosis are regular though, aren't they?'

'He gets pretty violent when he goes off. Keeps rabbiting on about demons tormenting him. It

214

worries me that he's been here four weeks and there's no sign of improvement.'

'So what do you think, Gwenda? Misdiagnosis? Change of medication indicated?'

'Possibly. He doesn't seem to be responding to the present lot.'

'Hmm, I wonder. Chronic psychosis, violent acting out, fixated delusionary visions. Those are all indications for the new stuff we've got.'

'Triloxyl? That's heavy stuff, doctor.'

'For goodness' sake, Gwenda. There's no-one else around. What's with the doctor stuff?'

'I just like to keep the two worlds a little bit separate. Helps me to know where my boundaries are, doctor.'

This with a smile to ease it.

'Well, then, nurse, what's the problem with Triloxyl?'

'Oh, come on. You've read all the literature, you know all the debate. They don't call it chemical lobotomy for nothing.'

'Emotive claptrap. It would never have been approved if there were concerns about harming patients. I seem to remember lithium getting a pretty bad press in its early days as well, and look how that's improved the lives of people. The fact is that Triloxyl produces mild inhibition of the broad range of emotional responses. The upside is that it seems to eliminate psychosis entirely, and be effective over the long haul.'

'But what's it like on the inside? Do we have the right to deaden people's emotional life so that the rest of us can get some peace? How is that different from what we used to do with lobotomies?'

'The difference is that the patient's brain is left intact and functioning. What right have we got to withhold medication which we know works? We can return quality of life for people, enable them to live in the community again. That's got to be an achievement.'

'So you're going to use it on Peter?'

'I think so. We'll run it past the rest of the team. But I suggest a trial — we'll review results in two weeks. You can keep an eye on him, and I promise to listen to your concerns. How's that?'

'As good as we can expect, doctor. Just one other thing.'

'Yes?'

'Without overstepping professional boundaries, I think I should tell you, David. Your fly's undone. We wouldn't want your emotional responses needing to be depressed, would we?'

'Arthur? Nah, he's away up the road, isn't he, Pete? Yeah, I thought I saw him going out. He'll be off raising the dead, I should think. But come in anyhow, padre. We don't get a whole lot of visitors here.

'Here, have a seat. Shift yer arse, Wal. Make room fer Kevin, that's right. Cuppa tea, Kev? Don't mind if I have a dak, do ya?'

'No on both counts. I won't stay long — I was just hoping to catch up with Arthur.'

'Well, that's a big job, that is, keeping up with our old mate Arthur. On account of him being the second son of God and all. Ya'd need yer skates on to catch up with him. Ah shit, Wal, don't eat the sugar outta the bowl with the friggin' spoon.'

'How's it going down here? Everyone seems happy enough?'

'Jeez, padre, they'd be happy here even if someone dropped a bloody A-bomb on the shithouse. Long as they still got their tucker at night, leastways. Nah, things aren't too crash-hot at the moment, I tell ya. I've just been told they're gonna close the place down 'cos of overcrowding. Reckon we've got too many to a room. Doesn't fit in with some poxy regulation or other.'

'What? Who's going to close it?'

'Some tight-arsed bitch from North Health, Barbara something or other. She came round a while back, doing an inspection. Didn't take much notice of it at the time. There's always some bunch of pencil-dicks crawling around the place. I clean the place up a bit and hide the beer when I know they're coming. But this time they've stitched me up good and proper.'

'What are you going to do? You can't close the place down, surely? There's nowhere else in Ponsonby that'll take men like these.'

'That's a fact, Kev, you hit the nail right on the head. I dunno what the hell to do. I can't just walk out on these blokes, eh. But I don't have the money to keep North Health off my back neither. I guess I'm just gonna have to sit here and make 'em throw me out.'

'What would it cost to make the alterations?'

'Well, we'd have to build on, see? To get more rooms. I think I'm allowed to stack 'em up two to a room, but that's the max. We'd be looking at something like, ooh, I dunno, forty grand? There's just not that kind of money in the business.'

'Look, Bob, I'm appalled at this. I can't believe that they would try and shut this place down. We need to get some sort of campaign going. Would you mind if I tried to organize something?'

'Suit yerself, padre. Be great if ya can get something going. These old buggers haven't got much going for them. I reckon we need all the help we can get. What've ya got in mind?'

The way he's walking in from the car says it all. She can hear it in the way he's shuffling. The box he's carrying as she meets him at the door confirms it. A whole career packed away in a cardboard box.

She holds him wordlessly. He slumps against her. At first she thinks his breathing is ragged. Eventually she realizes that he's sobbing. Silent, heaving sobs. She leads him through to the lounge, takes the box off him, lowers him to the couch. Kneeling there beside him, she strokes his forehead.

'They fired me, Marg. I'm finished.'

'No you're not, Brian. Your job's finished, that's all, your job. You're OK. I'm here.'

'I don't know what I'm going to do. I've built everything around that job, everything. And then it's all over in the space of five minutes. They made me hand my keys back, Marg. I had to hand my keys back!'

Another wave of pain breaks over him, and he begins sobbing again. Margaret continues stroking his head until it subsides. He lies there embarrassed. Without explanation she unzips his fly and reaches inside. It's an unconscious thing, an archetypal therapy thrown up from the swamp of her imagination. There are no thought patterns involved, just movement and sound. It's a form of nurturing, she supposes, strangely distant from her body. A form of compassion, like giving money to a busker.

There's a clock ticking now. You can feel the movement

of it as the great second hand sweeps across the face, scything through minutes as if they were stands of wheat. Arthur senses the current of it, adjusting his pace to catch the flow, to channel it, to use it.

He finds Digby on the usual corner. There's an inevitability about it all. Digby's a pawn, a bit-part player in a drama he doesn't know the name of.

'Arthur, my friend, how's that good lady of yours? It's a long time since I've spoken to a woman so full of charm, not to mention well proportioned. Make sure you give her Digby's regards next time you see her.'

'OK, Dig. Listen, I need you to do something for me.'

'If it's within my power to do, I would most happily do it, Sir Arthur. What was it you were wanting?'

'I need to borrow ten dollars.'

Digby's eyebrows descend at the same time as his pupils contract. Money's a serious subject, and becomes more so the less you have of it.

'In what sense, Arthur, do you use the word borrow? Do you mean take with the intention of repaying, or is it just a gentle way of asking for a hand-out?'

'I'll pay it back, Digby.'

'And when might that be? Before or after the apocalypse?'

'One week. You'll get it back in a week.'

'And then there's the small matter of interest . . .'

'Twenty bucks. I'll pay you back twenty bucks, all right?'

Digby's eyebrows resume their place, and a smile of sorts makes its way to his face. He extracts a well-worn $10 note from his back pocket, and passes it over as if it were fragile.

'A pleasure to do business with you, my friend. A real pleasure.'

For the umpteenth time, the photocopier jams. It's reaching the end of its natural life, and long runs of double-sided copying take it beyond its limits.

A few minutes later Kevin emerges from its bowels, bearing some concertinaed paper and toner smudges over the back of his hands. Photocopier maintenance isn't a course he remembers from seminary, though it would have been more useful than much of the other stuff.

While the machine churns again, he takes another close look at the handbill. It isn't particularly creative; rather more functional than inspiring. But it serves the purpose.

'Is Ponsonby Losing Its Heart?' the flier asks. 'A Public Meeting to Discuss the Closing of Local Boarding Houses', it announces, with details of time and location. On the back is an article from a local paper, raising concerns about accommodation for ex-psychiatric patients.

He's proud of it not because of its artistic merit, but because it represents action. *I, Kevin Connor, am doing something useful.* He has a cause, and one that is more tenable than selling people on the merits of a crucified saviour.

Now we're cooking with gas, he tells himself.

The photocopier immediately grinds to a halt.

'Hello. Can I speak to Brian, please?'

'Just a moment.'

That's unusual, she's thinking as she goes to wake him. *Not often that Brian gets phone calls from women.*

'Brian speaking.'

'Karen Bligh-Farnsworth here, Brian, from *Nightly News*. Mind if I ask you a few questions?'

'Well, I don't suppose so. What about?'

Karen draws a breath. This is the keypoint of the conversation. After a day of dead ends she's desperate not to lose this lead. It's all or nothing.

'It's nothing much, Brian. We've just been working on a piece about the Mitsuki fraud thing, and we wanted to confirm we've got our facts right. I understand you work for Global?'

'Well, I did do, up until this morning. What do you know about the Mitsuki deal? I thought it was confidential until the Fraud Squad had finished with it.'

Bingo. Jackpot. Lights, bell and buzzer. *You're in,*

you wicked witch, you're in. Important not to let the
excitement carry in my voice.

'Well, that situation's changed since it's gone
public, Brian. Otherwise I wouldn't be ringing you.
Our concern is simply to get the facts straight so that
we don't misrepresent the situation. We thought you
might be able to help us in that.'

'I'm afraid I've just signed an agreement which
precludes me from making any media comment on
the affair.'

'You wouldn't really be making any comment; just
helping us to get the story right. I can't see that there
would be any violation of your agreement in that. Did
you say that you've just finished up with Global? Over
the Mitsuki thing?'

'I imagine that much is fairly obvious. Yes, I was
the Loans Officer who approved the credit. I've
negotiated a settlement for departure, as they say.'

'I'm sorry to hear that. Now, our information is
that there was more than a million dollars at stake?'

'That's right. A million and a half, to be precise.'

'And Mr Mitsuki is nowhere to be found?'

'You'll have to ask the police about that. All I know
is what I've been told. The Mitsuki Corporation
doesn't exist, except on paper. Global doesn't expect
to get the money back. But I guess you know all that.'

'Yes, the substance, naturally. Look, Brian, how
about we come around and have a bit of a chat about

this? If we take any pictures we'll make sure your face and voice are distorted so that no-one can recognize you. And there, ah, there might be some money in it for you.'

'Well, I don't suppose it will do too much harm, seeing that you already know the bare bones of the story. Yes, all right. I'll give you a bit of background.'

He's aware that he's being suckered. But in the pit of his stomach there's a cold, hard anger directed at Dawson and his cronies. *Fuck the lot of them.*

He sits outside the shop, waiting. Anyone watching might think he was just having a rest at the side of the road.

They are all so blind and ignorant, Arthur's thinking, *but I will watch over them.*

This is the right place, he's sure of that. But now he has to wait for the right time, however long it might take. He's watching for a sign. He doesn't know what it will be, but he knows that he'll recognize it when it comes.

The day is rolling on under its own momentum. He's thrown in a cooling breeze to ease the heat. It ripples across the surface of the Waitemata and brings the smell of salt spray to the nostrils of boaties, tempting them out of captivity.

Arthur watches the people coming and going. Most of them ignore him, with no sense of who is in their midst. He's happy for it to remain so. For now.

A sparrow appears, and pecks at crumbs in among the cobblestones. It raises its head and looks at Arthur, puzzled. Then it flits into the air and hovers for a moment in front of the shop. At first Arthur doesn't understand. Then he sees that the bird is hovering directly in front of the automatic door opener, and that the door has rolled open.

It's all he needs. He strides in and up to the counter.

'I'll have two Lucky Dips, please.'

Waving the crumpled $10 note in triumph.

You can smell trouble coming, once you've got a nose for it.

Norm has had his hooter poked into the breeze since he first got up. *Plain as a dead fish, there's trouble on the wind*, he tells himself. It's only natural to prepare yourself for it. He takes another swig of the port.

It comes in the form of a police car. As soon as it pulls up in the car park, he knows the full plot. He grins to himself as he watches Constable Denning extract himself from the compact car given generously by several community groups. Behold the servant of the Lord. Or is it the other side? It's sometimes hard to tell.

'Morning, Norm.'

'And the top o' the morning to you, Denno. Come for your morning constitutional in the park, have you?'

'Wouldn't that be nice, now? But we haven't all got the whole day to ourselves like you have, Norm. Some of us have to work for a living.'

'We all have work to do, you mark my words. It's just that some get paid for working, and others for living. I prefer the living myself, but I'm happy to watch the likes of you working. If it's not your constitutional, it must be a social call, then. Would you like to take a seat next to me and share my refreshments?'

'Thanks for the offer, but it's a bit early in the morning for me. I'm sorry about this, Norm, but we've had a complaint about you.'

'A complaint? You've had a complaint about old Norm? Now what would the substance of that be, I wonder? It can't be my cooking, seeing as how I haven't been entertaining lately. And I don't suppose it's my brand of aftershave, on account of the fact that I don't wear any. Perhaps it's the cut of my clothes, then?'

'Come on, Norm. Don't do it the hard way. We've had a complaint about you drinking in a public place, and the allegation that you're sleeping here overnight.'

'You know I sleep here, Denno. So we better treat

that allegation as fact. As for the other, well, I may have been known to have a tipple from time to time. Cheers. Ah, it's thirsty work being interrogated by the arm of the law.'

'The complainant also alleges that you've been talking to young lads.'

'Where do you learn to talk like that? They must spend a lot of time teaching you how to speak as if you'd had half your brain cut out. Is there some sort of certificate in policespeak, Denno? As for speaking to lads, as you put it, that would be young David who comes round sometimes after school. He's interested in philosophy. He's been reading a bit of Kant, and I've been introducing him to Whitehead. You're familiar with Whitehead, are you, constable?'

'I've got a job to do, Norm, and I have to do it. I'm afraid I'm going to have to move you along.'

'Move me along? Along where, precisely? Along to another park? Along under the bridge with the rest of them?'

'Look, you know as well as I do that Bob'll take you in for a few nights. You'll have moved, I'll have done my job, and by next week you can be back again. Same as last time.'

'It doesn't ever strike you as pointless, does it, Denno? Packing all my stuff up and moving for a few days so that some prune-faced biddy can sleep happier in her starched knickers? It does me. I have to confess that from time to time I consider the essential meaninglessness of these little assignments of yours. But ours is not to reason why, eh? Just do our duty in making the universe a neater place. Tidy up the odds and ends, get them off the streets.'

'It's nothing personal, Norm.'

'No, it never is. Well, I can't spend time chatting. I'll need to be on to my travel agent to make plans. You don't mind if I don't show you out, Denno? I'm afraid it's my man's day off today.'

'You sure you know what you're doing?'

'I didn't give them much, Marg. They already knew what had happened. I just fleshed it out a bit for them. Anyway, they've promised to disguise me if they use it.'

'I'm surprised at you, just the same. It seems a bit out of character for you, talking to the media, bucking the system.'

'You can never tell what's in a man until you start kicking him in the guts. I'm not going to be their scapegoat without making some noise.'

'Good on you.'

There's a way of doing things. He positions the three candles carefully to make a triangle. They're from the bottom drawer, and Bob shouldn't miss them until the next power cut. Anyhow, it's a sort of investment.

He places the two Lotto tickets in the centre of the triangle. Arthur is fascinated by the shapes of the numbers, the patterns in them, the magic they hold. He studies them, trying to decide which one to put on top. In the end he lays them down side by side.

Breathing deeply, he lights the candles. He kneels in silence beside them.

It's there in the air, all the time. Luck, some people call it. Fate, magic, spirit; it's all the same. The trick is to tap into the mother lode and mine it. He throws his head back and sighs. He can sense it, taste it, smell it. Thick and heavy like fresh scones.

And now, yes. It is flowing through him. Tingling down his spine, coursing along his arms. His hands begin to tremble. He holds them out over the two pieces of paper. There is a physical sensation of release as he sloughs it off into the middle of the triangle.

Your will be done.

'Oh good, Karen. Hi. It's Kevin Connor here, from St David's.'

'That's right. How are you doing?'

'Great. Well, I have a bit of a favour to ask you. I dare say you remember Arthur, and the guys from the boarding house? Yes. Apparently they're under threat of being closed down, because they're not up to standard.'

'Well, the thing is, Karen, it's the best in a bad situation. No-one else wants to look after these people, so if Bob's place closes they'll only end up worse off. Anyway, I've taken the opportunity to call a public meeting to discuss it, and I wondered if you could come along to cover it?'

'This Wednesday, here. We kick off at seven-thirty.'

'Yes, certainly. I understand all that, but I just thought it was worth a shot. Why don't you think about it, talk to your producer, and get back to me?'

'Thanks, Karen. I really appreciate that. Keep the faith. Ciao. Sorry?'

'It doesn't mean anything; it's just a saying. OK, bye.'

How peaceful it is sitting out in the bricked courtyard. The trees filter out the noise of the traffic. The sun hangs motionless and merciless. Penny's glad of the sun umbrella.

An occasional breeze brings the mingled scents of the garden. She relaxes, allows herself to sink down into the pleasure of the moment. Warm skin, fragrant air, a good book. Tranquillity, she decides, laying the book to one side. A secret clearing in the jungle of life. A place to come back to.

It's not that I miss other people. I'm old enough to feel comfortable with myself. It's simply that there's no-one to share things with. Moments like this when you feel good about the cosmos.

I wonder if I've ever got over Margaret. Perhaps it's just nostalgia for a lost youth. We would talk into the early hours of the morning, and end up shattered the next day. She was so tender, so gentle. Cups of tea in the morning. Massages.

Companionship. That's what I'm missing. Dear God. Next thing I'll be taking up bowls and joining a travel club. Is that all I've got left? No point in fooling myself. It seems a hard ask, to face ageing alone. Silence even when you don't want it. Soon I'll start talking to the television.

Oh, stop it. Stop feeling sorry for yourself.

I'll make a really foul old lady. A genuine hag, I'll be. And enjoy it. You just wait and see.

'Look, I can't keep up with you. What's happening? You doing too much coke? Lost your judgment up your nose?'

Karen simply looks at him, and he unwittingly crosses his legs.

'OK, sorry, sorry. Bad call. Sore point. But you have to admit it's confusing for a humble producer to understand. The whole story is yours to start with. Then you won't go anywhere near it and I have to get Bill to take it over. And now you want me to do a follow-up? I don't get it, Karen. I admit it, I've lost the plot here.'

'There is no plot, Tim. It's called news judgment. Professional analysis. Has a story got what it takes to make it on air? I think this has.'

'A public meeting in a church to discuss whether a boarding house should close down or not? I mean, come on. It's got all the excitement of Camilla revealing she's not a virgin any more. This is a hard-news show, not bloody access television.'

'That's not what it's about at all. It's about Ponsonby, can't you see that? A whole tide of trendy migration attracted by the diversity of the community, and now pushing out the people who are different. Restaurant mile masticates the poor. Or if you want to do it the other way, it's a classic underdog-fights-city-hall story. Community care pogrom-style. Just let me cover it, and you can make a judgment on it. Come on, Tim, you owe me.'

'All right, but *only* because of cracking the Mitsuki story, not because I think there's any merit in a local-issue beat-up like this one. And you make sure that it doesn't interfere with any of the Mitsuki follow-up. Understood?'

'You'll make someone a lovely mother, Tim, you really will.'

'So what's it all mean, Bob? We going to have to shift?'

'No way, Pete. We'll fight the bastards to the end. This is our patch, and no turd-burgling bureaucrats are gonna shift us outta here.'

There's five of them round the table, slurping their tea and scratching. Bob and Pete, Wal, Sandy and Taffy.

'Ha, ha, got ya, ya big black bastard!'

Taffy crushes the flea between his thumbnails, relishing the crunch.

'So what you going to do, Bob?' Wal's asking.

'Shit, I dunno. I can hardly dish out shotguns to you useless pricks, can I now? Otherwise we'd be eating mince for a month. Maybe we could string all youse jokers' undies across the driveway as a first line of defence. At least that'd get all the flies out the house.'

'What's flies got to do with it?'

'Go back to sleep, Sandy. Fair go. Why the fuck am I bothering? We've gotta get something worked out, though. This vicar joker's got his meeting lined up for Wednesday, but I dunno what good that's gonna do. What we really need is some money.'

'Money? I've got some money. You can have that.'

'Yeah? How much money you got stashed away, Wal?'

Wal hunches his shoulders and cups his hand to

his mouth. When he speaks, it's in a raspy whisper.

'It's under the mattress. Twenty dollars.'

'Well, you're a dark horse, Wal, me old mate. Maybe we could all move into the Regent on the strength of that. Nah, ya bloody old queer, you hang on to yer money. We'll get out of this one somehow, no two ways about that.'

'What about Arthur?' Pete wants to know.

'Arthur? What about him?'

'I just thought he might be able to help. With the sort of connections he has, you know.'

'Connections? There's a few connections in his bloody brainbox that he needs to take care of before he worries about anything else. Nah, I don't think Arthur'll be any more use than tits on a bull. He's a good bloke. But if ya think God's gonna make a house call just so you bastards have got a place to live, I'd say ya've got another think coming.'

'Hah.'

Taffy has another flea trapped.

'Tonight on *Nightly News* we have the story of an audacious fraud allegedly perpetrated by a known Japanese con man. Global Banking has reportedly been duped to the tune of a cool one-and-a-half million dollars. Our reporter, Karen Bligh-Farnsworth, has the story.'

James Dawson finds himself turning cold. The

forkful of food remains poised in front of his mouth.

'Three months ago a Japanese businessman flew into Auckland, travelling under the name of Mitsuki. He had the air of success, wearing expensive suits and staying in one of Auckland's most expensive hotels.

'He was a property developer, or so he said. He spent time looking at potential sites, and talking to banks and lawyers. He was welcomed with open arms by those catching a sniff of some very lucrative deals.

'Several banks competed for his attention. Global Banking was one of those. Global had just adopted a paper at board level which called for building links with Japanese investment. They were proud of themselves when Mr Mitsuki opted to put his business through them.

'Tonight they may be ruing that decision. We have learned from an inside source that Global provided a credit line of one-and-a-half million dollars to Mr Mitsuki. This money has gone, and so has Mr Mitsuki. *Nightly News* has discovered that the man in question is in fact Hiroshi Yatama, a suspected con man wanted for questioning over a failed development in Germany.

'How is it, you might wonder, that a man can walk in off the street and persuade a bank to part with more than a million dollars, without even brandishing a gun? What sort of systems does Global have in place that such a fraud as that alleged can be carried out?

'We take you now to our mystery man on the inside of Global, who has been closely associated with the Mitsuki file from its earliest days. For obvious reasons, our source has asked that his face and voice be disguised. Global is keeping very tight-lipped about the whole affair, and has refused all our requests for comment.'

The scene changes to a shot of a man in an armchair. The pixels around his face have been enlarged to make a distorted blob.

James Dawson leans forward and stares at his large-screen television. He can see the black cuff links, with the distinctive BW in gold.

'Brian Wilson! You arsehole!'

Dear Arthur,

I hope this letter gets to you. I'm not sure what the arrangements are for mail at the boarding house, but I trust someone will make sure you get it.

I've been waiting for you to ring, but haven't heard anything from you. If it wasn't for my memories of our last encounter, I might be worried that something was wrong between us. But I'm sure your love is almost as strong as mine, and that there will no doubt be good reasons why you haven't been able to ring (not that I can promise to understand them!).

It's been very difficult for me to settle back to normal life since that astonishing night together. I'm still not sure whether it really happened, or whether it was part of some magnificent dream. Whatever it was, it has left me permanently changed. You have reopened in me something that got blocked up a long time ago, and I feel like a new person. For all the impossibility of it, I find myself hopelessly in love with you.

The trouble is that it's totally impractical. I think about you all day long, to the point that it's becoming dangerous. Yesterday I nearly chopped off two fingers while away in a daydream! I want to be with you, and would be apart from the small obstacle of a husband and two children. My life has suddenly become very complicated, and I don't know what to do about it.

My inclination is to take the easy way out and leave Brian. I would gladly get up now and pack my suitcase and leave. But what could we do? I can hardly move into the boarding house, and I don't know what other alternatives there are. I'm desperate to be with you, to talk all this over with you, to touch you, to look into your eyes . . .

It's in the writing of this sentence that she remembers with a gasp. He can't read. She starts to laugh but ends up crying. Eventually she takes the letter to the sink and burns it.

Perhaps it'll still get through.

They're still all sitting around the table with their multi-layered conversation.

'Arthur, me old mate, where have you been? Orright, don't tell me; about yer father's bleedin' business, I know, I know.'

'I've been fixing things for you, Bob.'

'Fixing things? Here, what've ya been doing with those bloody candles? They're for emergencies, they are. Ya know I get nervous when you plonkers start playing with fire. Ya'll burn the old place down, and then we'll really be in the shit.'

'I needed them for what had to be done.'

'Yeah, well, I don't want any sodding religious riddles, Arthur. Just put the candles back in the drawer, will ya?'

'I've got something for you.'

'What's that?'

'It's a Lotto ticket. It's a special one. This is what's going to save the house, Bob. You'll be able to pay for the alterations.'

'Yeah? Well, that's good of ya, Arthur. I appreciate this. I tell ya what, if we win, I'll go halves with ya, eh?'

'What for? I don't need any money.'

'Crazy fucker,' Bob's muttering under his breath. But he means well.

9

The moon diminishes.

It is no longer aligned with the greater light, and so its luminance wanes. Gradually, imperceptibly. Lunar winds of gravity shift and gust. It is inevitable.

Arthur tosses in his bed. He strains at the silence. There is nothing to be heard.

Ponsonby Road is quiet at 3.17 a.m. Moonlight slants across the streetscape, painting it as a spectral movie set. A scruffy tomcat pads the asphalt, ready for action. The night is warm and accommodating.

There are no stars visible, and no need for any. The city is self-sufficient.

Geranne sits atop a wooden parapet, looking down at the street. She yearns for it. There's something about the emptiness, the loneliness of it.

Is vacancy beautiful to humans as well? Do they appreciate this tragedy? Are they pining for our world as we do for theirs?

On the other side of the street, Burlain stands

behind the railing of a balcony. He's looking across at Geranne, and his eyes are full of sadness.

'Have mercy,' he mutters. 'Have mercy.'

He's feeling nervous, if the truth be told. In the middle of setting out the chairs, he stops to sit down on one. The hall is empty and very silent.

The television people will be arriving shortly to set up. There'll be action and echoing voices. For the moment there's stillness. He attempts to join it, envying the calm of indifference.

What if no-one should turn up? What if nobody cares any more? With the world looking on, will I be a fool again?

'*Be still.*'

Did I make that up? Do I invent the voice of God? Is it my psyche? Be what?

'*Be still.*'

'Wotcha, Norm. How's me best customer?'

'Yeah, good thanks, Bill. Or well, to be more honest. How's business?'

'Steady, Norm, steady. They all want their fancy bloody wines nowadays, so I've had to bone up on all of that. Bit different from the old days, you know. I used to think a man was a bit of a show-off if he asked for a foreign beer. Life was simpler then.'

'Ah, come off it, Bill. Next thing you'll be telling

me how they used to light the gaslamps on the corner. It's an old man's rusk, nostalgia is. I bet you're making a few more dollars now than when you started out.'

'Now listen here, you half-arsed wino, don't you go giving me lip. I've had the wife on me back wanting an overseas trip, so don't you go sticking your oar in as well. Fair go, a man can't get a bit of peace and quiet for quids.'

'No rest for the wicked, Bill. You should take your wife on a holiday if she wants one, you measly bastard. You've got enough tucked away to retire now and go travelling till they stick you in a box.'

'Yeah, and who's going to look after this then? Rob me blind, they would, if I wasn't here to keep an eye on them. No, "Shirley," I said to her, "we just can't make it happen this year. Maybe next year." She gives me the old cold eye, but there it is. Can't be helped.'

'You're tighter than the arses round the Business Roundtable, you are, Bill. Put some living back in your life before you haven't got one; take a few risks, for God's sake.'

'The only risk I'm taking is offering you credit out of the goodness of me heart. Now what is it you're wanting? A bottle of sherry?'

'That'd suit me just fine — a hip-flask if you don't mind. I'm staying at Bob's for a few days since Denno booted me out of the park, so I need to be a bit discreet.'

'I hear Bob's place is getting the chop, isn't it? I saw a poster about this meeting on tonight. You going along, Norm?'

'Nah, don't think so. It's for talking about us, not to us. I go with the flow, Bill. Not much chance of them closing the park, I wouldn't think.'

'Arthur! At last. I thought you'd forgotten me.'

'How can the moon forget the earth? You're with me always, Margaret, even if I don't call. There's been a lot happening lately, and I don't like telephones.'

'It's good to hear your voice, just the same. What have you been up to that's kept you so busy?'

'Delivering. Yeah, you could say I've been delivering. You know the story of Moses, how he freed the Jews? Well, that sort of thing.'

'You're not in trouble, are you, Arthur? I wish I could see you, touch you.'

'Trouble? Nah, not me. It's just that we needed a miracle here, and it took me a while to jack one up. But now I've got it all sorted, so there's no problem. How are things with you?'

'Strained. It's difficult having Brian around all day. He's off talking to a personnel company this morning. I feel sorry for him, but it's not enough.'

'You need to look after him, Margaret. He's growing up and he needs your support.'

'Mmm . . . When am I going to see you?'

'What about Sunday morning? Can you get away then?'

'It's too far away, but yes, that'll be fine. I sometimes go in to have breakfast with Penny on a Sunday morning. Where do you want to meet?'

'Come down the boarding house and we'll see what happens from there, eh?'

The lights are intrusive. They show up dirt which the cleaners would never find. Under their gaze, the hall collapses into two-dimensional tawdriness. Robbed of its mystery, if it ever had any. Like stripping the clothes off a pensioner for everyone to see. Kevin resents them, even though he invited them.

'Can I ask you to move just a bit, chief? Only I've got to get this cable run, see. Cheers.'

'Well, why not? I'm only the organizer,' he mutters to himself as he moves to the back of the hall. Karen has her legs crossed, shuffling through a bunch of papers.

'Thanks for coming. I don't think I really expected you to turn up. Is everything OK?'

'What's that?'

She surfaces briefly.

'Oh yes, fine, I think. We're just getting set up, you know. When do you think people will turn up?'

'Any time now, I should think. I've got no idea how many will show for it. It's a bit of an unknown,

243

really. I can't say I've ever organized anything quite like this before.'

'Mmm.'

She's absorbed in the research notes again.

He's looking at her.

'Karen . . .'

'Yes?'

'Nothing. I better get out to the door.'

'Not another bloody night out!'

'I'm sorry, but that's what I get paid for. I haven't heard you complaining about the size of my salary.'

'Yes, but Barbara, I mean to say. This is the third night on the trot. There's other parts of your life that you need to give some time to as well.'

'Such as?'

'Such as me, for instance. I thought we might have had dinner out tonight, caught up with each other.'

'Look, I'm sorry, Derek. It's not like I'm arranging things so that I can keep away from you. I'd rather be anywhere tonight than at this meeting. Some do-gooding vicar has organized a protest against the closing of boarding houses. You'd think the church would be on my side, trying to establish better conditions for the socially disadvantaged. Anyway, it was my recommendation that this particular hovel be closed, and I need to be there to defend it.'

'What time will you be home?'

'I shouldn't think it will go too late. People will see why it has to happen once they get the facts. It's well-meaning ignorance, that's all it is.'

She finally rejects the diamond earrings and decides on something a little more understated. She smiles at herself in the mirror.

From his vantage point above, it looks to Burlain rather like some sort of inorganic consumer of humanity. Light streams out from the open doors. People approach and are swallowed into the interior. He can see that more are coming.

High above Ponsonby, he continues his lilting call.

'Bob, good to see you. Did you bring any of the men up with you?'

'Yeah, as many as I could. Told them there was gonna be a big supper after with cream cakes. They're outside having a smoke.'

'We haven't actually organized much of a supper. Just a cup of tea and biscuits, I'm afraid.'

'Mate, I don't care if it's prune juice and birdseed. I only wanted to get the old buggers away from the TV set. They'll have forgotten already why they're here, let alone by supper time.'

'Thanks for coming early. Have you prepared something to say?'

'Whaddya mean? Written something out? I'm not

too good on the old writing, vic, but I'll say a few words if that's what ya want. Thanks for pulling this together, by the way. Looks like there's a few people turning up.'

'Let's just hope something comes of it. Now, I think I'll open the meeting and then get you up first to give us some background. How's that sound?'

'Box of fluffies. I better go and round the boys up before they set fire to the church. Old Wal gets a bit match-happy now and again, you know?'

Arthur has the dining room to himself. Apart from a few stragglers down in the TV room, all the others have gone up to the meeting.

I don't know what all the fuss is about. I told Bob I'd fix it for him.

Nobody believes any more. They limit themselves to what they can see. I want to take them and open their eyes to everything that's around them. I want them to meet you, Father. I want my time to come.

The hubbub of conversation bounces off the hard surfaces of the hall and fills the space. Kevin can't keep the smile off his face as they continue to stream in.

We're going to have to put out more chairs if this keeps up.

Eyes are periodically flicking towards the television cameras. It's good to know that this event is important.

After arguing with herself, Penny finally lays the book down and does her hair. She glances at the clock on her way out. *Just as well I haven't got far to go.*

He stands for a few seconds as the conversation subsides, and eyes turn to focus on the front. He feels the heat of the lights.

'Good evening, ladies and gentlemen. Thanks for coming along tonight to address an issue of vital importance to our community. I'm Kevin Connor, vicar of St David's, and I'd like to welcome you on behalf of our parish. Kia ora.

'I've lived in Ponsonby for many years now. When I first came, it was a very mixed community. People with different ethnic roots, with different lifestyles, with different levels of income. The diversity of the place was one of the things that attracted me. I suspect the same may be true for some of you.

'Where else could you find artists drying canvases on their veranda, Samoans putting down an umu in their back yard, students working on their cars on the street, psych patients out for a morning stroll and BMWs parked up on the footpath? There has been a traditional richness in the variety which constitutes our neighbourhood. This has produced a degree of tolerance and acceptance which is missing in many other parts of the city.'

He picks at a piece of imaginary fluff on his shirt. It's a distracting habit which his wife has told him about often.

'But many of us who have been attracted by all that Ponsonby represents, and moved into the area over recent years, have put pressure on the very aspect of the place that drew us in the first place. Ponsonby has got very white and very expensive. It has become harder and harder for the poorer sections of our community to survive here.

'How do we feel about that? Is it inevitable? Do we simply need to recognize that the tide is changing? That's the issue we need to be addressing tonight. The specific threat which has given rise to our meeting is the prospective closure of a boarding house in Shelly Beach Road. In order to give us some background to this, I've asked Bob, manager of the Harbour Lodge boarding house, to speak to us. Thanks, Bob.'

The row of men towards the back is set off from the crowd by a scattering of empty seats around them.

There's a constant murmur of muttering and vaguely guttural noises emerging from their midst. Frank has removed a good portion of the contents of his nasal cavity with his finger and is examining the result.

They look towards the front as Bob gets up.

'Yeah, gidday. I grew up round here — me old man ran the boarding house before I ever did, and we all lived upstairs. I've been looking after the place for the last seven years, since Dad died. It's not the flashest of places, eh. It's got a bit run-down over the years, but we don't own it, see. We just lease it, so there's not a lot of money spent on the place.

'We got twenty-seven men living there — well, twenty-eight really, 'cos Norm's staying with us for a while. Most of 'em have been there a good long while. A couple of 'em have been round since I was a little nipper.

'They tend to be at the rough end of the spectrum, if you know what I mean. Alkies, burnt-out psych patients, that sort of thing. They like it down Harbour Lodge 'cos they can be themselves, you know? Not too many rules and regulations, and I cut them a bit of slack if they get sick or fall behind in their rent or something. We give them a good feed and keep an eye on them, and they seem to like the way I run things.

'We've always got some government department or other on our backs. Fire regulations or building inspectors or someone. Most of 'em are decent enough, and even if we have a few barneys now and

249

again, we can usually talk things through and make a deal of some sort.'

He scans the crowd for Barbara Harmon. He saw her coming in, bitch. For the next bit he fixes her with his eyes, throws out the challenge.

'But now we've got a letter from North Health telling us that the men are overcrowded, and that we can only have two to a room. Orright, we've got 'em stacked up three to a room most cases now, but that's the only way the numbers work, see? The blokes are happy enough.

'The fact is there's no way we can do it, not without a whole lot of money which we haven't got. So they've told us they're going to close us down. Well, I really don't give a . . . What I mean is, there's other jobs I could do if it came down to it. But what about these fellas, eh?'

He looks out to his faithful tribe, encompasses them with a gesture.

'Where will they go if they get tossed out? Most of 'em wouldn't fit in with the crowd at other boarding houses. "What about a rest home?" Missus Harmon there asks. Well, I'd like to see that, I really would. The other residents would be out the back door so fast they wouldn't have time to collect their pearls.

'I've always thought of meself as a reasonable sort of a joker. But I can't just stand by and see these blokes chucked out on the street for the sake of some new bloody regulation. I dunno what anyone else can do, but I hope some of you might get in behind us and help us to stay open.'

There's a smattering of applause, not wholly enthusiastic.

Wal sticks his hand down the front of his trousers and scratches. A well-dressed woman nearby watches, and tries to avert her eyes. Wal gives her an exaggerated wink.

Kevin opens the meeting for discussion.

Barbara Harmon rises to speak; makes her way to the front where the television lights are shining.

'Kia ora. Barbara Harmon from North Health. I was part of the review process which evaluated Harbour Lodge, and I wrote the letter which Mr Davies has referred to, setting out our requirements.

'There were a number of points we raised in the letter, including our unhappiness with the standard of cleanliness and the potential health risks created by current food-handling procedures. Some of these items have been the subject of earlier correspondence with Mr Davies. The most serious point, however, has already been alluded to.

'Under our new regulations for boarding houses, there is a specified minimum floor area required for each resident. This is not, as Mr Davies implies, a petty imposition. It is a standard introduced to protect the wellbeing of boarding-house residents, who are often exploited for commercial gain. We consider it essential for the mental health of residents that they have sufficient personal space.'

She surveys the crowd. She's speaking their language. They're travelling with her.

'We are certainly not seeking to drive these people out of Ponsonby, or to turn them out on the streets. I find such suggestions personally offensive. Our only concern is to achieve the best quality of life possible for a group who have suffered various misfortunes. The fact of the matter is that Harbour Lodge is currently substandard, and no licence will be issued until conditions are improved.'

There's a long burst of sustained applause.

Pete has a bad coughing fit, and looks in vain for somewhere to spit.

A man with a cellphone stands.

'Jim Purvis, chairman of the local community committee. Let me say first off how pleased I am to see such a good turnout of Ponsonby people. I find it encouraging to live in an area where people still find some importance in local issues.

'It seems to me that we need to clarify the issues here. I think a lot of us would agree with the concern expressed by the vicar in opening the meeting tonight. We're proud of the diversity of Ponsonby, and we want to fight to retain it. Our community committee has been talking seriously about this very issue in recent months.

'But the troubles of Mr Davies' boarding house seem to me to be something of a red herring. From what Ms Harmon has just told us, there are some legitimate concerns about the way the operation is managed. I can't help wondering if our concern for the poorer sections of our community wouldn't be best expressed by supporting North Health in their attempt to raise the standards of care.'

'You mean we should kick them out of their beds so that they'll be better off?'

Bob can't help himself. Penny is one of the few who giggles at his interjection.

Kevin calls for order and suggests that all comments be addressed through him as chairman.

The voice is faltering, hard to hear.

'I've been living in Ponsonby since I was ten years old, and I'm seventy-two now. Oh, sorry, my name's Mavis. Mavis Dickson. I've seen all sorts of things over that time. People come and go. Buildings come and go. There's hardly anyone left now who remembers what Ponsonby used to be like years ago.

'Used to be trams come up College Hill, there did. The churches were full every Sunday. I remember this place, St David's, when it was in the old buildings. A lot more tasteful it was then, in my opinion. And then we had the Islanders coming in. The Chinese greengrocer up in Three Lamps, he couldn't get the taro off the ships quick enough before it was all sold out. People used to worry then. Gang troubles, there were.

'Students coming in, with their noisy parties, wrecking good houses. And then there was the lunatics, too. Oh yes, I know it's not fashionable to call them that these days, but it's what I grew up calling them. Straight out of Carrington they used to come, though even that's closed down now. We've had them all, coming and going.

'I used to know my neighbours in the street. We didn't live on each other's doorstep, but we were there when things went wrong. Good decent folk, they were. All gone now. I don't know anyone now. The cars come and go, and I see the light from the television in the night, and sometimes the noise of a dinner party. But no-one much says hello.'

A significant cough emerges from the front row. As gently as possible, Kevin asks if there is another point to be made.

'Oh dear, rambling, am I? Well, you have to have some privileges. The only point I have is this. They've

254

all arrived and they've all left again. There was no use worrying about it then and there's no use worrying about it now. The yuppies — is that what you call them? — they'll be on their way too, if you give them time. Give them time, they all go. That's all.'

Bill finds something hilariously funny, and can't stop himself chuckling in his deep voice. Whether it has anything to do with what's been said or not is anybody's guess. Bob yanks on his sleeve and the noise gradually subsides.

Penny speaks.

'I wanted to respond to what Jim was saying earlier on. I appreciate that he doesn't want us getting sidetracked from the issue of the diversity of Ponsonby. It's just that I doubt we can see the closing of another boarding house as being a red herring in that context. This is not the first boarding house to close in Ponsonby, is it? There used to be a lot of them.

'I don't know why the others have closed — perhaps because they became uneconomical to run. We do know why this one is about to close, and Barbara has given us her very substantial reasons for that. Most of us don't have much to do with boarding houses, I should think, and even less to do with the people in them.

255

'We're happy to let people like Bob run them. It's not the sort of environment we'd want to live in, but it does seem to be a home of sorts for the men who've been there over the years. I can't help wondering if we don't have some responsibility to help Bob get round this situation, and continue to do what he does. Otherwise it seems a little hypocritical for us to bemoan the changing nature of our community. Is it only the idea of diversity we like, and not the people who are actually different?'

'Hi, I'm Christine and I think that woman made some good points. As far as the boarding house is concerned, I can't help noticing that some of the residents are here with us. It seems ridiculous to be talking about them without asking what they think. I was wondering if one of the residents might like to give us their view of things.'

Bob groans and puts his head in his hands. After a few seconds' silence, he nudges Pete.

'What? Yeah, OK. I'm Pete. This is Wal next to me, and then that's Bill and . . . oh sorry, Bob, sorry. Jeez, look, I'm not too sure what all this is about. What did you want me to say, luv?'

'Can you tell us how you feel about the boarding house closing?'

'Here's the thing, see. We don't even like to talk

about it as a boarding house, you know? It's sort of like home for us. We might be a bit rough round the edges, but it's like a big family for us. Some of us came from big families in the old days, so we like it like that. Bob here, he's a good bloke. A good bloke. If the place gets a bit untidy now and again, that's our fault, not Bob's. He does his best.

'We get good tucker down there, better than a lot of places I been. And Bob lets things slide if you get a bit short of money. He tells us off, but his bark's worse than his bite, really. Now as for closing the place down, I don't know what you mean. How would you feel if someone came into your house and said they was going to close you down?'

'How about the overcrowding?'

This from the back of the hall.

'Things are a bit tight down there, but that's all right. When I was growing up we had to sleep two to a bed, so three in a room seems pretty good. It wasn't us who was complaining about the rooms, Bob, honest it wasn't. We want to stick with you.'

Bob puts out his hand and claps Pete on the shoulder.

Barbara's lips are pale from the way she's pressing them together.

'My name's David, and I work in the area of psychiatric aftercare. Most of you will know that

257

there's been some huge changes in mental health policy in the last decade. We've made a real effort to return the mentally ill to the community, rather than punishing them twice by locking them up for their illness. Returning people to the community is a bit of a euphemism, really. The fact is that there's not much of a community to return them to.

'The end result is that, for a lot of people, we lose track of them after about six months out of hospital. Many of them end up on the streets. Some of them find their way into boarding houses such as the one which Bob runs. Now there's no doubt that the operators of some of these houses are unscrupulous. They exploit their residents for the maximum return.

'I'm speaking from a position of experience when I say that Harbour Lodge is not like that. The manager appears to have an extremely good relationship with his residents. At the risk of cutting across the bows of my esteemed colleague, Barbara, I venture to suggest that we should do all we can to retain this boarding house within our community. I suggest we open a fund for making the necessary alterations to the house.'

The response includes much murmuring and the endorsement of some applause.

A slight woman is getting to her feet. Kevin has seen her somewhere before. *Where was it, now?*

Oh shit.

'We're all trying to be very tolerant here. Talking about differences and how we appreciate them. Well, there's some differences we can do without!

'A former resident of Harbour Lodge, he . . . It was years ago now. She was only six, a beautiful girl . . . Innocent eyes. Everyone said she had innocent eyes. He . . . he molested her. She killed herself later on.

'I know you can't bring back the past. But you don't have to forget it, just the same. He was a child molester, a pervert. He got put back into this precious community you're all talking about. And he destroyed my daughter. Took her away from me.

'If they want to close down the boarding house, then I say good riddance to it! Do you want to carry on putting the whole community at risk? For what? So you can feel good about how tolerant you are? I wish they'd never closed the asylums. They were there for a reason; for our protection. And now we have no protection at all.

'Close it down, I say. Get these people out of our community, and back into a proper hospital where they belong. Before anyone else has to go through what I've been through.'

Pete has tears rolling slowly down his cheeks.

The murmuring has broken into open conversation

now, and the sounds of disagreement can be heard echoing around the hall.

Kevin can feel it slipping away.

The television cameras continue to watch. The sound man is pretty sure he caught it well enough.

Wal picks the moment to belch, a deep, sonorous report which rips through the confusion and reduces it to quiet.

Kevin gets to his feet to try and rescue something, but it's already too late. A man in a suit is speaking, his face flushed.

'Excuse me, I don't know that woman's name, but I'm pleased she's brought us back to reality. I'm as happy as any of you to have different types of people around here, but there has to be sensible limits, doesn't there? I mean to say, are we going to invite criminals to come and live in Ponsonby so that we can be even more cosmopolitan?

'I'm not convinced, actually, that Ponsonby is really the best place for the recuperation of these type of people. They may be better off out in the country somewhere, where life is less stressful. This is an expensive suburb now, and I can't imagine it's easy to live in for poorer people. I've noticed lately that there's been people begging on the street corners. It's not necessary, and it doesn't do anything for the restaurant trade, to be frank.'

Ah, thinks Digby, *now I recognize you, you tightarse bastard.*

'If we're going to be talking about the Ponsonby community, then the real issue I want addressed is parking . . .'

The whole thing is falling apart before his eyes. Comments are being thrown from all over the place. Kevin tries to speak but is too late again.

'Look, I'm in real estate, Tony Villers. I've got to say that I agree with the previous speaker. Ponsonby may not be the best place for boarding houses any more. I turned one over to a developer last year, and once he'd done the place up, the capital gain was out of this world. I mean you could have bought four boarding houses in South Auckland for the money.

'Now this place we're talking about is in Shelly Beach Road. With all due respect, that place has got to be worth a mint. You have to ask whether the present usage is the best bang for buck. And another thing, without stepping on anyone's toes. The properties either side wouldn't be sorry to see the boarding house close, I can promise you that.'

Chaos reigns. The noise is deafening. People are shouting. As Kevin stands, he can see two people pushing and jostling with each other.

Wal's sitting with his head between his hands, trying to stop the noise.

Bob stands and yells.

'Ah, fuck the lot of ya. We don't need to sit through any of this crap. Who the fuck d'ya think yer talking about? A bunch of animals? Ya think we're running a soddin' zoo down there? These guys sitting here might have their problems, but I'd rather share my house with them than most of you lot. You, ya parasitic real-estate prick, yer head's so far up yer arse that ya'll need to pick yer nose through yer belly button.

'Ya pack of poxy, poncy, self-righteous tossers. All of these blokes started out in life the same as you did. They had families, they had hopes, they wanted to do something with their lives. Things went wrong, that's all. They've got as much right to live wherever the fuck they like as you have, even if they don't drive BM fucken Ws or eat at restaurants. Most of you only turned up in Ponsonby in the last five minutes.

'Well, ya can stick yer meeting. Is Ponsonby losing its heart? That's what the poster said, wasn't it? Too late, I say. The heart's been cut up an' put in packets with fancy fucken bows on, so it can be sold in the latest trendy shop with an Italian name.

'C'mon, boys, we're off home. There's no place for us here, that's for fucken sure.'

Karen is despising herself for how exultant she feels, seeing the nod from the cameraman that he's got it.

Chairs are being tipped over. There's an edge of violence to the clamour.

Kevin is calling out vainly for order. He finally gives up and slumps into a chair.

Barbara is trying to keep the smile off her face.

Wal's muttering about the cream cakes as he follows the rest of them out of the door.

Burlain continues his watch from above.

The crowd is vomited out from the hall, and great waves of hostility buffet the air.

Indigestible.

The night air is still warm, but something's changed. It isn't as embracing as it was earlier. There's a feeling of stuffiness which makes it hard to breathe.

There's a brittleness to the echoing of footsteps on the asphalt. Car engines growl with the menace of guard dogs as they're kicked into life. As the people disperse, they're tearing shreds from something and carrying it away with them.

The great double-hung eyes of the villas seem to droop in sadness. It's as if there were a wailing and a keening just out of reach of human hearing.

At least that's the way it seems to Penny as she makes her way home.

Dawson says the redundancy payout's cancelled.

Brian has just got off the phone. Margaret picked it was something serious.

'But he can't do that, can he? Why?'

'He recognized me from the *Nightly News* thing. He says that I signed a contract promising not to make any media comment, and that seeing I've breached that then my money's out the window.'

'Did you sign that?'

'I don't know. I think I probably did. I didn't really care what I was signing by that stage of things. He's probably right, Marg.'

'What are you going to do? What are we going to do?'

'I'm going to fight him. I'm going to get a lawyer and put him through the hoops in the Employment Court. I'm not lying down for Dawson ever again. What d'you think?'

'Good on you, go for it. We'll need to try and generate some income, though.'

'I think that might be all right. The guy I went to today from the personnel place, he was brilliant. I was only thinking of jobs in the banking sector. But he asked me why, if that was what I was committed to. The funny thing was, when I stopped and thought about it, I don't really like banking at all. We started on a process of working out what my gifts and talents were. I've got to go in again on

Friday to do some profile tests. He reckons I should be able to change fields if I want to, head off on another track. I'm excited about it, Marg. I haven't felt this way since, I don't know, since we were first married, I suppose.'

She's looking at him with curiosity. You think you know someone, and then they come out and surprise you. There's something stirring within her. Admiration?

Arthur is walking, praying for the city with every step.

He stops at the top of a hill, looks out over the darkened streets. The city is as close to peace as it gets. He sends a blessing out to it.

In the distance there is a Coca-Cola sign making a neon declaration. He watches it, intrigued by the alternating red and white. *Those colours. Of course.*

There is a shift in the deep vaults. Current is flowing, connections are being made. Arthur is seeing what he sees, but he sees *beyond* it at the same time. Many streams have reached a junction, and Arthur alone stands in the river. He *understands*.

He must have cried out in his excitement. Two men walking on the other side of the road are looking at him to see what trouble might be brewing.

Red and white. Red and white. Coca-Cola.

They troop into the dining room. Some of them sit at the table; others lean around the walls. The trip home has been quiet.

'Well, shit, there's no need to look so glum, ya misery moochers. Anyone'd think that smoking had been outlawed. We don't need to take any notice of those shitheads with their flash cars and diverse fucken communities. We're home! I'll look after ya, ya sorry excuse for humanity. We'll be right. Now, Wal's been yabberin' in me ear about supper, so what say we break out some ice cream?'

The anxiety slips from the room. Smiles sneak around the crowd. Hearts are opened as easily as the freezer; aroha spooned out like ice cream from the huge tub. The men from the TV room sense food and come sniffing.

Bob's at the centre of it, where he belongs. Dipping his hairy, unhygienic arms into the plastic container, barking commands as he makes sure there's enough to go round.

'Whaddya reckon, Bill? This'll put some lining on yer arteries, eh? Keep ya warm in the winter. That's the story, get into it. Nah, sorry, mate. It's hokey-pokey or sweet fuck all, I'm afraid.

'Here, piss off, Bill, you've already got yours. Ya think I'm as silly as you jokers, that I don't know who's had some and who hasn't? Have to be a bit faster than that to fool me. Come here, Taff. Get some ice cream down ya. You too, Morrie. Stop playing with yerself and get yer hand round a spoon. An' try and keep it on the plate, or ya'll be licking it up off the floor, next to that pox-ridden cat.

'Go on, shove off, Wal, you've had some as well.'

But Wal's not wanting more. His empty plate is hanging in his big hand, dripping onto the floor. There's a big ring of ice cream around his mouth. His eyes are shining. He's walking towards Bob.

'Whaddya want, ya goofy bastard? Piss off.'

Wal wraps his arms around Bob, and plants a slobbering ice-cream kiss on his cheek.

Bob grimaces and wipes it off with his sleeve. They're all laughing and clapping, and Bob's laughing too.

'Mad, the whole bloody lot of ya, that's what. That old biddy was right, they should've locked yas all up years ago. Don't go thinking we're having ice cream every night, 'cos we're not, see?'

There's a knock at the door. Pete goes out to see who it is. He comes back in leading Kevin. A sorry vicar, if ever there was one.

'I've just called in to apologize for that fiasco. I really am deeply sorry for the attitudes you've been exposed to. I wish I could do something to make up for it, but I've caused enough trouble with my meddling already. I'm sorry, Bob, sorry for the hurt to you and these men.'

'Ah Jeez, Kevin, get off the grass. You're not responsible for the whole bloody world, even if ya think ya are. That's life. Bastards are bastards, and they'll be kicking the shit out of the likes of us until the end of time. Now ya can waddle around feeling sorry, or ya can join us for a party. We're celebrating something, only we've forgotten what it is. Isn't that right, boys? If yer really lucky, Wal here might give ya a kiss.'

Amidst the noise and laughter, Kevin is pushed into the middle and someone puts a plate in his hand. He looks at it in puzzlement, and slowly begins to smile.

10

It's late by the time he gets back to the boarding house. The lights are out, but you can always get in through the door round the back, if you know the way.

They're all in bed apart from Morrie, who's wandering around in the darkened TV room, muttering to himself. Arthur doesn't mind. He likes being on his own.

In his hand he carries an empty Coke can, a treasure rescued from the gutter. He places it on the mantelpiece as if it were a trophy. Which it is, in a way. Stands back and looks at it. Red and white.

There he is, rummaging around in the junk drawer in the kitchen. *Ah, I knew it was here. I knew he wouldn't have thrown it out.*

It's a Christmas decoration, a gaudy picture of Santa Claus with red glitter on his cheeks. Just as he remembers it. This, too, goes up on the mantelpiece, next to the empty can.

Now then, we see it. Red and white, white and red. *The connection.*

The Real Thing. The Father of Christmas. *Yes.*

Tim has a smile all over his face. He'd be tempted to kiss her if he wasn't so frightened of her.

The end of the live stuff feeds through to the monitor, and the technician turns it off.

'Well, what do you think? Is it good or what?'

'Sensational, Karen. Absolutely sensational. We can edit that up into a bloody good little drama, and it'll have all the pull in the world.'

'Can we hold it for a week or so?'

'Hold it? Why the fuck would we want to do that? This is live news, baby. Strong, immediate, in your face. And it's exclusive. We want it up there on the main bulletin, where the ratings happen.'

'I want to doco it. Cut in some of my earlier stuff, give it a bit of background. Story line — where do you go when nobody wants you any more? We've got good stuff, it's gutsy; we can sell it, Tim, I know we can.'

'You think? Who gives a toss about psych patients?'

'Come on, Tim. We're talking Mr and Mrs Public here, not urban sophisticates like you who've had a compassion transplant.'

'It'd need an ending. Something dramatic to give it a hook, a way for us to sell it with the promos.'

'Yeah, I'll work on it. Just give me a week or so? A done deal?'

If only there was some way of getting a competitive advantage out of her, he's thinking. *What's in it for me?*

She takes her time going through the file notes. Best not to miss something and then regret it later. Partly to keep him fretting, if she was inclined to be honest.

'Well, nurse, what's your professional opinion?'

'Professionally? I'd have to say it looks pretty good. The indicators are positive, psychotic episodes seem to have stopped, physical condition about as good as it's ever been. No obvious *medical* side effects.'

'Why the qualification?'

'Have you looked into his eyes, doctor?'

'What's that supposed to mean?'

'I think there's less of him at home than what there used to be. It's like looking down a deep well these days, and you can't quite be sure if that's a man you see at the bottom or just a trick of the light.'

'That's your professional opinion? Come on, Gwenda, you can't be serious.'

'No, it's not my professional opinion. I gave you that earlier. You asked me to elaborate on my hesitation about side effects. It's an intuition, a gut feeling. The sort of insight you've told me to look out for in the past. But I won't record it, doctor, and it won't appear in any formal evaluation. It's just an observation between the two of us.'

'You really think he's flat?'

'Have you heard him laughing lately?'

'Mmmm.'

'If it went so badly, why are you so happy?'

'I went round to the boarding house afterwards and had supper with the men. They were having a great time. You'd have thought they'd just won the fight and been told they could stay. It was great, Linda, I really enjoyed myself.'

'I'm glad it was you and not me. I hope you had a shower before you came to bed. Dylan, get your fingers out of the milk. Oh no, look. Tell him, Kevin.'

'Cut it out, Dylan. What do you mean by that remark about a shower?'

'Well, you know. There's fleas and goodness knows what else in places like that. You can't blame them, poor souls, but I expect they don't wash very often. Oh, for goodness' sake, stop him, will you?'

'No more, now, you hear me? Or I'll take it away. They treated me like one of the family, you know. I felt more at home there than I do in any of our church services. They're real people, Linda, with no airs or graces or pretence. What you see is what you get.'

'Oh, honestly, I've had enough. Are you just going to sit there and let him get away with that? Go and get a cloth now, Dylan, and clean it up. Here we go again, making saints out of anybody who's not part of your flock, and demons out of the rest of us. I know, God's living there among the poor, I've heard the sermon. Just so long as you don't expect me to go with you to that filthy old place.'

'It's not a filthy old place; it's their home, where they live. Pick that up out of the rubbish bin and put it in the sink. You know better than that. And leave your sister alone. Anyway, I don't know what's going to happen to it now, honestly I don't.'

She wakes as the light seeps into the bedroom. The pale pink walls release their colour as the morning strokes them.

Alongside her Brian is breathing heavily, twitching as he navigates his dreamworld. For her it has been a dreamless sleep, as far as she can remember.

The quiet is pervasive and accepting. She welcomes it into her interior, and all is at peace. Without moving her head, she surveys the bedroom. It is satisfying, and all her own doing. The honey kauri glows under her gaze. The pictures, chosen with care, pick up the colours of the walls and the drapes. The room is tidy, orderly, calm, beautiful. It is her space, even if she has to share it. Where she loves to come to at the end of the day and wake up in at the beginning of the next.

Margaret scratches absently under one arm, then slips a hand under her satin top and massages one breast. It's partly a half-hearted self-examination, mostly just for the sensation of touch and the soft waves of pleasure. It's one of those mornings when you can luxuriate in yourself.

They made love again last night. Not that she intended to or even thought about it beforehand. Just gone along with it and enjoyed it in the end. Is it a betrayal of Arthur? It doesn't seem so. Though Arthur's definitely a betrayal of Brian.

The nipple swells under her fingers. *I shouldn't have started thinking about Arthur.* The other hand brushes lightly over her pubic area. Not with any intent. Just for the memory.

Tomorrow morning I'll see him. I feel nervous, almost.

Brian begins to stir. She resents the prospect of her space being invaded. *Poor Brian. I must try to be kind to him.*

Even if I can't sleep here, no-one can stop me getting the grass under my feet. Inspecting my property. Now look at that rubbish. You don't get that mess when I'm on station.

The morning air has that damp freshness about it, like someone's kept it in the fridge over night and just taken the lid off. Already the lick of the sun is warm, and most of the dew has gone. Norm rests a while under a big oak tree, an old friend of his. He leans back into the trunk, allows the strength of it to hold him. He digs in his pocket and finds the makings of a cigarette.

I still need something to lean on, even at my age.

He twitches out the strands of tobacco, moistens the finished product with his lips, and fits it to the corner of his mouth. The first hit causes tears to well up in his eyes, and a dizzy nicotine rush in the back of his head. A wet, lumpy cough cringes at the back of his throat. He tries to hold it down, but eventually gives in to the inevitable. With the fit the phlegm rises and he has to spit.

Wooh, that's better.

Still hanging in the sky like someone forgot to take it in last night, the moon. Fading away, and ghostly white in its daylight guise. It looks enchanting, hanging down there over the Westhaven boats. Against the Coca-Cola sign. City of Sails.

From an upstairs window of the old house, Arthur's looking at the same scene. *Well, will you look at that? Red and white. Red and white.*

The Saturday breakfasters sprawl over the footpath.

They are the admirers of Ponsonby, the tenants of her easy grace, the connoisseurs of eggs Benedict followed by latte, the commentators on every nuance of social trend. They're splendid here in the sunlight, like pretentious flowers opening to waft their fragrance over the ridge.

The old streets tolerate them as a dog becomes fond of its fleas. There's room for all.

But the hard surfaces ache for the touch and blessing of John. Where has he gone with his love?

And Joe's Bargain House and Hydra and the Gluepot. Where have they gone, and why do the gaps still feel empty, even though they've been filled? And the runny noses and the leaking of oil onto the road and the smell of cabbage. The old are allowed their memories.

There's a queue outside a small machine on the side of the road. People are taking their turns at doing things to it with their fingers. In return money slides out between its thick metal lips. They take it and leave, making room for the next in line.

The breakfasters are engrossed in their consumption.

Byzantium is packed. Which is why Karen agrees to a table outside. She hates being *recognized*, especially on a Saturday morning when all you want is espresso incognito. Even making sure that Trudi takes the more exposed seat doesn't provide enough shelter. *This public life which I love to hate.*

Trudi is valiantly finishing off her smoked salmon bagel. There's a streak of cream cheese at the corner of her mouth. Karen reaches across to wipe it away with a finger. Their friendship goes back into the primeval swamps of memory, where images of innocence lurk.

They are minor rituals, these encounters over coffee. There's not much in common now, with Trudi ankle-deep in motherhood and domesticity. But she remains mercifully unimpressed with fame, preferring her secret knowledge of Karen with pimples and pigtails. A session with Trudi is like returning to your homeland after years in exile. Just so long as you don't have to live there any longer.

'And the children? You're enjoying the children?'

'Most of the time, yes. Not that you're really interested, you never have been. I doubt whether you could even tell me what their names are.'

'I, uh . . .'

'Look, it doesn't matter, Karen. You don't have to like children, and you don't have to pretend with me. I don't take it personally. I know you're happy for me to be happy with my kids, and that's enough. I can't for the life of me imagine you as a mother; that's not for you.'

The annoying thing about Trudi is her somewhat fey insight. Karen was fifteen years old when Trudi first told her that she was headed for a public life.

'I'm sorry, Trud. I should know better than to play games with you. I am pleased for you, though, pleased that you're settled and happy. You always said you'd get pregnant to the first bloke with enough money to give you a good time.'

'Yep, that's me. When Gregg turned up in a Porsche, I just lay right down and opened my legs. It's all a matter of knowing what you want, and what it takes to get it.'

'And things are all right with you and Gregg?'

'No, not really. About a month ago, just after Sarah was born, I found out he'd been bonking the receptionist. Men can be so pathetic. I told him he had three choices. I could cut his dick off and put it down the waste disposal, he could keep screwing his teenage fantasy and I would take him to the cleaners in the family courts, or he could grow up and go on being my husband. He's decided to have a go at being mature, but I'm not sure yet whether he's capable of it.'

'Oh Trudi, I'm so sorry. You don't deserve that.'

'Bullshit, Karen. It's just life and what happens. I don't expect any special favours on account of my radiant personality. I'm committed to Gregg, and in his own way he's committed to me. He's just a naughty boy who wants a spanking from his mother. Now he's had a telling off he feels much better about himself. It's been hard for me and my self-esteem, but I'm through the worst of it now.'

'Is there anything I can do to help? I don't know what to say . . .'

'You were never a Mother Teresa in the field of compassion, love. That's all right. You just keep paying the bill for these little get-togethers of ours, and I'm happy for you to be challenged in the empathy department. Anyway, what's been happening in your sordid little life? There's a shining in your eyes that I can't quite put a label on. So what is it? Man, woman or vegetable?'

'No relationships, Trud, and no drugs either. Honest.'

'What then? There's something in your life that wasn't there last time we met. You know you can't hide things from Auntie Trudi.'

'Look, this is in confidence, right? You breathe a word and I'll send the boys round to get you. I've, um, I've had a sort of experience thingy.'

'What sort of experience?'

'Well, I don't know really. A wonderful experience. I was in a church for a funeral, following a story. And then it just hit me, all golden and warm and light-filled. It was like the best sex ever, without a partner.'

'Trust you to compare everything to sex. So it was a *religious* experience. OK, that makes sense.'

'Was it? That's what I'm scared of. You know me,

Trudi. There wouldn't be a less religious person around. I've got no time for all that mumbo jumbo — men dressed up in women's clothing and abusing little boys out the back somewhere. I've got no desire to become a part of all that.'

'Tell me how you felt when it was happening.'

'It was as if there was someone there with me. Someone who knew me through and through, someone who could see all the bullshit and posturing, and yet loved me. I felt loved like I've never been loved. There was no demand in it, nothing I had to put across or give up. Just love.'

'Oh well, that's definitely not a religious experience then, is it? Most likely something you ate, I should imagine.'

'Listen, I'm the cynical one in this friendship, OK? There was this Maori guy, a psych patient that I interviewed for a story. He thinks he's the second son of God. He was speaking at the funeral, and when I looked at him in the middle of this, this experience, it seemed like he had light streaming out from his face.'

'There's a connection there, Karen, I can feel it. I don't know what any of it's about, other than you having a private encounter with God. But I do know that what you just said about the Maori bloke is really important. You have something to do, a role to play.'

'You think so? Bloody hell. This is so weird and complicated. I could do without this in my life, I really could. I wish I could forget it all and get back to being a bitch. It's the only thing I've ever been really good at.'

She wanders from room to room, hoping to see something which will provide distraction. It's all lovely, as she wants it. But empty. Each room is as vacant as the next, and there's no voice to fill them. Penny's tempted to say something out loud, to bounce her humanity off the walls. But who knows where that will lead.

The mood is unintentional and unwanted. *I'm not a depressive person.* Even the garden can't do the job today. Beauty, goodness, warmth; they're all flat and unimpressive. Nothing has enough reality to stand out in the fog of sadness which surrounds her. It's like gravity reaching for her, making the weight of her life oppressive and unbearable.

She lies along the sofa, picks up the remote and begins channel surfing. Rugby, black-and-white film, talk show, music video. Nothing. *Like my life.* Something happening but nothing of consequence. She punches the off button to exert some control. The silence has never left, merely been masked for a few moments.

The magazines on the coffee table have been read,

but she flicks through them anyway. An unsolved murder in Hamilton. How a woman made a success out of a computing career from home. The inevitable article on relationships, with photos of the couples. One's a lesbian couple. She refrains from reading the text, but the picture's enough. They're sitting on a swinging love seat, and the photo's been taken as they're laughing together. She holds the magazine close so that she can see their eyes more clearly. They're genuinely happy, and there's an easy familiarity with each other.

Why must everything good die? What sort of a game is this where you don't dare hope any more for fear of the pain? What is it about me that makes it impossible to hold the things I reach for?

The name keeps flashing in the background like a neon sign through the window. You try to ignore it but in the end it defeats you. Without even going to the window, she knows what the sign says.

Margaret.

It's a way to pull punters in on a late Saturday afternoon. A country-and-western karaoke session. There's hardly a country-and-western fan in sight. They're here for the send-up, to laugh at themselves and the ridiculousness of the music and the sentiment of it. The favourite is *Stand By Your Man* done as a duet by gay couples, with all the urban sophisticates hooting and hollering. There's money in mockery.

Colin is one of the stars. Here he is, dressed as usual in Elvis retro, wrap-around dark glasses a standard accessory. They start chanting his name and clapping as he makes his way towards the front.

'Col-in.' *Clap clap clap.* 'Col-in.' *Clap clap clap.* 'Col-in.' *Clap clap clap.*

He dismisses them with a wave, but by the time he makes it to the stage his smile has grown wider. He stoops down so that his mouth is directly over the microphone.

'Thank you all, brothers and sisters, and a happy new year. I can only say to you what my mother used to say to me. Keep your mind out of the gutter and your hands above the table. Ha ha. Thank you very much. I'm going to sing you a song in a minute, just as soon as I finish this smoke. I've got a joke for you. Ha ha. Thank you very much. I'm going to start now.

> *There was an old soak from Madrid,*
> *Who was less than a twenty-bob quid.*
> *He showed off his willy*
> *And girls thought him silly*
> *To expose what was better off hid.*

'I made that up. Ha ha. Now I want to sing for you.

Colin's eyebrows descend to mark the solemnity

of the occasion. The crowd's whistling and cheering. 'Go, Colin.'

The voice is slightly off key, but it has a rough quality that matches the song. The hooting slowly dies down as the audience is drawn into the song. It's gone quiet. There's only Colin's cracked old voice, stinking as it does of hard times and cheap wine.

In the corner a middle-aged gay man has tears rolling down his cheeks. When Colin finishes, the whole room is silent for a few moments before the applause begins.

'That's all. Thank you. Don't clap, buy me a beer. God bless you, and as my mother used to say, don't play on your own. Ha ha.'

The hype is terrific. The heat of the lights, the music, the cameras; Burlain loves it all. The essential gaudiness of it all. There's nothing that he knows of in heaven to quite match this.

Geranne isn't so taken. She's nervous and unsettled by the whole business. It takes her a while to adjust to new situations, and this is quite unlike anything she's been involved in before. So many things are happening at once that it's hard to keep track of them all. But there's no doubt where the centre of attention is. It's on those two people behind the desk, where all the cameras are pointed.

'You really think we should be doing this?'

'Why not? It's our assignment, isn't it?'

'Yes, but it means more direct involvement than we usually have. Isn't that against the rules or something?'

'We don't have to worry about rules. Shacinda told us, so we do it. Unless you want to explain why we did something different.'

'No, OK. I guess somebody must know what they're doing, even if we don't.'

'Right, it's just about time. Let's do it.'

It's a mixture of satisfaction and sadness to reach the end of the bottle. He misjudges the distance to the veranda floor and the empty bottle clatters as it falls over. Norm belches in appreciation of the world.

Colours languish in the late-evening light. The air strokes your cheek with the tenderest of fingers, and rides saltily up the lining of your nostrils. *If I was God, I'd be out here strolling around. Taking the evening air and smoking a pipe.*

But seeing as how I'm not, I'll just sit here and be thankful.

The strained and creaking floorboards announce Arthur's arrival. He sits in the chair next to Norm. He's rubbing his fingers across his palms, and jogging one knee up and down on the ball of his foot, making the floor shake.

'What's up, Arthur? You look more worried than you ought to be.'

'I'm OK, Norm, I'm OK. Just one thing and another, that's all. Getting the times right, sorting out the seasons, that sort of thing. I don't want to get this wrong.'

'And what is it that's pressing so heavy on you, Arthur, my son? You look like you're carrying the salvation of the world.'

'Nah, it's just my father's work, just getting that fixed up. Sometimes it's hard to sort his voice out, you know? Like someone's talking quietly in a crowded room, and there's all these conversations crowding in on you, and you're trying to sort one out from another.'

'You do better than most. I wouldn't know God's voice if it was coming at me through a pair of headphones. But I'm feeling all right, just the same. Living out here in his backyard does me fine.'

'Tell me, Norm, where does Father Christmas come from?'

'What?'

'Santa Claus, you know. Where does that come from?'

'It's mostly just a story, I think. But he's supposed to be from up north somewhere — the North Pole, isn't it?'

'I'm from up north, you know that?'

'A bit further north than that. The story grew up around an old fella who used to hand out presents to poor people. Saint Nicholas, I think he became.'

'He just gave them away, for nothing?'

'Yeah, I think so. That's where the whole idea of giving presents at Christmas came from.'

'I like that. It's good to give, Norm. That's what God does, you know? Gives things for nothing.'

'And sometimes takes them away again.'

'Shit! What was that?'

'What was what?'

'The light — didn't you see it? The whole sky. And the house; it was like it was on fire, it was glowing so bright.'

'I didn't see anything, and I'm the one who's been drinking.'

'Don't worry about it. One day you'll learn to see. That's it, though, I bet. It's happened.'

'What?'

'Wait and see, Norm. Wait and see.'

In Howick Margaret and Brian are taking the evening air. They stroll along the wide and manicured footpath, past houses of plaster and brick. Low walls and flowerbeds are territorial markers. The occasional dog gives a perfunctory bark to earn its keep.

Brian is relaxed and expansive. He's untroubled. He notices things for the first time.

Margaret is tense and confused. Her heart churns its way through the feelings; anticipation, despair, friendship, betrayal, passion, uncertainty. Her inner world is consuming all her energy, but Brian seems not to notice.

'What do you want to do, love?'

'What do you mean?'

'Well, if you had free rein; if you could wave a magic wand and make things the way you wanted them, what would you choose?'

She panics temporarily, as if he could see inside her and know the jumbled images flashing across the screen.

'Oh, I don't know. A Caribbean island, servants. That sort of thing. What about you?'

'I feel like doing something important. I have no idea what, but something that's worthwhile. You spend your life moving pieces of paper around, keeping appointments because they're in your diary. And then all of a sudden it's taken away from you, and you think, so what? What difference did it really make whether I was doing it or not? How is the world any different for my having passed through it?'

'It's a big world — hard to make an impression on.'

'Yes, but I've never even tried. I've settled for too little. To tell you the truth, I'm glad that this has happened. It's woken me up, shaken me. I just hope that it's not too late, that I still have a chance to do something useful. I've been preoccupied, Marg. I haven't been seeing things clearly. I haven't given you all that you deserve.'

Margaret is walking quietly, her eyes fixed on the ground. She sniffs and wipes her nose with the back of her hand.

'What is it? Margaret? What's wrong?'

'It's nothing.'

'Come on, love. Don't shut me out. Tell me, what is it?'

'It's nothing, Brian, nothing. Don't push me, please. I'm just having a bad day and I need some space. I'll be all right tomorrow. Just let it be.'

Sunday morning is never Bob's best time. A lie-in just makes him aware of how tired he is, and how impossible it will ever be to catch up. So most of them are giving him a wide berth.

'Who put that fucken Santa up on the mantelpiece? Yer a bit ahead of yerselves, even for you crazy pricks. And who left this bloody old can lying around? Fair go, I got to do everything round this place.'

He deposits the can in the rubbish bin, and returns the Father Christmas to the drawer.

'Arthur.'

Wal delivers the word as if it provides a solution to the mysteries of the universe.

'What?'

'Arthur. He was tellin' us all about it yesterday. Something about the colour of it. I didn't really follow him, truth be told.'

'Ya wouldn't follow a fanny if it was waving welcome signs at ya! Not that there'd be much to follow if it was one of Arthur's stories.'

'Gidday, Bob. How're you doing on this great morning?'

Arthur's filling the doorframe, with a triumphant smile all over his face. In one hand he carries a newspaper, which he holds high.

'Here it is!'

'Yeah, the Sunday newspaper. Bravo. Well done. Ya wanna medal or something? Just stick it on the table and I'll look at it later.'

'No, you don't understand. This is it. What we've been waiting for.'

'It's not that long since last Sunday, Arthur. And ya don't even read, so I dunno what yer getting all excited about.'

'The Lotto results; they're in the paper.'

'Oh yeah. But I never got time to get a ticket yesterday, so it's no good to me.'

'I gave you a ticket, remember? For the boarding house.'

'Orright, yeah, ya did. Now what the fuck did I do with it?'

Bob hauls out his wallet and thumbs through the contents. Eventually he extracts a fairly crumpled ticket and lays it on the table.

'OK then. Chuck us the paper over here and we'll see if we're millionaires, eh?'

He pulls a pen from his pocket and starts checking the numbers in the paper against the ticket. Arthur's standing over him with a gigantic smile. The other men in the dining room have gathered around in a small circle to hear the verdict.

'Nah, no good, mate.'

Arthur goes pale and rocks back on his heels.

'What d'you mean? Check it again, I know it's right. Go on, check it again.'

'Yeah, orright. Don't get ya tits in a tangle. Nah, still no good. The best we've got is two numbers in one row. Have to try again next week.'

Arthur's face crumples. His huge head lowers in shame. There are tears in his eyes. Pete reaches out a hand and places it on his shoulder. He jumps back in fright as Arthur lifts his head suddenly and calls out in a strangulated cry which ends in a kind of maniacal laugh. Once started the laugh goes on and on. Arthur's shoulders are heaving up and down, and great gusts of laughter are surging out into the room.

Bob's seen this before. Over the top. I better ring the bloody hospital. But Arthur's gasping, holding on to him, trying to say something through the laughter.

'Ya what?'

'The wrong ticket! I gave you the wrong ticket! I've got the other one here.'

He reaches into his pocket and produces a folded slip of paper. Still laughing, he raises it to his lips.

'Here, don't slobber all over it, ya big plonker; give it here so's we can have a look.'

Some of the others have joined in with Arthur's laughing. They're not sure why, but it seems the friendly thing to do. Bob takes his time, shifting his eyes from the paper to the ticket and drawing little circles around numbers. He lays the pen down and sits there quietly. The cackling subsides.

'Well, I'll be fucked.'

'What? What is it?'

'Second division. Only three winners. Fifty-six thousand dollars. Arthur, ya tin-arse fucken dark horse, you. Yer a rich man. Ya hit the bloody jackpot. Ya won!'

'Nah, don't be silly, man. It's for us. It's for the boarding house. I told you God would get us out of this one. This is a deliverance, like Moses and the children of Israel. We're safe. We can stay!'

The sort of noise that rises from this demented crowd is like your worst fears of a lunatic asylum. It's a high-pitched, ululating babble of voices, part laughter, part cheer, part wail. Wal's jumping up and down on the spot. Morrie's running round and round the table with hands in the air. In the middle of it all, Arthur stands beaming. Strong and relaxed as an upright lion. Bob sits shaking his head, his eyes wandering back to the numbers to make sure he has it right.

Unseen in the corner, but considering themselves very much part of the action, two angels are holding hands and laughing.

'Well, Geranne, any doubts now?'

Eventually Bob stands and embraces Arthur. His arms only get partway round the bulk, but it's enough to convey what he wants. Arthur enfolds him, wraps him up like a small child. Bob becomes self-conscious and backs away.

'Well, what are we standing around here for like a pack of Presbyterians in a pub? Let's break out the beers and get some food together. We're going to have the mother of all parties, oath we are.'

She can hear the noise as soon as she gets out of her car on the street, and it seems to be coming from the house. As she walks up the drive she begins to get apprehensive. The thumping could be anything. A fight? But there's music playing, and there's no edge of violence to the din.

I thought he might have been out here to meet me. God,

I hope he's remembered. I'm such a fool. This whole thing is ridiculous. What on earth's going on in there?

Margaret finds her own way in, still apprehensive about the noise which is tumbling out from the dining room. She stands there in the doorway, trying to make sense of it all.

Arthur and Bob are standing on the table in the middle of the room. All around them men are shouting and yelling and shaking cans of beer to squirt or throw over the hapless pair. Smiles are rampant. She begins to smile herself, caught up in the mood of the old house.

Digby spots her, and makes a beeline for her. He takes her by the hand and leads her into the room.

'Margaret, my darling, it's been too long since you've graced our house with your beauty. Come in, come in. Would you like to dance a little?'

'What's going on, Digby? What's this all about?'

'It's your boy, Arthur. He's got a big prize in the Lotto, and he's giving it to Bob to do the alterations on the house. They won't be able to close us down.'

'Arthur? He's won money?'

'Yeah. Beats me as well. But then there's no accounting for luck, is there?'

Norm sits in a corner with a sausage roll in one hand and his bottle in the other. Beer's all right but it doesn't quite do the trick these days. He's happy to be part of the celebration, though he feels safer sitting down. Not so far to fall.

From a corner of his eye he's watching Arthur. Something about his eyes that reminds me. And the way he's rubbing his hand on the side of his trousers. Up and down, up and down.

Norm's worried about him.

Still, he's happy enough having saved us all, and what with Margaret at his side.

It's around lunch time that Kevin arrives. Bob has rung the church and left a message on the answerphone, seeing as how the vicar was busy doing whatever he does on a Sunday morning. Only seems fair to bring him in on the good news after everything he's done.

Bob grabs him and pats him heartily on the back, quite a few beers gone.

'Kevin, me old vic, how the hell are ya? Come an' have a beer or a cuppa tea or whatever you jokers drink.'

'Seems like it's always party time down here. I'll have a beer, thanks, why not. So this is straight up, then; Arthur's won Lotto?'

'Straight as a giraffe with a stiff neck, vic. Though he hasn't won it, strictly speaking. Just second division, but it's enough to see us right. So whaddya reckon, eh? Ya must've been chucking the odd prayer up to old Huey or somethin'.'

'Funny you should say that — we prayed for you all this morning in the service. But the deed had already been done by then, looks like.'

'Ah well, every little bit helps, I always say. But whaddya make of old Arthur over there, eh? I'm starting to think maybe he is the second soddin' son of God. He'll have my vote for the job, anyway. Here, look out. Looks like he's going to make a speech. *Hoy!* Shut up, you lot! That's better. Arthur here wants to say a few words, so let's give him a fair go.'

Arthur climbs up on a chair, slightly unsteady to be mounting the table by this stage. He has a beer can in one hand and a lamington in the other. He clears his throat, marae style.

'Kia ora, te whanau. We're all having a good time here on account of us being able to stay here and not have to move. That's good, but let's not forget how it happened. I bought us that Lotto ticket, but it was only 'cos my father told me to, and he did all the rest. That's God, my father, if some of you still haven't figured it out. He's a pretty good guy, my father, and he decided he was going to save you. Now I know some of you think I'm a bit mad, but this is proof that what I say is right, you understand?'

He pauses and looks at Margaret. Hung up for a few moments on her eyes.

'So I don't want you to forget what's happened, you know? My father is your father too, and he was looking out for you. See, he loves you, that's all. Simple as that. He loves you. So don't you go forgetting that.'

There's a perfect stillness across the room.

'I'm not always going to be with you, see. There's going to be some pretty ugly stuff coming up. But that's still coming. Meantime we're safe and we're happy. But I want you all to remember this day, and remember what Father God has done for you, and remember your old mate Arthur. And just so's you do, we're going to have a toast. All right? So raise your cans, and drink to God who loves us.'

'To God who loves us.'

The chorus of mutters stumbles to a ragged end. Arthur climbs down from the chair. The conversations gradually resume, but a little more subdued. Digby makes his way over to Arthur.

'Yeah, that was good Arthur, what you were saying. Very good. There's just one thing I've been thinking about.'

'What's that, Digby?'

'It's just that, if you're thinking of going away . . . you won't forget that twenty dollars, will you?'

The old house is making the most of it. Soaking up the noise and happiness into stiff old boards.

Flooring and joists creaking under the jumping and dancing. Windows shining.

Many things have happened here. Meals, arguments, births, business deals, suicides, seductions, even a fire. But not that many miracles.

Many people have lived here. A banker, several traders, a doctor, a Member of Parliament, a caterer, an insurance broker, and the present lot. But nothing like the second son of God.

And so it is that the kauri and the brass appear to glow; that the cracked and peeling paint does its best to be respectable; that the doors swing back on the hinges to allow easy passage.

'It's what you had to wear today, Margaret. That blouse.'

'You like it?

'Red and white. It's special.'

II

They sit out on the veranda. Margaret is remembering another time sitting outside. Arthur leans his huge head back and sighs. He's smiling. She reaches over and strokes the side of his face. It's the gesture of an old married couple.

'I've missed you so much, Arthur. I'm thinking about you all the time, and dreams . . . I wish we could be together more often.'

'We're together now, Te Kare, and that's good. Maybe there will come a time when we can't be together, and then this moment will seem special.'

'Mmm. But I want to be together properly . . . intimately. You know what I mean?'

'Nah, I don't know what you mean, woman.'

'You big sod. I want you naked and next to me, I want you inside of me, on top of me, all over me. I want more of you than I can get.'

'It's a bit tricky, eh. Getting together like that. It has to be the right time and place. You're a queen, Margaret; you got to be treated right.'

'I've been thinking. About that money. Fifty-six

thousand, wasn't it? Well, Bob said he only needed forty thousand to do the place up.'

'So?'

'The other sixteen thousand. We could use it. Make a start for ourselves.'

'What d'you mean?'

'We could get out of here. You could get out of the boarding house. I could get out of my marriage. We could go somewhere, run away together.'

She's looking down as she speaks, drawing imaginary circles with her finger on the arm of the chair. Her heart's beating faster than normal. There's a silence, a gap. Arthur sighs again, more deeply this time. When she raises her eyes, she finds him gazing at her with sadness. She wishes he would not speak.

'It's not my money. God gave it for a reason, see. For the house, for the whanau, for the men. We can't use God's money for ourselves, or something bad will happen. And you can't leave Brian. What about the children? That would be a wrong thing to do, Margaret, and I don't want you to do wrong things. Not for me or for anyone.'

'What the fuck are you talking about? You come into my life like a hurricane, leave it smashed to pieces, and then tell me I have to stay in the wreckage? I'm in love with you, Arthur. I taste you on my breath when I wake up. You're with me everywhere I go, in everything I do. My thoughts circle round you like a dog tied to a stick. I feel you in my limbs, in the marrow of my bones. You shove yourself into every one of my dreams. I wake at night panting for you. And now you say I should stay in my marriage? I can't do it, Arthur. Don't push me away.'

'It's for a purpose, can't you see that? After everything I've told you, you think this thing is just about us, about you and me? I love you too, Margaret, but there's things that have to be done, and they've got to be done the right way. It was Father God who brought us together . . .'

'Sod God, Arthur; sod the old bastard. I want you, not God. I want to be with you. I can't go on living in two worlds like this. Let me come to you, Arthur. God'll let you. Someone else can do his will for a while.'

Arthur groans. There are tears in his eyes.

It's a short walk from the boarding house to the park. There's a bit of stuff to carry, but it all fits in a big plastic rubbish sack that Bob's given him.

Leaving the house isn't as easy as it was once. You can get to like the feel of bed springs under you, and good solid walls to keep the wind out. Even the company, from time to time. There's worse places to live.

But the solitude and open spaces are home. The

301

freedom a man has to do what he wants when he wants to do it. The sense of being in touch with the majesty of life as it flaunts itself before your eyes. The smell and the cold and the discomfort which remind you every day that you're human, scratching for survival on the face of the earth.

It's what Norm has come to late in life. One option among many. A homeless alcoholic, who pities those who pity him. If he were to go for comfort, to take some simple luxuries, things might get lost. God may no longer speak to him from among the trees. He might begin to clench his open hands. He might forget that he was broken, and pretend to be whole. He might lose his capacity for awe.

So he smiles to himself as he arranges his things in the foyer of the toilets. As he places his worn Bible on top of the blanket. As he sits down and smokes a cigarette.

Be it ever so humble, there's no place like home.

The evening falls like a stunned bird.

From somewhere over the Waitakeres, dark clouds have crowded the sky. They roll ominously, grinding their way towards the ocean. An occasional seagull calls a warning. The swirling blackness hangs over the city.

Sometimes, flashing through the gaps, the golden sickle. A new moon.

Perhaps there will be a reaping.

'So what did she say?'

'She had no choice, really. As long as I'm doing the alterations they ask for, they've got no comeback. When it's all finished, we'll meet their requirements for space. So it's a done deal. Ya should've heard her chokin' on the humble pie. She was flappin' around like a fish with a hook in its gut. She wants it all in writing, of course. But we're here to stay, and not even old titanium-tits Harmon can shift us. Here, drink yer tea, vic, before it gets cold.'

Kevin takes a generous pull at the dark brown liquid, forgetting for a moment about the sugar. It takes a lot of self-control to keep the grimace off his face.

'It's a pretty remarkable story when you think about, isn't it? You might even say miraculous.'

'I don't care what the bloody 'ell ya call it, as long as it still ends up deliverin' the moolah at the end of the day. Have to admit that it's got me going, though.'

'How do you mean?'

'Well, a man hardly likes to talk about it with the likes of you around. Just the possibility that there might be more to life than sex and sandwiches, I s'pose.'

'Is that a nod in the direction of God?'

'More like a wink from a blind horse. I'm a hard bastard, ya see, vic, I don't have much time for any of that stuff. When ya've scrubbed the blood off the side of the bathtub for the umpteenth time, all that religious carry-on seems a bit flaky, ya know what I mean? But this last lot's so far over the top that even a cynical prick like me can't help but wonder.'

'It makes you think about Arthur, doesn't it? And him being the second son of God?'

'Nah, it doesn't make me think that far. I've told ya before, Kev, Arthur's a nutter. A fruit loop, a crazy; a big-'earted, good-natured, solid-gold dingaling. I remember growing up with some of these blokes. I used to believe their stories. There was this one old geezer, Keith. He had the idea that the Russians had planted something in his brain, and they were sending messages to him. Scared of getting caught, he was. So he got me to be his messenger boy. He'd write all this crap down in code, and then get me to deliver it for him. I had to take it to this certain grate in the road, and post the bit of paper through the bars. Sometimes I'd wait there for half an hour, trying to see in and find out who was collecting the message. Eventually he started screaming in the night, and then he got a hot iron and pressed it against his ear to try and seal his head up. Fuck of a smell for days afterwards. It's no good buying into their fantasy worlds. It just screws ya up in the long run. Ya just got to remember that they're mad and you're not. No good all of us going down the shithole, is it?'

'But Arthur's not in that category, surely? He makes sense when he speaks. There's a . . . there's almost a spiritual quality about him sometimes. He's so convinced that God has singled him out. On one level I agree with you that he's just deluded. But on another, I can't get the thought out of my head — what if it were true? He said he was going to save the boarding house, he bought the Lotto ticket, and lo and behold the house is saved. That's pretty amazing, really. None of us is making that up. It was a kind of miracle, and Arthur performed it.'

'It's just the way things happen. These people live half their lives on a different plane, in cuckooland. Sometimes they get in touch with stuff that we don't have access to. I've seen it happen before. But it doesn't make Arthur the second son of God any more than I'm the Queen of Sheba. Take my advice, mate. Don't get sucked into anyone else's fantasy. Yer own are all ya entitled to.'

'I remember when Arthur first came to see me. He wanted me to tell the world that he was here, that the second son of God had arrived. I dismissed him straightaway. It's not as if I've had nothing to do with psychiatric patients before. But even then, there was some special quality about Arthur that I just couldn't get out of my head. And there's been other things going on, things that keep pushing me back to Arthur. I'm not so sure about him as you are, Bob. I think we should take him seriously. At least give him a bit of a chance.'

'You give him whatever ya like. I'll give him thanks for the Lotto ticket, a bed and a feed whenever he wants it, and a wide berth to his religious mumbo jumbo. Be careful what ya hitch yer horse to, vic. That's all I can say.'

People don't realize what news is. They think it's reality, fact; a little window through which they can see what's really happening. But events are only the raw material of the news makers, as paint is to an artist. Putting it together, that's the craft. Chopping it up, changing it, weaving it together in new patterns, linking one event with another so that it unfolds a story. It's in the edit suite that the news is created. Until then it's not *news* at all. Just a stream of things that have happened.

Karen has had the knack since the first time she tried it. The ability to find the narrative line, to create drama, to build tension. She follows some basic instinct — an almost visual sense of how it must hang together. Producers have learnt to keep quiet and go with her.

This is her best work. She doesn't need anyone else

to tell her. It flows, it moves, it breathes. Everything about it, even the camerawork, contributes to the natural gliding progression of the piece. It glows like art film rather than doco. The pathos, the tragedy, the slow build to those dramatic scenes in the hall. Even Karen can't watch it without being moved, without the story getting on the inside of her. It's as if some new quality has been released within her and found its way into her work. A lightness, a grace almost.

But there's still something missing. The ending. A dénouement, a conclusion which does justice to such a fine piece. She's been through the footage time and time again, but there's nothing there. Or nothing adequate.

I have to find it. Or make it. I'm not going to ruin this with anything substandard. I owe it to Arthur.

The thought has arrived before she has time to track it. *Arthur.* From the beginning to the end. The loop, the connection. *Yes, that has possibilities. I need to talk to him again. Where to find him? The boarding house?*

'Margaret?'

'Arthur! I didn't expect to hear from you so soon.'

'I wanted to say sorry. I don't want to hurt you.'

'It's all right. I'm just all over the place right now. I don't know what I want.'

'You're wonderful, Margaret. You're everything a woman could be. Even if you weren't the Queen of Heaven, you'd still be a queen. Your face shines with aroha. You make people happy wherever you go. I love you.'

'Whoa! What's bought all this on? Don't feel you have to stop, though. I need all the hype I can get.'

'You don't need anything more than what you've got, because it's in your heart. Do you understand that? That you have something amazing on the inside? Do you know how special you are?'

'When you tell me, I believe you. Oh, Arthur, I still want to be with you.'

'You will be. I can promise you that. Only it might not be as soon as you think. There's some things that have to happen first. You understand me?'

'I'm not sure. What sort of things?'

'Secret things. Not much that I can talk about. But you know that blouse you were wearing when you came over?'

'Yes, the one you liked.'

'Well, that holds the key. The red and white. Think about that. That's all I can tell you.'

'Sorry? I don't follow. I'm not sure what you mean.'

'We can't say too much on the phone. But I'll give you one more hint. Santa Claus.'

'Santa Claus? Are you all right, Arthur? You haven't been drinking, have you?'

308

'I've already said too much. Just trust me, and listen carefully inside your head. When the time's right, it'll all come clear to you.'

'Please, Arthur; it frightens me when you talk like this. Don't, please don't.'

'It's OK. Everything's OK. Everything will work out. Just concentrate.'

There's a click and a ringing in her ear. She stands there for some time listening to the tone before she realizes that he's hung up. It makes her feel stupid. She quickly replaces the phone in its cradle and slumps into a chair.

What does this mean? What can this possibly mean? It's all so confusing. I have nothing to hang on to; nothing to tell me which way is up. I'm so afraid, so terribly afraid. And this sick feeling in the pit of my stomach. I feel so sick.

Can you hear it?

It may be the wind in the power lines. Some piece of machinery away in the distance. Perhaps it's somewhere on the inside of your head.

A high-pitched whining or wailing. It has an almost human quality about it, but not quite. Like a mother crying for a dead baby. Like a child frightened in the night. Like a victim calling in pain.

There it is again. Ringing out along Ponsonby's ridge. Two angels are covering their ears.

Can you hear it?

On afternoons such as this one, Penny loves to walk. To feel the sun on her face and the breeze nuzzling her hair. To have the time to take it all in. To cogitate with your feet.

With no particular destination; perambulating in Ponsonby. Down the side roads, observing people as they stitch together their ordinary lives. Washing cars, scratching in gardens, painting windowsills, reading on verandas. She feels loose and at ease. Part of it all, but responsible for none of it.

She doesn't quite know how she found her way here to the reserve. It was all a matter of turning one direction rather than another. But she's glad of her instinct, which has brought her to grass and trees.

There's a vacant park bench calling to her. She sinks onto it, aware for the first time of weariness in her legs. Penny leans back against the wooden slats, feeling the comfortable weight of the afternoon pressing against her. She breathes in, absorbing the whole day into her lungs; savours it, and exhales the leftovers.

A sparrow investigates from a safe distance, nodding its head to one side in the attempt to make sense out of the intruder. Penny smiles. Noting the absence of any crumb-producing material, the bird flits on.

She sips at the park with her eyes, luxuriating in the green. The great trees move sedately in accord with the wind. The whisper of their leaves reminds her of the surf sliding up the sand at the end of its effort. With her eyes closed she can almost smell salt in the air.

A scraping sound draws her attention. It comes from the squat concrete building under the trees — the toilet block. And now she can see. A man, seated in the entrance. Drinking from a bottle in a brown paper bag. His clothes are worn but surprisingly neat.

She watches him with the detachment of distance, allowing her mind to wander. *How old would he be? What's his name? How did he come to be here on this particular afternoon?*

Was he once as I am? Did he worry about his future? Perhaps he still does. Or is he free now, released by the gentle balm of alcohol? Concerned only with the tasks of daily survival? She reaches out with her mind, trying to enter his experience by remote control.

There's nothing there, other than the calm of the afternoon with its narcotic warmth. He's reading something, she can see. Pausing every now and again to close his eyes.

I could take him home. Give him a bath and a good meal. Put him in the spare bed with clean sheets. Bring him a cup of tea in bed.

And then what? She laughs at herself, and her impossible fantasies. There's no point of connection. They might as well be on opposite sides of a great chasm. There are no bridges any more. *He'll sit there with his bottle and his book, and I'll get up and make my way towards home.* Comfortable and alone. Secure and isolated.

Penny remembers when she first moved into Ponsonby. The excitement of the place. The mix of people. Exotic languages tangling with each other. Wildly colourful clothes; everyone trying to assert their identity. Smells, the origin of which you could only wonder at. Toad Hall and Ivan's and Betty Wark.

We all belonged here, then. There was a place for all of us. Ponsonby loved us. But something's dying. We've all grown hard, indifferent, separate. Perhaps it never existed. Maybe I projected my dreaming onto the place. So why do I feel so betrayed?

With a rush all the pieces fall together. What must be done. It's so sudden and so obvious. She sits there, stunned. Scared to breathe for fear it may disturb the clarity. *Of course.*

Finally she rises to go, this time with purpose. She looks back at the man, only to find that he's watching her. Penny smiles as she turns her back.

Why can you never find a card which says what you want to say? Kevin rejects another and returns it to its place on the shelf. It's for the birthday of a parishioner. You need to be careful with the message that you choose. The faithful are adept at reading more into the words than intended. Or less.

It's his peripheral vision which deciphers the large blob passing the shop window as Arthur.

Kevin is jamming the current card back into the wrong slot and running out the door.

'Arthur!'

The head turns. The smile of recognition provides light for a small developing nation.

Kevin is trotting up to him, placing one hand on his shoulder.

'Arthur, it's good to see you; I've been wanting to catch up with you. How about we go and have a coffee together? There's something I wanted to talk to you about.'

A brief flash of concern dents the beatific smile. Kevin guesses at its source.

'It's OK; I'm paying. Let's just wander up to Atomic, shall we?'

'That sounds good, vicar. I'm not too busy just at the moment. I think I've got today pretty much under control.'

They stroll up the road to the café, chatting about the plans for the boarding house. Arthur opts for a table in the garden out the back, and Kevin organizes the coffees.

Arthur is continuing his impression of a saint, exuding grace and serenity like a wide-eyed Indian holy man. The coffee leaves a frothy wet mark on his ragged moustache, which he removes with a sleeve.

'You ever think about the poor, vicar?'

'You mean poor people around here?'

'Jeez, there's not too many of them nowadays. Nah, I mean real poor people overseas, with their twiggy little arms and pukus that stick out. Kids with flies crawling up their noses.'

'I suppose I think about them now and again, but not as often as I should. Our parish supports a child in Somalia, so that's a bit of a contact.'

'Whaddya think of it? Why does it happen? Why do these little kids die in their mothers' arms? What's God doing about it?'

'Why're you asking me?'

'You're a vicar. You have to talk to your people and tell them what God's like. What d'you tell them?'

'I don't talk about it very much, I'm afraid. Poverty's not something the congregation wants to hear too much about. It just makes them feel helpless. The times I have addressed it, I've said something like God's provided us with enough food and resources to go round, and that it's our responsibility to make sure it happens.'

'Is that what you believe?'

'It's as close to it as I'm likely to get, yes.'

'You think that's it? God's made a big farm for us and all we have to do is share out the kai?'

'Well, that's a bit of a simplification, but . . .'

'You think God's not there with those kids? You think his heart's not breaking? You think they don't haunt him day and night, those big eyes looking at him? So why doesn't he do something, eh? You think he has to wait around till we decide we're going to fix it up for him?'

'I don't know, Arthur. I don't know enough about God to answer those questions.'

'What about Jesus, then? Why did God bother sending him to you if it wasn't to give you some answers?'

Kevin stares into his coffee cup, pushing some bubbles around with his teaspoon. He can't bring himself to look Arthur in the eye.

'You didn't get it, did you? You didn't fucking get it, any of you. So now he sent me, and we've got to go through this whole thing all over again. You think this is easy? You think we can just go on like this all the time?'

When Kevin brings himself to look, he can see the huge, heaving sadness in Arthur's eyes. It's like looking into a swamp of pain, where rotting dreams sink slowly into the sludge. Seeing straight into a heart which is weary of suffering. Almost as if Arthur were not there, as if . . .

'I'm sorry, Arthur. For myself and for the rest of us.'

The silence waits.

'What I wanted . . . It's probably too late . . . I was going to ask you if you could come and speak at church this Sunday. Do you remember when we first met, when you wanted me to announce you? I still don't know that I can do that. But I can make a space for you. A chance to explain to a wider group of people about God, and about yourself. Not a sermon — we don't really have sermons any more — just you talking to the people. It's not much, I know, but if you thought you might do it, I'd be honoured, Arthur, I really would.'

Arthur's smiling again and his eyes are shining. It makes the sun come out from the cloud it was lurking behind. A shaft strikes the fern bush behind Arthur's head and gives the effect of a green fingery halo.

Your voice will be heard in the halls of religion, and it shall echo down the generations.

'Yeah, OK, that would be good. That would be real good. Me in a church. Man, I think I better have a smoke on the strength of that one.'

Even the way he comes into the house makes a statement. Margaret is immediately wary. She fills the kettle with water and turns it on as a safeguard. She still hasn't got used to him being around during the day.

He loosens his tie, slings his briefcase onto a chair and looks about.

'Margaret?'

'In here, love.'

She's fussing at the sink, rinsing a clean cup. He comes up behind her, wraps his arms around her, nestles his head in her neck and kisses it. She stifles the shudder as her flesh recalls that other approach from behind.

'I've done it, Marg. I've damn well done it.'

'That sounds positively dangerous. Do you want a cup of tea?'

'I want a stiff whisky, but I'll settle for a cup of tea. Don't you want to know what it is I've done?'

'Of course I do. Let me start again. Brian, what is it that you've done?'

'I've changed careers. I had an interview this morning, and they liked me so much they made an offer straight off. You're now looking at the Human Resources Manager of Brent Industries.'

'Brent Industries? The electronics place? That's wonderful, Brian, I'm so pleased for you. But what's a Human Resources Manager?'

'It's a glorified personnel officer; someone who handles staff. I'm really excited about it, Marg. It's a whole different ball game. The tests I did show that I'm good at working with people, so this is perfect. And the firm is wonderful — bright, energetic, progressive. They believe in their own products and they got me very enthusiastic about being part of their team. But the best part is the salary.'

'What?'

'Fifteen thousand more than I was getting at Global!'

He embraces her, lifts her off the ground and twirls her around. She laughs; genuinely pleased at Brian's happiness. He puts her down and kisses her.

'That's great, Brian. I'm thrilled for you. Let me get this cup of tea organized and we can sit down and talk about it.'

The clatter of cups and gurgle of hot water are soothingly familiar. In domesticity there remains a comforting continuity. It's a ritual to provide meaning in a splintered universe.

'I haven't been so excited about anything for years. This means everything to me, Marg. It's a new lease of life; a whole new chapter. We can start everything again, you know what I mean? Something's happening — don't you think? There's something completely different come into our lives.'

'What d'you mean?'

'Just a few weeks ago I was a boring banker locked into a dreary firm that drained the life out of me. We were drifting, you and I. Don't pretend we weren't, Margaret. I don't notice much but I knew things weren't right. The trouble was I didn't know how to fix it. I thought I was trapped, destined to live the rest of my life like it was some sort of duty. And then out of nowhere, from what seemed like a disaster, there comes this new chance. It's like someone's woken me up, and for the first time I've realized that I've been asleep. But no more. I'm awake now, and I'm going to stay that way.'

She looks at him, trying to work out what it is. Gradually it comes to her. He looks different. The physical shape of his face has changed. He could have been through plastic surgery. His skin has colour, and there's a new softness and depth to his eyes. The dark folds have disappeared. His mouth now lifts up in the corners instead of down. *Remarkable. When did it happen?*

'Yes. I think you're right, Brian. I think you have genuinely changed. For the better.'

'I did something last night that I haven't done since I was a boy.'

'What?'

'I . . . I wrote some poetry. It's not very good, but it felt good to write it.'

His voice is quiet and shy. She notices that his cheeks have coloured. He is self-conscious, embarrassed, anxious to admit such a thing. Margaret simply stares. Too much to adjust to in too short a time. She reaches out a hand and very gently touches his face, feeling the heat.

'Would you like to read it? It's nothing great, really it's not. Just a few thoughts.'

She traps his lips lightly between her fingers.

'I'd love to read it. Be quiet and go and get it.'

As he trots off to find the poems, she wants to crumble, to fall apart under the weight of it all. Instead she draws a deep breath and holds it.

It is with a violent jolt that Norm snaps into wakefulness. His heart is pounding and the sense of dread is so present that he could reach out and part it with his hands. His whole body is wet with sweat. All of his muscles are rigid, and he dare not move while the dream is still so strong.

They had been walking down a broad avenue, the two of them. On each side there were huge oak trees, dappling the sunlight as it passed through them. There was a warm wind at their back, and ahead of them a great but indiscernible light.

They were chatting as they walked, enjoying each other's company. Norm had the feeling that it was Arthur who knew where they were going. He was happy simply to walk alongside, to bask in the warmth of that huge heart.

Arthur was talking about something important. His voice rolled along the avenue, booming richly among the trees. He remembers it so clearly.

'This is the way we all have to come, Norm. People

are frightened of it, but there's nothing to be afraid of. You see the light, how steady it is. That's where we're headed. I wish I could go all the way with you, lead you home and introduce you to everyone. But there's some things I have to do first, that only I can do. You understand that, don't you?'

Norm had nodded, scared to interrupt the voice.

'It's not far away now, d'you see? The light is very close. The light is coming into the world, Norm. Coming for good. You have to hold on to that and remember it. Sometimes when the light comes it casts shadows in front of it. Don't look at the shadows, look to the light that's coming. I'm counting on you, Norm, I'm hoping . . .'

Arthur turned and looked into his eyes. He stopped, and his face fell. Norm could tell that he had seen something, found something in his eyes which shouldn't be there. He searched in his own heart, trying to locate whatever it was that Arthur was fixed on. But there was nothing.

'No, Norm, no . . .'

As he watched, it happened in front of him. One side of Arthur's face began to droop, as if the bones were beginning to soften and could no longer support the flesh. Slowly, excruciatingly, great globs of protoplasm gathered and began to roll down the face. Like molten wax it ran, falling away until it revealed the white bone underneath.

But only one side of the face. The other side was still as it had been, looking at Norm. From nowhere a crow alighted on the top of Arthur's head and began to peck at the chalky white skull. The skull crumbled, and fragments of it began to fall to the ground. In the gaps there was nothing but blackness.

Arthur swayed on his feet and began to stumble. Norm reached out to hold him, but it was too late. The great bulk of Arthur dragged Norm down with him, and then they were falling and falling, the one good eye still staring accusingly. There was a horrendous crash as they hit the ground, and Norm was instantly awake.

It could be just the usual alcoholic dream, but this one had a different feel.

What does it mean? Arthur in trouble? Arthur falling apart? What was it that he could see in me?

It is raining on this morning. A gentle summer rain which shrouds the world and causes steam to rise from the road.

A kaumatua in West Auckland shields his eyes as he looks to the sky, seeking the meaning of these tears.

He recognizes some of the faces as he looks around them. People that Arthur has passed or smiled at on the streets of Ponsonby, without knowing they were members of this church.

The way they're singing from their books puzzles him. Like they're doing something they don't really want to do but think it better to get it over with. The organ plays alongside them, as if in competition. He can make out the words to most of it, but there's no spirit, no wairua.

As the song drones to its end, the people sit down without any prompting. He's left standing there for a few moments, alone in the crowd. As if he didn't stand out enough already.

From the front, Kevin's smiling at him. Arthur plonks himself down on the pew quickly, causing it to shake alarmingly. From the end of his row, a woman in a green dress is giving him a very dark look.

Arthur pulls a stained hanky from his pocket and blows his nose loudly.

'Friends, I have decided to do without the homily today. Not because I was lacking in inspiration, but because I feel constrained to introduce to you someone who has some valuable things to say. I have only known Arthur for some months, but in that time I have come to count him as a friend and a person of genuine spiritual insight and wisdom. Arthur is a local Ponsonby resident, and some of you may have seen him without having the opportunity to speak to him. This is a new and different setting for Arthur, speaking to us this morning, but I know I can assure him of your support and encouragement.'

A couple of meaningful throat clearings raise some doubt as to the vicar's assurance.

'Arthur, thank you for coming to be with us this morning. I invite you now to come and speak to us.'

Arthur stands at the front, careful not to trespass on the altar area. He looks out at the selection of humanity before him. He senses the mana of the occasion.

'Tena koutou, tena koutou, tena koutou katoa. Thanks for the chance to be here today, and thanks especially to the vicar for the invitation.

'I have some things to tell you today that might sound a bit strange to you people, but I offer them in aroha, and I hope you'll take them the same way.

'All of us come from God, eh. I don't suppose I have to convince you lot of that. We all belong to God, we're all his children, and that makes us brothers and sisters of each other. Just because I've got a brown face and most of you are Pakeha, that doesn't mean we don't have the same father.'

The woman in the green dress sniffs loudly.

'God made all of us with an idea in mind. Some of us have things to do. Some of us are made just to be who we are. The hard part about life is to work out what's the idea God had for your life, and then to be it or do it. Lots of people end up not finding that, and they always feel like something's missing.'

Kevin is nodding in appreciation. A weary older woman lifts her head and listens more closely.

'While we all come from God, some of us get marked out in a special way. God did that to me. I didn't look for it, didn't ask for it, but I got it anyway. God just spoke to me one day, and he says, "Arthur, you're the son of God."'

Somewhere there's a rather sharp intake of breath.

'Some of you might be thinking this guy's mad — he thinks he's Jesus or something. But like I said, I didn't choose this. Many times since I heard that voice, I wish it could have been someone else. But it's hard to argue with God, you know what I mean?

'And all of us have some special idea for our lives. But with me, God gave me a message that I have to pass on. There's a lot of other stuff I have to do as well, but we don't need to talk about that. I've been given this thing to tell you, and now I'm passing it on to you. What you do with it after this is up to you.

'It's pretty simple, really. Here goes. You were made out of love and made for love. You were made to love God and to love each other. All of you running around in circles trying to get things or make a big impression, and you're missing the point about life. God's been waiting and waiting and waiting. There's been some good stuff going down. Here and there, you know. Patchy. But there's been a lot of bad stuff as well. A lot of hurt, a lot of pain, a lot of suffering. God's got tired of the whole thing. Tired like you wouldn't believe. And so he said to me, "Arthur, you tell them that it's all over. I've had a gutsful. I'm going to wind it up before it gets even worse." '

There is a profound stillness over the congregation. They are held by the voice, carried along by something in this huge, scruffy man. Kevin has his eyes closed, and is smiling.

'Me here, Arthur, I'm the second son of God. If you trust me and listen to me, I can show you the way to go from here. There's still time and space for you to learn. But you have to trust me.'

Towards the back, somebody is whispering to the person next to them. David is sitting to one side of the church, next to Gwenda. He's glaring at Kevin.

'There's this other thing too, while I'm here. I'm not sure if I should be telling you this, but I might as well. Some of you will be hearing other voices in your head besides mine, but I want you to shut them off. You have to learn to sort out the voices; that's what I've had to do.'

There is a hint of anxiety in Kevin's face; downright disdain in that protruding from the green dress.

'See, here's the thing now. You know Santa Claus, don't you? I'll bet all of you know who Santa is. Did you know that he's also known as Father Christmas? Where d'you think he got that name Father from, eh? Who's the Father of Christmas?, answer me that. It's God, isn't it? God the Father, that's who.'

The murmuring sweeps like a wave across the surface. It has an angry tone. The first person walks out, making a display of it.

'No, listen. Father Christmas and Father God are brothers, you see? That's what's been revealed to me. Just like there's two sons of God, there's two fathers as well. I'm the first one to have seen that, to have been told it . . .'

The rumble of complaint swells and breaks open. Kevin is feeling *déjà vu* as he staggers forward for the rescue. *What did I do to deserve this?*

Arthur looks on, bemused.

'Norm, what the hell are you doing here? I thought we'd got ya packed off to yer home in the wild? We better chuck another spud in the pot.'

'It's all right, Bob, I'm not here to stay. There's just something I wanted to talk to you about.'

'Go fer yer life, Norm. I'm all ears.'

'It's Arthur.'

'Arthur? He's away out somewhere; should be back soon I . . .'

'I'm worried about him. I was watching him at our little party the other day. I think he's going off. I've seen him when he's been sick before, and I recognize the signs. This thing about red and white, you know? He was on about that just before he ended up in hospital last time. I can't be sure, but I thought I should say something about it.'

'Funny ya should say that. I was just looking at him this morning, wondering the same thing. No probs, Norm. Thanks for telling me. I'll get on the blower, take him in for an assessment. Doesn't pay to muck around — I've learnt that the hard way.'

'Thanks, Bob. I feel a bit guilty, going behind his back.'

'Nah, don't be stupid. Yer doing the best thing by him. Oh yeah, that's right — while yer here, we stuffed up with the Income Support payments, so there's a bit of spare cash owing to ya. I put it in an envelope here somewhere. Not a helluva lot; thirty-odd dollars from memory. Still, ya can't complain about that, can ya now?'

Father Patrick wanders across to the window and stares into the distance for some time. He turns and comes back to stand beside Kevin's chair.

'Did you ever consider that you might have engineered this?'

'Hardly. What would I want to create this sort of

328

chaos for? I can do without all the hassle, frankly. I've had a gutsful of church politics.'

'Precisely. And now a whole group of people are calling for your resignation. Isn't that what you wanted? To have other people make the decision for you? So you can leave and blame the small-mindedness of the congregation?'

Kevin recognizes enough truth to hold his silence.

'Do you belong there any more, Kevin? Is your heart there? Do you love the people? Be honest with yourself, man. There's no-one here you need to fool.'

'No, Father. No. The answer's no. God have mercy, no.'

There's a lot of traffic on the road. Bob doesn't like waiting for anything, and waiting behind cars is the worst of the lot. He slaps his hand on the dashboard and curses.

'There's no hurry, Bob. Time doesn't go any faster or slower because you fight it.'

'Yeah, thanks for the lesson, Saint Arthur. If this bastard in front of us doesn't get a move on, he won't have any friggin' time.'

There's a gap in the conversation. Arthur watches the people out of the van window. He likes driving around.

'Arthur?'

'Yeah?'

'About the boarding house, and the money and that.'

'What?'

'I just wanted to say thanks. Ya know.'

'You already did, mate. It was nothing. Thank God, that's all. Hey, where are we going?'

'The hospital.'

'The hospital, good. Who's sick?'

12

Pink. Great clouds of the stuff, streaming from the walls. Hard, straight walls. He can see it, but it's like watching a movie on a screen. Arthur's struggling through the pink fog, trying to divide it, to find a way through. He keeps slipping back, fading. Floating in this tide of pink with nowhere to stand, nothing to hold on to.

And then there's a woman, glowing in white. An angel? No, a nurse. A nurse? Why would a nurse . . .?

'Arthur? Can you hear me? How are you feeling this morning?'

He begins to speak, but his lips are a thousand miles away, and he can't reach them to make them work. A soft moan emerges from the distance, and a string of dribble slides from the corner of his mouth.

'You haven't been too well, Arthur. We've given you something to calm you down and help you to sleep. We're going to be keeping you here for a few days until you're feeling better. The doctor will be down to look at you later. Meanwhile you might as well get some rest. All right?'

Again he reaches out from the centre, trying to make it to the surface. This time a rough grunt emerges, and the dribble continues its journey down his neck. But the white has gone, and now there's nothing but unrelenting pink again.

There's a great silence. At first he can't make it out, almost welcomes it as peace. And then he remembers. What it is that's missing. The voice of God.

Like a crab shell washed up on the beach, with the insides rotted out of it. Empty. But the fog is rolling down again, and he no longer has the energy to resist it. He allows himself to be enveloped by it, feels himself falling.

'I can't believe you've done that! Straight up? Fifty milligrams of Triloxyl before you've even had a chance to diagnose him?'

'Look, I talked to his caregiver who brought him in. I did a quick assessment and I made a decision. It's not like this is the first time he's been admitted. He's got a record that goes back for ever. Delusional psychosis. We've been having good results with Triloxyl and I thought it was indicated by his history.'

'Come on, David. This is me you're talking to, remember? I know about this paper you're writing, and I know what they're paying you to write it. You're looking for results, aren't you? Wanting to see what happens when you hit a patient with a high-end dose straight up, to see if it's a way to push people through the ward faster.'

'That's an oversimplification, Gwenda, and unfair. I've assessed this patient and applied my professional judgment in what I consider to be his best interests. It's true that I'm interested in his progress, and it may be that his case is pertinent to the paper I'm preparing. But that's *not* my prime motivation in prescribing Triloxyl. Last time he was admitted we didn't have it available as an option. The possibility exists that this could be the key to giving this poor chap a normal life, and clear up these episodes completely. It would be unfair to deny him the benefits of a new and effective medication.'

'The fact is that we've never used it first up before, and I'm pretty sure no-one else has. We're on new ground here, and none of this has been through the committee or accepted as a clinical trial. He's a person, not some sort of guinea pig!'

'Don't be ridiculous. That's a cheap shot and a total overreaction. Apart from what it means to me that you don't trust either my word or my judgment, I think you're completely out of line. Would you talk to any other doctor like this?'

'For God's sake, David, it's because I'm close to you that I'm able to raise it. Don't dismiss me because I'm overstepping the boundaries. I can't stand it when you get priggish like this.'

'I don't think there's much point in pursuing this conversation. I'm his doctor, I've made my decision. We'll be monitoring his progress and if there are any problems we'll reconsider. But for the meantime the case is closed.'

This morning it's just not working.

The sun still washes the street; the punters are occupying their stalls and toying with their cups; strands of ethnic music compete and blend; but it's not working.

The flow is missing. It's like a drummer who has suddenly lost all sense of rhythm in one hand. What was pumping yesterday is a jangle today. Muffins are heavy and indigestible. The coffee has an oily taste. The talk is edgy with desperation.

Ponsonby experiences the unimaginable; a moment of self-doubt.

Nothing has changed. Everything is different.

Every so often a significant grunt emerges from the newspaper. Brian is working through it with a pen in one hand. Occasionally he mutters and makes a mark on the paper. Margaret refuses to be distracted, and gets on with cleaning the oven.

'Marg?'

'Hmm.'

'I've been thinking.'

'What?'

'Can you stop that for a minute and come and listen?'

She emerges reluctantly from the interior, sighs and strips off the rubber gloves. Pushing her hair back with a forearm, she sits at the table opposite him.

'Well?'

'You know how you've always liked the sea? I've always thought you're like a different person when we go away on holiday near a beach somewhere.'

'What's all this about?'

'You remember a couple of years ago when we were camping up at Whananaki? You used to go off on your own in the evenings and sit on the beach. I came down one night when the kids were in bed, and you were still sitting there. The moon had just come up, and you had your face lifted to it. I hung back in the pohutukawa, watching you. I can still see it now. It was like you were part of the thing, somehow, in a way that I never could be. I felt jealous of you.'

'I don't remember.'

'I never said anything about it. It was like you were untouchable, somehow; like you were a goddess and I was a dull plodder lurching about the place. I loved you and hated you at the same time. It was like you were mine, but you were beyond me. Anyway, the point of all this is that being near the sea seems to light you up like a candle.'

'There's something magnetic about it. Ever since I was little, the sea would heal me of anything that was wrong. You're right; I feel completely different when I can smell the salt in the air.'

'I've got some money I've been putting aside over the last few years — a bit of an emergency fund, you know. Anyway, with this new job and the extra income and everything, I was wondering whether we shouldn't check out buying a beach house. What d'you think?'

'A beach house? You're joking, right? We couldn't afford that, could we?'

'I've been checking out some prices here, and I reckon we could manage it. Things might be a little bit tight in the short term, but nothing we couldn't cope with.'

'Tell me you're serious about this, Brian. I don't even want to begin thinking about it if it's not a possibility.'

'Of course I'm serious. I wouldn't have mentioned it if I wasn't. I think it would be good for all of us to have somewhere to get away to, a place we can relax in, read some books, watch the sea, eat crumpets by the fire.'

'Where? Where could we afford to buy? It wouldn't want to be too far out of Auckland.'

'Depends what you want, really. As long as you don't mind a place that's a bit run-down, we could look at places like Sandspit, Leigh, Mahurangi; or on the other side, maybe Karekare or Muriwai.'

'Muriwai? Seriously? We could buy a beach house in Muriwai?'

'Well, judging by the prices here, I think we could, yes. Not the top of the range, by any means. But something that's got a view of the sea.'

Margaret takes a deep breath and savours it for a few moments. Her eyes are cloudy. She looks across at Brian, who has a wry smile and slightly raised eyebrows. *Who is this man? Why have I never noticed him before?*

Dear Parish Council,

I have consulted with the Bishop, who will shortly be contacting you. However, I thought it best to offer some personal explanation for the matters he will be discussing with you.

Since Sunday a week ago there have been various concerns raised relating to my offering of the pulpit to a visiting speaker. Some of these concerns have been taken up with me directly, and I have discussed my perspective on the events with those who have approached me. I understand that a number of complaints have been received by the Council, and that as a result there has been informal consultation with the Bishop.

At this stage I have no wish to enter into discussion concerning the incident at the heart of the present discontent, nor to defend myself against the various accusations which have ensued. The event is now past, and I see little value in raking over the coals. It does disturb me somewhat that Council has seen fit to contact the Bishop without first providing opportunity for me to answer charges against me.

Be that as it may, my chief purpose is to inform you of my resignation as vicar of this parish. I have discussed this at length with the Bishop, and he is in agreement that this is an appropriate course of action. He is working with me to investigate future venues of ministry, and will outline for you the process which is to be followed in electing my replacement.

I would not want my resignation to be misconstrued. It is not an angry reaction to the criticism I have received in recent days, although that may have helped to hasten my decision. My resignation is the culmination of a long process of thought which I have been working through in conjunction with my spiritual director. After much soul-searching, it is apparent to me that my contribution to St David's is at an end, and that my moving on will bring new possibilities for growth and development for the congregation.

My time among you has been fulfilling and enriching. I trust there will be opportunity over the coming period to express my thanks and appreciation to you all.

However, some recent events outside the life of the congregation have occasioned something of a crisis of faith for me. In this situation, and with considerable personal uncertainty as to my suitability for ministry, it would be unwise to continue in my present position. I feel both relief and a new sense of freedom having made the decision to conclude.

I would be grateful if you would convey my resignation to the congregation in the appropriate manner. I will of course undertake my usual responsibilities during the transitional process, and be available to discuss any ensuing issues. For the upcoming Council meeting, however, I think it best to absent myself and allow you the freedom to discuss events with candour. I therefore wish to tender my apology for that meeting.

Please be assured of my best wishes for the parish, and my appreciation for the work we have shared together in recent years. There remains a deep sense of regret in my leaving St David's.
Yours faithfully,
(Rev) Kevin Connor

The last time she was near a psych ward it was in that other place. Carrington. With its air of medieval squalor. This is much brighter. New and pleasant. Carpet on the floors, not so much echo.

Karen makes her way to reception, where the woman is engrossed in a telephone conversation.

In the far corner is a man in pyjamas and a dressing grown. He's a young man, perhaps twenty-two. His head hangs forward, and to one side. His eyes look up from under thick black brows, watching Karen. She finds it unpleasant.

What's best? To ignore him? To acknowledge him? She turns to offer a smile of encouragement. His dressing gown drapes open. Her eyes are drawn to the black slash in the front of his pyjama bottoms. Emerging from this hairy aperture, a flaccid penis hangs in full view. The man seems unaware of it. He simply continues to stare, rocking gently from foot to foot. She turns away, embarrassed and unsettled.

The woman behind the desk holds a hand over the phone, giving attention briefly to Karen.

'Karen Bligh-Farnsworth. I phoned earlier, about Arthur.'

'Oh, yes. A special visit. You're a relative, aren't you?'

'That's right. Sister-in-law. Can I see him?'

'I'm sure that's fine. Just take a seat, will you, and I'll get someone to take you along to the ward.'

Karen waits. There's only one magazine on the table, a weekly publication about cars. She flicks through it with sufficient absorption to shield her from the man with the eyebrows and the dick. *Why doesn't somebody do something with him?*

Eventually a surly man in a white jacket appears. Whether he's a nurse or an orderly isn't immediately apparent. He seems to lack the power of speech, communicating with nods and grunts. Karen follows him down corridors.

Keys hang from a chain at his waist. All the locking and unlocking creates a feeling of panic in Karen. Entering a place which it's hard to escape from.

They arrive at a room which, Karen assumes from the tone of grunt, has some connection with Arthur. There's no opportunity to ask, as the white jacket moves on.

He's stretched out on top of the bed, on his back. Snoring so loudly that the room seems impenetrable. Pink seems inappropriate, somehow.

It occurs to her to turn and flee. But the story demands that she proceed. She sits on the side of the bed and shakes his shoulder. His great frame absorbs the motion without response. Karen applies more strength, and begins to call his name.

She's rewarded with a splutter and a corresponding heave of his body. She shakes again and calls again. His eyes open lazily, but they're glazed.

The world is still full of pink, but now this fuzzy outline of a dark-haired woman is in the centre of it all. She seems to be calling his name.

Karen is appalled. The eyes have nothing in them. Or very little. Just in the middle, in the black pupils, it's like looking down a telescope the wrong way. There may be something at the bottom of it all.

He's fighting now. Fighting to make it up from the depths, fighting to get some words out of the darkness, fighting to remember why he's drifting in this sludge.

'Arthur, do you remember me? My name's Karen, and I'm from television. We've talked before, d'you remember?'

She sees the flicker of recognition as it flashes across his eyes. His lips open but no sound comes out. He's obviously drugged to the eyeballs.

Arthur can see her. She looks worried about something. Television. He has a vague picture of a flashing box in the corner of the room. What's the connection? There must be some connection.

'I came to see you because I wanted to talk to you. But it doesn't look like a good time for you to be able to talk. Perhaps I'll come back when you're feeling a bit better.'

He summons everything he can find to draw on, and pushes it all towards that distant mouth, trying to get it to work.

'No!'

The sudden exclamation frightens her and makes her jump. Her heart is pounding in her chest. *What if he gets violent?* But his eyes are speaking, reassuring her, pleading with her. Karen has the weird feeling that she actually understands him.

She reaches out a trembling hand and brushes the hair away from his forehead. It's a simple gesture of tenderness.

His arm is so heavy. It's full of lead and hurting. He extracts it in slow motion, moves it with huge effort until his hand is able to find hers. A soft mumble spills from his lips.

'What was that? What did you say, Arthur?'

She bends close to his mouth, trying to make sense of the inarticulate sounds.

'I love . . . I love . . .'

'What, Arthur? What do you love?'

But he's gone again, his eyes closed, the breathing heavy.

She sits there for a few moments, feeling strangely emotional. *Poor bastard. What the hell am I going to do for a story now? You've let me down, Arthur. And I thought you were the key to the whole thing.*

There's a confident knock at the door. On her way to answer it, Penny looks again at the kauri panelling glowing in the late-afternoon sunlight. There's an awful finality about this whole thing. *God, I hope I'm not making a huge mistake.*

She doesn't have much time for agents. But they have their function, like abortionists or dentists. Best just to get on with it. She ushers him in.

A young chap, Brent. With the arrogance of too much money and not enough pain. They all look young these days. And he seems to know his stuff.

'Well, tell me the bad news.'

'No bad news to tell, I'm afraid. I've finished the appraisal, and talked with some of my colleagues, and we've come up with a strategy for sale. With your approval, of course.'

He opens the leather-bound folder on his lap and extracts a piece of paper.

'We've put it all together for you here. That first figure is what we consider a realistic price for your property, given current market conditions. The second figure is the one we recommend that the house go on the market for, which will give us room for negotiation.'

'You're serious? The house is really worth this much money?'

'Absolutely. I can give you a schedule of what similar properties in the area have sold for if you like. The market's very positive at the moment, and we would be very happy to market your property for you. We're very confident of our estimates, and I'd be very surprised if we ended up going below our estimate there.'

'Goodness. That's a lot more than I'd expected, I have to tell you.'

'We have forty buyers on our books wanting a

place in Ponsonby, and this house is just the sort of thing they're looking for. Can I ask you, out of interest, why you're selling?'

'I need to leave. Ponsonby has been good to me, but I've changed and Ponsonby's changed. It's very much a spur-of-the-moment thing, to be honest. I just know I have to move on. I'm too comfortable here. I'm going to travel overseas for a while. When I come back, I'm going to live somewhere different. Dunedin, perhaps. Or else out in the country. I don't know.'

'I can't say I understand, but I'm happy enough to work with you in selling a place as lovely as this. If you're prepared to sign with us, of course.'

'Oh yes. I'm as ready as I'll ever be. Things have to come to an end, Brent. Sometimes they have to end before anything else can start again. Now, show me where I'm supposed to sign.'

'Thanks for coming in, Gwenda. Take a seat.'

'Am I going to need one?'

'I really don't know. What I'm interested in finding out is why, according to the chart, this patient didn't receive his medication this morning.'

'I'm sure you've already been informed that I overrode your instructions and told the staff not to administer it. I considered it detrimental to the patient's health.'

'My God, listen to yourself. Who the bloody hell do you think you are? How much pharmacology have you done? Do you think nurses should take over the prescription of medication?'

'I have some responsibility for the care of patients on my ward, and I took what I considered to be appropriate action to preserve the safety of my patient.'

'This is all about Triloxyl, isn't it? Even though we've discussed it up hill and down dale, you've still got this irrational fear of what is an approved medication. Well, you've gone too far this time, Gwenda. You simply can't make up your own mind which of my clinical directions you're going to follow. I carry the ultimate responsibility for patients' welfare, and I'm afraid this is going to have to go on report.'

'You don't have to report it if you don't want to, David.'

'Of course I bloody do! It's my job. This isn't some lovers' quarrel where we can argue the toss over who's right and who's wrong. We're professionals with responsibility and accountability. You've made a mistake and you're going to have to face the music.'

'Have a look at him, you self-righteous prat! He's out of it, gaga, drugged into oblivion. He came in here capable of rational conversation, and we've knocked him out with some new-fangled version of horse tranquillizer. I don't believe your assessments are based solely on clinical indicators.'

'And what the hell is that supposed to mean?'

'You're angry at him because he disrupted your precious church service! He embarrassed you, and when he showed up down here, you decided to teach him a lesson.'

'That's ludicrous, Gwenda, absolutely ludicrous! I won't listen to this! Get out of here right now! Get out!'

'It's a very little man who can't face the truth, David. You disappoint me.'

'Go!'

This time when he wakes, things are different. He knows where he is, and why everything has been so murky and sluggish. The fog's still there, hovering somewhere off the coast. But for the meantime it's receded, and he can see almost clearly.

What did I do? It must have been something if they've put me in hospital. I can't remember. I can't stay here, though. There's things have to be done. Margaret . . .

The one word brings a flood of longing and regret. He wants to have her near him, to hold her, to speak to her, to calm her. *I can feel again!*

'Hiho, Arthur.'

It's Norm, all dressed up and wearing a tie.

Carrying a scrunched paper bag that doesn't have a bottle in it.

'I brought you some chocolate, Arthur. Thought you might like something sweet to chew on. All right if I come in for a while?'

'Ka pai, come in, man, come in.'

Even Arthur is surprised at the croaky sound of his voice. But at least it's working again. Norm pulls up a chair beside the bed.

'It's good to see you again, my friend. Bob and all the boys send their love, and say they're waiting for you to get back home. You're not looking too bad for a Maori.'

'Hey, I look better than your white face does. I don't know why I'm in here, Norm. I was just trying to remember how I got here, but it won't come. What happened? What did I do?'

'Nothing to worry about, Arthur. You were starting to get a bit sick, that's all. Bob brought you in and they decided to keep you in here.'

Norm's taking a special interest in the bedspread, toying at it with his finger and regarding it closely.

'What's up? What's the matter?'

'It was me told Bob that I thought you were going off. I didn't think you'd end up here, Arthur, honest I didn't. I was worried about you, that's all. Going on about Santa Claus all the time. I didn't want you to get really sick. Ever since John, you know . . .'

'Hey, Norm. It's all right. It's OK, brother, it's OK. I'm going to be all right. But I need to get out of here. There's a whole lot of things I have to do, you know? Things could really fall apart if I'm not around for a while.'

'I'm sure they won't keep you in for long. It's probably just a matter of sorting out your medication or something.'

'Yeah, well, I've stopped taking medication now. I don't need it any more. It just gets in the way.

'Look, I need you to do some stuff for me, OK? Get in touch with Margaret for me, and let her know where I am. Tell her I'm OK and that I love her. Tell her she's the queen, OK?'

'OK, Arthur.'

'Then out the back of the boarding house, in the old tool shed. There's a big parcel wrapped up in a plastic bag. I want you to find it and see if you can find some way for Margaret to get it, and make sure she knows it's from me.'

'Will do.'

'And then I've got to tell you some stuff that I want you to remember. Can you do that for me, Norm? What's your memory like these days?'

'Pretty good. I can remember most things.'

'OK. Here goes, then. I'm the second son of God, Norm. Don't you ever forget that. Whatever else happens, don't ever forget it. Maybe I haven't always got it right, but most of what I've told you has come straight from God. I know you believe in God, Norm. But lots of people are struggling, feeling hurt and hurting each other. They need to find God — that's what they need most of all, but they don't know how. That's all I've been doing; trying to make it easier for them. But they're so blind, Norm, so bloody blind. They can't find their way, a lot of them, so they give up. Tell them not to give up. Tell them if they can't find their way to God, then God will find a way to them. Tell them not to give in or give up. To keep on looking for love even when they get shit upon. You tell them, Norm.'

'You can tell them yourself, when you get out.'

'And I will. I will. But in the meantime I need some help, and I want you to tell people what I told you. You're a good friend, Norm, a good man. I love you, man. I'm tired now. I need to get some sleep, you know?'

'Sure, Arthur. Get some rest. I'll take care of that stuff for you. See you later.'

She drums her fingers on the desk while the ringing tone drones on. That last look of Arthur's is haunting her. Something in his eyes. What? Karen's remembering the time in the church; what she saw in him then.

'Hello? Bob? Karen Bligh-Farnsworth here.'

'Yes, that's right. The bitch from *Nightly News*. Look, I'm sorry we got off to a bad start. I think I probably misjudged you.'

'Well, I'm doing what I can. Listen, I wonder if you can help me out with a couple of things. First up, I just wanted to follow up on the boarding house — how're you getting on with the threatened closure?'

'You can't be serious. He did what?'

'So everything's OK now? You can get the alterations done? The men can stay?'

'But why on earth is he in hospital then? What happened?'

'Well, he didn't look too good when I went in to see him. Any more drugs in him and they'll be bottling his blood for anaesthetic. I hope you're sure about taking him in there. I couldn't get any sense out of him.'

'A message for me? Are you sure?'

'Well, yes, television lady — I guess that's me. Tell my story? What the hell does he mean by that?'

And now the time has come.

How ordinarily it comes. How commonplace the seconds passing. How uneventful the arrival. How unheralded. How unnoticed. How suddenly.

But it moves in only one direction. There can be no turning back. Not ever.

His eyes spring open. There is a man in the room. A man with a white beard. The man is wearing a white shirt, with flashes of red on the shoulders.

Red and white! Red and white!

The man has a needle on a tray.

Arthur sees, and sees it all. He has seen it before. He will see it always. Around the man there are demons. The demons are entering the man, one after the other. He turns and smiles at Arthur, and Arthur is looking into the eyes of the devil himself. Each one of the man's teeth is silver, and they are shining in the light. He reaches down and picks up the needle, and it turns into a sword in his hand.

Arthur launches himself at the man, going for him with two hands around the throat.

David hears the bell ringing and leaps to his feet. He can already hear the shouting and banging, and races towards it.

In the middle of the corridor a tremendous battle is raging.

There are four men grappling with Arthur, being tossed aside with remarkable ease. Arthur is yelling at the top of his voice.

'No! No! No!'

Heads and limbs are crunching against the wall. Two orderlies arrive on the scene and join the battle. The tide is turning. Arthur's flailing is reduced as they each begin to get a part of him and hold it down. He's pinned to the floor now, and bucks ineffectually like a fish in the bottom of a boat.

'All right,' gasps the nurse with the white beard. 'What do we give him now?'

Burlain has hold of Geranne, whether for his own comfort or that of hers he is no longer sure. They are appalled and oppressed by the violence. Each blow and cry seems to bruise them.

It isn't how they understood it to be. Not how they want it to happen. Not at all.

But for now they are helpless to intervene. Trapped into watching what they never wanted to see. Their own cries of anguish fill the ether, but fail to move human eardrums.

'Give him phenobarb, one hundred!'

'You sure? He's had Triloxyl.'

'Just fucking give it to him, before he gets loose again.'

The nurse fumbles as he prepares a new syringe.

'OK, guys. Here goes.'

One of the orderlies has Arthur's pyjama bottoms pulled down. They strain to hold the big man still while the needle is inserted.

'Done!'

They wait for the blood to reach the brain.

Arthur sees the last cord break free. There is nothing left to hold him now, and he is drifting upwards, floating.

There is music playing, such music. And underneath it a chant in his own language. It is the chant for the welcoming home of a warrior hero.

The light is shining, and there is cheering and shouting.

He suddenly arches upward, so that his back no longer touches the floor. The men holding him down are lifted effortlessly. He stays there, arched rigid, for a few moments, gurgling. Then there is a thump as the body collapses to the floor.

How quickly he begins to turn blue.

'Arrest! Arrest! Get out of the fucking way!'

But it is too late, David. It has always been too late. From the beginning of time it has been too late.

The second son of God is dead.

In Ponsonby, the sun moves behind a cloud, and a sudden chill darkness falls over the street. People shudder for no particular reason.

In the boarding house there's a loud cracking bang. Bob looks towards the ceiling and curses. Wal pisses his pants in fright. Pete is swamped with sadness, and turns his head to look for the cause of it.

Margaret is standing in the lounge when she drops to the floor like a stone. Her gut is gripped and squeezed. She remains there on her knees, moaning.

On the slopes of a hill in the far north, a giant totara creaks and sways and finally topples to the ground. When the crash has finished echoing through the air, there is a deep silence. Who is to say why the tree has fallen?

Silence.

Bob's pissed off. The parking round the hospital's godawful, and he'll be buggered if he's gonna pay to park. He wishes he'd have come earlier when there's not so many people around. And now they're shagging him around at the desk.

'Look, love, it's not that complicated, ya know? Just tell me what room he's in and I'll find me own way down there, orright? Not like this is the first time I been here.'

'I'm sorry, sir. You'll have to wait here for the doctor. Just take a seat and he'll be here shortly.'

'Ah, fuck me gently. Things never change, do they?'

'I'm sorry?'

'Never mind, love. You get back to yer magazine; I'll be OK. I've got nothing better to do.'

When David sweeps through the door, his face is

still ashen. He finds Bob pacing up and down.

'Mr Davies, David Jorgensen. Would you mind coming through to my office?'

'Look, I've just come down to see Arthur. I don't want to naff around, see, 'cos I've left the van on a yellow line and some Nazi'll tow it away if I'm too long.'

'Please, Mr Davies. We need to talk and this is not the best place for it.'

Something in his eyes convinces Bob to follow up the carpeted hallway. The office is plain, the desk loaded with papers and books.

'Please, sit down. I'm afraid there's no easy way to do this. The fact is, Arthur had a major cardiac arrest just an hour ago, and he didn't make it through. He's dead. I'm sorry.'

Bob simply stares intensely into the eyes of this man with his white coat. He's looking for some sign that it's a joke or a trick or a mistake. But there's nothing there.

'What the fuck are ya talking about? There was nothing wrong with his heart — I brought him in 'cos I was worried he was going off, that's all. And now yer tellin' me he's dead? What the fuck did ya do to him? Ya killed him, ya bastard, didn't ya?'

'Look, I understand that you're upset, Mr Davies, but ridiculous accusations are not going to help anyone . . .'

Bob is on his feet and around the other side of the desk before David has any idea of what's happening. He grabs the lapels of the white coat in his two fists and lifts the doctor clean out of his chair. With the momentum he swings David up against a book-lined wall. A large volume falls from the top shelf and strikes a glancing blow on the frightened man's head.

'Listen here, ya pox-ridden little prick. I could kill ya now, ya little fucker, ya understand that? I could snap the bones in yer neck. Yer a murderer, that's what ya are. The smell of death's coming out yer throat. What have ya done to my Arthur? What have ya done to him? He was a man when I brought him in here, a big fucken man, more than a man. How can he be dead? What did ya do to him, ya bastard, ya rotten death-dealing bastard? What did ya do to Arthur?'

And then the strength has gone from him, and he buckles to the floor, still holding the doctor. There are big rough grunts gulping out of his mouth, and tears running down his face. He rolls his head from side to side, and still the awful noise echoes around the room. Bob's grip stays locked onto David's lapels, and the doctor's been dragged, startled, to the floor.

They're like this when Gwenda finds them. She prises Bob's fingers loose, one at a time. Then she lifts him to his feet, supporting him. Very gently, she leads him from the room, away to where Arthur lies. David is left lying on the floor, gasping.

She ushers him through the door of the room, and then she's gone. This is a white room, and Arthur's covered in a white sheet. Just his great brown head protrudes from the top, and his long hair splays out onto the pillow.

Bob makes his way over to Arthur, blurred through the tears. He runs his fingers over the face, brushes them through the hair. It is Arthur and not Arthur. But there's a hush in the room, like when you go into one of those huge cathedrals and there's no-one else around. He sits in a chair beside the bed. He reaches under the sheet to find a hand, and holds on to it. The hand is cold and rigid.

'I'm sorry, Arthur. I didn't mean it to come to this. I want ya to forgive me, Arthur. Wherever ya are, ya bastard, I want ya to forgive me. I love ya, man, and I'm pissed off at ya for doing this. I can't believe ya've gone. I won't let anyone forget ya, Arthur. I'll tell them all. You wait and see if I don't.'

But no answer comes from those stiff lips.

A shaft of light fills the room, and makes a little shining patch on Arthur's forehead. It seems to Bob like a sign of some sort.

The tears find a path through the stubble and drip from his chin. Apart from this silent trickling, Norm is entirely still. He has turned to stone, and there is no blood in him, no breath, nothing at all to suggest that this man remains alive. Apart from the pain which crushes his chest like a boulder.

How long has he been sitting here on the concrete? There are no markers any more; no units of measure which mean anything at all.

There is no sobbing. No movement of the shoulders or wrenching of the diaphragm. No groaning from his throat. Just the continuous issue of tears, flowing down like rain on a window.

The images of that dream come again and again and again. Arthur's face. The one accusing eye. The falling.

Beside him there lies an empty half-bottle of whisky. It is as still and as useless as Norm.

An intermittent plopping is the only sound in the whole of the universe. It is caused by the tears falling onto an envelope lying open on Norm's lap.

The envelope contains three crisp $10 notes.

Margaret turns and begins to make her way back down the beach. She must have come miles along the black sand. It has grown late, and the colour is draining from the sky.

The breakers pound into the shore, but their fury is lost on Margaret. They can't touch her where she is. The gulls swoop over her head. She is partly aware of the coldness of the wind, which fires stinging particles of ironsand into her face. But it does not come near the coldness on the inside.

There is a great, gaping chasm somewhere, which echoes down into eternity. Its name is Arthur.

For the first time she lifts her head from the sand, and stumbles in shock. There, risen over the sand hills, swollen and menacing.

Huge and glowing in satisfaction.

The moon.

The insatiable moon.

On the eighth day the sun did not rise.
It didn't rise the day after.
God was neither alive nor dead.
The darkness of the Void,
Mountainous, mile-deep, civilized darkness
Sat on the earth from then till now.

James K. Baxter, 'The Maori Jesus'

Afterword

It's Wal who leads her in, muttering to himself as he goes. She's very nervous, eyes darting in all directions for hidden dangers.

'Here he is. That's Bob there, that is. Bob, this lady wants to have a word with you.'

He's sitting at the table, with the newspaper open in front of him. But his eyes are unfocused. His shoulders are slumped. He lifts his head towards this intruder, with no warmth.

'Look, I'm sorry to barge in on you like this. You don't know me. My name's Penny. I saw you up at the meeting about the boarding house.'

Consciousness kicks in and his eyes narrow. She's well dressed in a casual sort of way; must have been quite a looker in her day.

'Yeah, that's right. I remember ya spoke, didn't ya? On our side, too. Jeez, we didn't have too many friends up there that night, that's a fact. Here, have a seat. Bob Davies, I am; and this here's Wal. Get the lady a cuppa, Wal.'

'No, it's all right thanks. I won't stay long.'

'Suit yerself. The place is a bit of a mess, I'm sorry. Only we've had a bit of a wake here, see. One of our blokes died in hospital, and it's knocked us around a bit.'

'Arthur?'

'Ya knew him?'

'No, I have a friend who's a nurse at the Conolly Unit where he died. Gwenda. She was quite upset about the whole thing — she rang and talked to me about it.'

'The redheaded one? She was good, real good. She treated him with a bit of dignity.'

'She said he was from here. I didn't know him at all, though I met him once. He was — he was very close to another friend of mine, Margaret.'

'Is that a fact? Margaret, eh? I haven't seen her since he died. Arthur thought the world of her, ya know.'

'She's very upset, to say the least. It's a bit awkward, you know, with her being married.'

'Yeah, I thought that might have had something to do with it. Tangled webs and all that. Anyway, love, what can I do for ya?'

'It's the other way round, I think. You see, I've just sold my house in Ponsonby for rather a lot more than I expected. I wanted to do something useful with some of the money. Ponsonby's been good to me over the years. Anyway, I've got a cheque here for fifty thousand dollars, and I want you to have it to do the alterations to the boarding house.'

'Well, I'll be fucked. Excuse me, missus, only it's a bit of a shock, ya know? Why would ya want to give it to us?'

'I'm not sure that I can explain it. I feel like I've been caught up in something. But I'd like you to take it and use it to keep the boarding house open.'

'That's the thing, ya see. We don't need it any more. Arthur sorted it all out for us, so we've got enough to do all the work. I hope it doesn't sound ungrateful, but I couldn't take yer money under false pretences, like.'

'Arthur had money?'

'Nah, not a penny. It's a long story. But he saved our bacon, I can tell ya.'

'I'd like you to take the money anyway. As long as you use it for the men in some way. Make the alterations bigger, buy them new beds, have a party, whatever.'

'Look, I couldn't take it off ya, love. It wouldn't seem right.'

'Please. For Arthur. Even though I didn't know him, I feel like he's tied up in the whole thing somehow. This is where the money belongs. Just make sure that these men get the benefit of it. I'd like to think this boarding house is going to stay around for a while.'

Bob is taking the cheque and smiling. Wal is

happy because Bob is happy. He gives Bob a hug, and looks tentatively towards Penny. She takes a step backwards and then begins laughing at herself. They are laughing together. With Arthur.

'Tonight we want to stretch the bounds of television. The theme of this evening's programme is mental health. But we will be going beyond facts and figures, beyond medical specialists and government policies. This is a story from the inside of the system, where people live and die under the stigma of psychiatric ill health.

'I'm Karen Bligh-Farnsworth. Tonight we bring you the story of a man who suffered greatly at the hands of the authorities, and eventually died in their care. His crime? He believed himself to have special significance, to be the second son of God.

'We will be talking to some of the people whose lives were touched by a delusional psychiatric patient who was as intriguing as he was confused.

'A boarding-house resident who lived in poverty amid the newly rich of Ponsonby, this astonishing character has had a profound effect on many who knew him. Because of him, a household of derelict men sleep tonight in safety and security.

'Was he insane, as he was classified? Or did he perhaps have insights and abilities which call for a different sort of evaluation?

'You be the judge. Tonight we bring you the story of Arthur, second son of God . . .'

As Karen previews the tape, she understands that something bigger than her is taking place. And it all goes back to that morning in the church. *I must have inhaled.*

She tries reading the eye chart while her doctor puzzles over the information in her file. Margaret is pleased with her eyesight. It's far better than Brian's, who should have glasses but won't face the fact.

'I'm sorry, Mrs Wilson, but I'm having a little trouble here. There seems to be some sort of confusion with our records. You used to see Dr Wadsworth here, is that right?'

'Yes; I was his patient up until last year when he retired.'

'Hmmm. And your middle name is Anne?'

'That's right. What's the problem?'

'Well, I've only seen you a few times, but there's parts of your file here which simply don't reconcile with these last results.'

'I've never been aware that there's been any problems before. I haven't had any really significant medical problems. Just the pregnancies, and then I had my tubes tied. Mostly I keep pretty healthy.'

'I'm afraid we're going to have to get the tests done again, in that case. I'm not sure if the tests themselves are suspect, or whether they've got your results mixed up with someone else's.'

'Why? Is there something serious? I'd prefer it if you'd tell me what's going on.'

'Oh no, nothing serious. It's a mistake, obviously. There was nothing showed up in the blood tests at all, so you can relax on that score. It's just the urine sample — most peculiar.'

'What?'

'Well, according to these results, you're pregnant. But that's impossible.'

Two angels are high in the sky. They're laughing and laughing, and the sound of it reaches to heaven.